Nils' Passage
Tales of the Faerevold
By
J. Daniel Stanfield

Syringa Press, Inc.

To Mary Alice,

I've surround you.

J. Daniel Stanfield

24/50

Nils' Passage
© 2011 by J. Daniel Stanfield

ISBN: 978-0-9831827-1-9

Printed in America

10 9 8 7 6 5 4 3 2 1

Editor: Bob Spear
Interior Design: Bob Spear
Cover Design: Jeanne Ritter

PUBLISHED BY:
Syringa Press, Inc.
2109 High St.
Leavenworth, KS 66048
913-648-4058

STERNZCO

Old Man Winter held Iskago tight in his frigid grasp that year. On this particular morning, the rising sun rode low and hidden in the dancing snow. The frigid wind drove the heavy wet snow helter-skelter down and between the dirty streets. On the ancient city's sidewalks, the bundled bodies and gray faces of the intertwined commuters were nearly indistinguishable against the dancing snowflakes. Within this mass of plodding humanity, Nilsson Sicharis shuffled forward into the blowing snow, head-down, crouched over, and shivering against the sharp winter. He did not resist the crowd's undulations as his fellow pedestrians pushed and propelled him along the icy walkway.

Nils was a middle-aged man quickly approaching the end of his prime. He was of average height with curly black hair sprinkled with the beginnings of gray that stuck out akimbo from a threadbare woolen cap pulled tight over his head and ears. Nils was covered from head to foot against the blustery sharp winter. He wore scuffed shoes, a plain tattered overcoat, and a long scarf that surrounded his neck. His fingers tips protruded from holes in his mittens. Any passerby who happened to see him plodding along would have described him, if they had bothered to, as a man neither tall nor short, nor fit or yet excessively overweight. His shallow cheeks and dull eyes betrayed a man, one might politely say, "A bit down on his luck."

His face was rounding, slightly pudgy and carried a deeply carved fatalistic expression of perpetual melancholy. If someone had noticed Nils trudging his way within the swarm, they may have seen a visage that displayed all Nils held deep inside his soul. Anyone who looked closely enough in those days could clearly make out he was a man deeply haunted by some vile, inner demon. If one were to catch a fleeting glimpse of him while he worked through some problem deeply in his mind, that person may have caught an occasional flicker cross his oft-bedeviled demeanor. In those glimmering seconds, one could catch a faint reflection of what Nils had once been, wished he was, and yet in the vast, ever growing power of STERNZCO, was not.

Unique among his fellows, he supported a rather unremarkable pair of wire-rimmed eyeglasses. Rare in the Republic but required due to the combination of his severe myopia, plus the lack of money required for the corrective surgery common amongst the elites as well as the burghers. To be without financial means was no great dishonor. Indeed, many scions of the great elite families had fallen onto hard times during the bleak and dark days of the Great Collapse. Nevertheless, the spectacles were the outward sign of his poverty as only the most impoverished and destitute of the Republic's vast citizenry could ill afford the procedure. Yet, the sight of one not taking the least steps to address such a visible sign of physical weakness was an affront sufficient to raise the bile in one's belly. For like all societies, a certain rabble haunted the back alleys of Iskago's bars and whorehouses. These were the lowest caste that spent their Troy Sterling satisfying addictions to the various concoctions that tamped down pain.

Like any other old, crowded, and very dirty city, Iskago's core was a mix of architecture and design that reflected its heritage. Entire city blocks held structures built during past eras that bespoke of financiers, merchants, and artisans looking proudly out of the shiny windows of their sturdy stone buildings. Now, in the days of the Republic's Great Collapse only the dim reflection of the red eyes of some feral animal stared hungrily behind the grimy and often boarded up window fronts. Other sections of the downtown area hosted a plethora of tall skyscrapers made possible by new materials and modern technology. In the center, rising to the sky, an ancient and immense office building stood silent and impassive to the passing swarm of people at its feet. Its granite base covered a square mile, and its sheer sides towered over the rest of the buildings within Iskago's central core. Larger and taller than anything else, at one time it was Sternz Place, in honor of its builder and founder of The Sternz Company, Joshia Sternz. Now it was STERNZCO, and the building now known simply as The Tower.

Nils' Passage

Nils was a quiet man, one not prone to the sudden violent outbursts of his fellow boozers and losers. An old, non-descript cat was his lone companion. The feline shared whatever happened to be the meal of the day. Nils drank alone, tall glasses of copious amounts of the ice-cold vodka he kept in the freezer. A combination of the smell of rancid alcohol in his sweat and an abnormal reticence rarely provided opportunities for him to speak to his neighbors at his work, nor in the apartments of the building in which he lived. Even when stoned cold drunk and returning to his home from Klinger's Bar, he made so little noise in his daily routine of life that later Ms. Beebleton, the local gossip who made the gathering of minutia her life's work, remarked after his death, "Now, what was his name again? Are you sure he lived here?"

As the undulating crowd reached the corner of The Tower, Nils drifted away from the main mass of commuters and joined a smaller group that swept him up the building's granite steps and through its massive glass doors. He slowly moved in line through the security checkpoint, and like everyone else, submitted his meager belongings to the electronic scanners and allowed the guard to search his person. His ratty hat and overcoat, the muffler and mittens, and even the wired rimmed eye glasses went through the scanners. At the opposite end of the gauntlet, Nils secured his things. He then made his way across the wide marbled floor of The Tower's great lobby to one of the drab stainless steel elevators. At the first one's opening, he pushed his way in with a pack of other STERNZCO workers. Their blank eyes did not register when the elevator door closed in front of them. Nils thought to himself, *What a pain.*

><

Dominare Avery rode alone in the back of an opulent motor car; its ancient rubber tires the certain sign of great prestige and wealth. The pale sun shined on the limousine's ruby red boot and passed through the rear window reflecting the polished profile of his chiseled, athletic face. He was tan, vivacious, and had a firm, square jaw. Yet, his face held the soulless, piercing dark eyes of a shark. Dominare, or Dom, as he preferred to be addressed, was a man in his early thirties whose very demeanor communicated the extreme confidence that came from his finely honed skills in the art of gaining and wielding power.

The limousine's tires splashed snow and muck from the pavement as it passed the last of the freezing commuters nearing The Tower. It turned from the icy road and into a covered parking area reserved for the STERNZCO top brass within The Tower's side, and stopped. Security guards flanked the entrance. One hurried to the car and opened the passenger door. Dom exited the vehicle. His polished shoes gleamed as he firmly placed them on the ancient cobblestones of the Executives' private driveway. He wore a dark grey silk suit, a black fedora, and fine buff-colored calfskin gloves. A brushed camel hair coat of tan lay neatly over his ensemble.

The guard had failed to move away from Dom's exit out of the vehicle at a pace to suit Dom's mood that morning, causing Dom to force his way past the man's extended leg. With a low snarl, Dom brusquely pushed the man aside and strode into the building. He crossed a marbled threshold and carelessly scanned his identification card past a security scanner. STERNZCO workers and guards stood sheepishly aside as Dom strode evenly through the building's wide foyer. When he reached the single elevator with a gilded door trimmed in red, on cue, the elevator's door opened for him. A richly uniformed operator bowed to one side as Dom imperiously entered. He stood in the middle of the plush elevator as the door closed, his dark eyes smoldering.

At the Executive Level of The Tower, two elevator doors opened simultaneously to reveal a modern reception area set at the juncture of Dom's office and two long corridors. Branching perpendicular in opposite directions along The Tower's width, the corridors formed the top of a T. At its base, an attractive receptionist sat behind a switchboard; ensconced among the polished wood, sparkling glass, and gleaming stainless steel. A computer and key board stood to one side of her. A headset with a chrome earpiece and microphone rode primly on the tight roll of her red-blond hair. She sat at attention and held her hands neatly in her lap as the two men exited their respective elevators.

The red polish of her perfectly manicured fingernails reflected Dom and Nils as they walked next to each other toward the reception area. They stopped their progress once they reached her domain. Without looking at Nils or inhaling his fetid body odor, Dom spoke, "Ah, Nils old boy. Be a good chap and see that the DENVER data gets posted to my files."

Twenty-something years in the Legions and pushing five at STERNZCO had taught Nils many things. One of which was how to respond to demented despots. In a low professional tone, Nils replied, "Yes Mr. Avery, right away, and with a copy to the other departments?"

Dom icily retorted, "That will not be necessary. The annual performance evaluations are coming up. We wouldn't want any issues to get in the way of a bonus or perhaps a promotion?"

Nils lowered his eyes and replied deferentially, "Yes sir, Mr. Avery."

With the exchange between the two finished, Nils turned onto one of the corridors and shuffled down a long hallway. Dom lingered before his gilded-haired thane for a brief moment and slowly moved his lecherous eyes over the outline of her ample breasts, and then onto the form of the Nils. The receptionist did not fail to notice how Dom allowed himself to wallow in his lust. One clear thought leapt to her mind, *Dirty beast! Is there no end to your depravity?*

Before she could conjure more notions of her disgust for the man, Dom regained mastery of himself and strode past the receptionist, and then through a set of richly carved wooden doors. Since his ascent to the High Daemon's chair, Dom gave no thought to his slave's reaction to his passing amusements. To be sure, he did not hesitate to use sex as a terrible bewitchment of others for since his initiation into to the Coven, Dom had learned the delights of the flesh as a means of power.

Once inside his office, he perfunctorily glanced at the paintings, sculptures and other pieces of rare and very fine art, which decorated his spacious office. Rich leather chairs faced a large desk of aged teak that set in front of wide windows. A well appointed bar and book shelves lined one of the walls. All these despotic trappings silently bespoke the central message Dom wished to convey, *Be wary all ye who carelessly enter for great and terrible is my occupant's power.*

With any thought of his serfs neatly tucked away, he easily moved toward his desk. As he moved, Dom nonchalantly took off his coat, hat, and gloves. These outer vestiges of prestige he carelessly placed on the back of one of the chairs. Like a monarch placing himself on his throne, he majestically lowered himself behind the desk in a plush, leather chair. The day's issue of the *Bourse Ledger* lay neatly on his desk. He lazily turned on his computer and began his work as all thoughts of the receptionist washed out of his mind. Dom was in high spirits that morning and thought to himself. *What such fun!*

This morning, the old guard presented Dom the opportunity to practice his second great talent, terror. In the Coven, Dom had also mastered the application of fear. He exclaimed aloud to empty furniture, "First up, I fire that slouch of a guard! How dare he stand in my way? Next thing, get the old man to buy off on DENVER. And then, the best for last, dinner with Lis-Yan and our Master."

With a few deft strokes on the keys, he completed the act. Twenty minutes later the guard found himself sacked. In those days of the Great Collapse, work of any kind was scarce. Having lost his job of thirty years and with no hope of finding another, the veteran and former guard made his decision. No longer able to provide for the love of his life, the old man did not go home nor stop off at Klingers. In the midst of the swirling snow that stampeded through the city that morning, he stepped off the curb and directly in front of a speeding tram. His death was instant, and ruled an accident. This small blessing allowed the Legionnaire's Assurance Fund to pay his widow the Troy Sterling required to maintain her in the small cottage that lay in the rural outskirts of Iskago.

In the middle of Dom's musings, the receptionist had silently entered his office. Saying nothing, she carefully placed a cup of hot coffee on a small coaster near The Great Man, and then picked up his discarded garments and hung them in a small side closet. Without notice from the rising power within STERNZCO, she silently returned to the reception area and closed the doors behind her.

It had not been the first time she had found Dom busily ruining someone's life. However, she had learned early on with Him not to comment nor inquire. After she returned to her desk, she sat demurely at her designated work space, attending to the menial tasks that filled her days within The Tower. On many occasions, as she sat in the box Dom had decreed for her, she reflected how both men and women were attracted to him. None could say if it was due to the perfection of Dom's athletic form or to the supreme confidence that seemed to exude from the man. Perhaps it was both.

She herself had been more than eager to couple with him, and this knowledge seemed to grate most insidiously on her soul. For when she first came to STERNZCO, the combination of her intelligence and business acumen, as well as stunning beauty landed her a position working for CEO Bolton Masters. She eagerly connived with Dom in the old CEO's demise, but was completely crushed when Dom refused to forward his recommendation for the oft-promised promotion and substantial pay raise it would have entailed. What had begun as pride and ambition became survival during the Great Collapse. Her one focus that now numbed her soul and memories of those times she had submitted herself to Dom's lust for, *What?* She thought.

Dom did not easily let go of his victims once he was finished toying with them. This was especially true for those such as the receptionist who were particularly talented and useful to his schemes. As in the Coven, he had quickly moved far up the power hierarchy of The Tower, and had easily dissuaded the other executives from taking her on, keeping her firmly in his grasp. In exchange for the job she so desperately needed, she had resigned herself to Dom, and now was His property, His alone. He had decided this doom for her, and to this, she resigned herself.

She had a paying job with credits enough to get by on. She did not consider, nor comment, nor inquire as to what He did with or to anyone anymore. Even the sickening sight of Dom so brazenly craving for the broken down and drunken Nils did not give her power to speak. That evening after work she found solace in the fact Dom had not found fault with her that day. She could still pay. For one more day the magistrates had not come to force her nor Bolton's child out of the one-room flat they shared with five others, and onto the frozen streets.

Nils was also one of Dom's many possessions though not a thrall. Nevertheless, as the receptionist, he had long ceased giving umbrage to the CEO's Executive Vice President. When he reached the far end of the long hallway, Nils entered a narrow office. Between the battered gray metal shelves that lined its plain walls, Nils hung his shoddy outer garments on a nail that served as a hook. He then wove himself through an obstacle course made of piles of boxes, crates, and data disks that reached near the ceiling and filled most of the space. He made his way through the closeted maze to a tiny metal desk covered with stacks of files that framed an ancient computer and key board.

Once at the small desk, he folded himself into a plain chair behind his workspace and retrieved a bottle of vodka from deep within one of its drawers. After spilling some of the liquor into a plain coffee cup, he took a long swallow. This action temporarily pushed the unremitting vision of Seti Four to the compartment in his mind that allowed him to focus on his work. He then began to scan the labels of one data disk after another until he found the one marked DENVER. He placed it on top of the mess on his tiny desk.

He then removed it from its cover and inserted it into the computer. Once its contents began to display on the monitor, he began to read the data disk's memorandums, charts and graphs. Each described the terra-forming project upon which the current CEO had designated as the sole grand strategy to pull STERNZCO, and perhaps the rest of the Republic, out of the Great Collapse.

Even in his advanced besotted state, Nils was thankful he was a superior analyst. Hunched over the STERNZCO business of the day, and like the receptionist, he was also grateful of the wages he earned at STERNZCO. For he recalled how after leaving the Legion Marines, Fredric Sternz had found him sitting in a pile of garbage and his own excrement in the alley behind Klingers.

Nils had picked the worst time to leave the Legions, right as the Bourse Houses had all failed, Republican Troy-Sterling had become near worthless, and the Great Collapse begun in full swing. That morning he had had a lead on a job at the old country club where he had once worked as a boy. It was not much, but it would provide room and board, and if he hoarded it carefully, enough Troy Sterling for the pills he needed to drown the demon that haunted his sleep. However, when he arrived, the manager took one whiff of the stench of him, and that was that.

Nils ended up in lying in the trash behind Klingers. He resolved himself to existing between stints of begging handouts, and soup at the Salvation Refuge. On those days when he managed to be semi-sober, he pushed a broom at Klingers. As he lay sprawled out amidst the sewage and in a most inebriated state, Fredric Sternz appeared above him. Silhouetted in the gleaming sun through Nils' dirty spectacles, a hand reached out from a silk suit. When Nils took it, things changed. Soon he found himself in the small apartment and the first hot bath and shave he had had in months. With Ms. Beebleton's ceaseless snoopy nose closely examining the delivery of food, and suits, ties, shoes and coats came all with a terse note inscribed, "*In lieu of wages to be earned, F.S.*"

In the beginning grim days of the Great Collapse, the firm under Fredric Sternz was a rare place of hope, joy, and light in the Republic. The Tower's denizens knew of the great suffering that transpired outside of its walls, indeed how could they not when the despair of the millions of homeless and starving was everywhere to see. Yet within The Tower, Nils came to the firm knowing no one, not even his benefactor, nor nothing of business.

He began his career in the parking garage, pushing a sweep broom across its oily floors and cleaning out the trash bins. Later, he received his first promotion, moving up to the basement post room. There he sorted and then delivered the various packages and items throughout The Tower. In addition to quickly mastering these menial tasks, he also learned the function of every department and division, as well as getting to know the persons in charge at STERNZCO.

He chatted about any subject with just about everyone who worked in The Tower. He came to know them all the clerks, janitors and maintenance men, the young girls in accounting, the toughs who worked security, the Vice Presidents and their talented Executive Directors waiting their turn for a go at the brass ring. Soon, he could describe STERNZCO's expected revenue, expenses, and profits, marketing and sales strategies, investments, mergers, and acquisitions. He also had intimate knowledge of who was sleeping with whom, and who was on the way up the corporate ladder or out the door. In short, within a few years, the only person who knew more about STERNZCO than Nils was Bolton Masters, the CEO himself.

Most of all, he was able to function on his own, and sleep long and sound without fear of the nightmare that had haunted him for so long. He got off the booze and pills. He even began to eat decently. Once again, he visited the gym on a regular basis for some much-needed exercise at the ancient form of swordplay Gunnery Sergeant O'Connor had taught him so many years ago.

He was 36 when he left the Legions a broken man. When he hit his early forties, he had been clean for so long he had forgotten what it was like to be haunted or stoned. He had been moved up to an Executive Director's job under Fredric Sternz, and based on a long record of outstanding work was eagerly anticipating a move as a Vice President of one of STERNZCO's many subsidiaries.

Upon the day, CEO Bolton Masters brought Dom onboard and the pervasive sense of hope that permeated the firm began to dim, and then darken. Fredric Sternz moved to another assignment at the blossoming Mars operations. Surprisingly and without explanation, Dom took the Directorship Nils had been aiming for. This, in itself, did not bother Nils; there were plenty of other opportunities in The Tower for him. Soon though, in place of superlative comments, Dom seemed to find constant errors in Nils' work. Daily, Dom excelled in pointing out Nils' smallest failures to his superiors and colleagues in public venues; always emphasizing that only through his personal attention to detail and timely intervention had Dom saved the firm from Nils' evident incompetence.

For the rest of the firm, it was as if Nils had ceased to exist. Whatever confidence and congenial words the other managers and staff had once shared quickly dissipated as the rising sun burns off fog. Rumor had it Nils was not moving up in The Tower, but was on the short list for sacking. Things deteriorated for Nils when Dom became Executive Vice President to the Chief Operating Officer. Dom, who possessed the keen ability to spot faculty and aptness, early on recognized Nil's talent and had him moved into the closet at the end of the hall. Dom was clearly the man of the hour within STERNZCO, mysteriously and quite rapidly replacing the firm's heir apparent, Fredric Sternz. Under the watchful eyes of the red-blond receptionist, the inner darkness fell again on Nils.

The small insults and injuries to his reputation Nils could easily endure. He had suffered far worse. Then one evening as he slept and from deep within Nils' soul, the demon of Seti Four returned with a wicked vengeance from its long hiatus. Within the United Republic Service Ship (U.R.S.S) *Sergeant York,* Gunny O'Connor was standing close by an infirmary bed, firmly holding his Captain's unhurt left hand, saying something Nils could not hear.

Nils, standing next to the grizzled veteran, turned his gaze from the badly wounded Marine and to the old non-com. In a white-hot blinding flash, Gunny O'Connor disappeared. As many times before, at this point Nils was held firm in the demon's grasp; feeling a blackened claw digging deeply into his left hand. He cried out and struggled to free himself, yet the more he tried to pull himself away from the ghoulish form, the deeper the claw dug into Nils' flesh. As he wrestled with the hideous form that firmly held him, the weaker Nils became. Even his screams for help began to fade away as the fiend drew Nils toward the hideous form of its burnt and broken visage. In the nightmare, Nils gathered the remainder of his Legionnaire's strength and managed one last defiant battle cry. As it had been when he first found himself conscious in the *Sergeant York,* Nils awoke from the nightmare in a soaking sweat.

That night Nils once again began to rely on alcohol to stifle the demon. He had half awakened still in the nightmare. With himself and Gunny O'Connor silently watching together, one of the Fleet Surgeons laid his hand on the Captain's heavily bandaged right arm and said, "I was able to fix the broken bones in his legs and this arm, and with a snip and cut here and there, take care of most everything else."

Then pointing to the Captain's heavily bandaged face the Surgeon said, "These wounds will take some time to heal."

In the haze of the wicked hours between midnight and dawn, Nils lay in his bed; the memory of Seti Four now began to play itself over and over before his now waking eyes. Attempting to fight the demon, yet always failing, thrashing his sweat soaked covers away from himself, Nils got up from his drenched bed, hurriedly dressed himself and found his way to an all-night store and bought three bottles of vodka. He was well into the second one when he returned to his apartment. The next day he woke up after two in the afternoon, two empty vodka bottles lying at his side. Nearly everyday from then on Nils managed to keep Seti Four tucked deep away in a drunken fog. He barely cleaned himself or ate. When his money began to run out, Nils took what he could for his fine clothes and other things.

Fed up with Nils' lack of grooming, basic attention to hygiene, and the ripe stench of booze that emanated from his worn clothing, Dom requested Nils' dismissal through the Directorate of Personnel. After two weeks had passed and still finding the old drunk at the tiny desk at the end of the hall, Dom checked with his sources in personnel. It seemed a note had come from the Office of the CEO regarding the matter. Dom read the tealeaves, and determined Fredric Sternz still had some power to hang onto the sodden tramp.

Dom conceded the minor defeat and kept Nils on. With the eventual rise of Fredric Sternz to CEO, and unable to dispose of Nils, Dom took great joy from the fact he had managed to restrain the drunk in the small room down the hall. For Dom eagerly applied Nils' superior business skills to whatever tasks were required. Yet Dom always took credit for all of the success, and ever laid the blame for the smallest setbacks upon Nils. With Dom's ever-watchful receptionist monitoring the elevators, Nils was close enough to be under Dom's constant control and yet far enough away to not be an obvious embarrassment to STERNZCO's rising star.

It had become mid-day and Nils stopped typing and looked up at the wall clock displaying 12:00. He returned the now nearly empty bottle of vodka to its place in the desk drawer. He pushed his chair away from the computer and slowly unwound himself from behind the tiny desk. He stood, stretched his back, and retrieved a small brown bag from one of his coat pockets, proclaiming to himself, *Strange it takes more to get me drunk these days. Lunch time.*

He silently left his cubicle and winding his way out of the maze of crates and folders, shuffled through the office corridors. The other employees worked silently. Neither they nor Nils greeted or talked to each other. Within STERNZCO, the only sounds emanating from the cubicles and small office spaces were those of the steady click-click of computer keys and the low hum of office machines. Indeed, the place reminded Nils of a very large library with its quiet patrons. Nils walked along in his solitude until he turned into the cafeteria. Even within the dining room, the STERNZCO ordinary people kept quiet. Nils found an empty corner table. There he sat alone and fished a plain sandwich out from the brown bag. Along with his co-workers, he ate his lunch with a steady, melancholy purpose.

Far at the opposite side of the cafeteria was a space roped off with thick cords of crimson suspended by a series of short and brightly gilded poles. This was for the exclusive use of the STERNZCO upper executives. Rarely did one such as Nils dare approach this area. He, like his colleagues, knew his place in the firm and kept it. He sat at his small table and observed as Dom sat within this corporate holy of holies at a large, opulent table loaded with several varieties of fine food and drink. A bevy of strikingly beautiful women and equally handsome men surrounded him. Snippets of their light discourse floated throughout the cafeteria and over Nils' table. Nils thought it sounded like the sharp chatter of birds in the park. Nils knew better than most the lethal venom Dom and his entourage dispensed with their words.

At the head of Dom's table, the wizened form of the CEO sat in quiet majesty. Deep wrinkles covered his now aged face. From beneath a thicket of grey hair and eyebrows, his piercing blue eyes curiously surveyed Dom and the collection of courtiers. On one side next to Frederic Sternz, and closest to Dom, sat an extremely lovely woman. On the other sat a young lad of about fourteen who closely resembled the tall taciturn man sitting beside him and opposite Dom.

The man was strikingly out of place. He had made an odd attempt to dress in executive style, wearing black trousers, blue shirt, a yellow stripped tie, grey jacket with thin red stripes, and a pair of highly shined black dress shoes. Nils instantly realized what he most certainly was, a veteran recently out of the Republican Legionnaire Marine uniform. He also recognized him as his former Regimental Commander of the Seventh Marines.

Colonel Randal Clark, now with your son visiting with the Big Guy, thought Nils.

In his hands, Fredric Sternz held the DENVER file.

"Ladies, gentlemen," The CEO began.

"These are the projections for our newest project. In no small measure, I thank Dom for the superior work he has done to date. And I must say, I agree with the assertion there may be great opportunity for profits."

Dom's sycophants, on cue, parroted the CEO. They flashed false smiles and slapped the table or the backs of their companions with the palms of their hands exclaiming, "Profits, profits!"

The young lad stood from his seat and attempted to mimic them, but after a quick scowl from his father, he quickly sat down. With a sharp, quick glance from Dom, the group fell silent and the CEO continued, "Profits? Yes, but not without some risk. Dom, do you have any ideas?"

With a smile of supreme confidence Dom enthusiastically stated, "There are some very intriguing possibilities."

He then scanned about the group, noted Nils and then settled his gaze on the lovely associate sitting near him. In his most polite voice, Dom commanded more than asked as he posed the question, "Ah, Beatrice, can you be a good lass and fetch Nils here?"

Beatrice was tall, and her fair complexion, deep blue eyes and honey-blond hair were some of the features that made her, in the patois of the time, a hottie. She had high cheekbones, full, firm breasts, a narrow waist, a well-formed posterior, and long, athletic legs. These attributes alone would have been enough to set Beatrice apart from her colleagues at the table. Nevertheless, these aspects, striking as they were, did not make her the envy of Dom's eyes. Beatrice was as superbly intelligent as she was strikingly beautiful. She was also more articulate and bolder than Dom's entourage.

Yes, for all of these things and more, Dom, passions for un-restrained power burnt his soul the more to possess her.

Dom had learned well the lessons of punishment and reward. To him, a person's fear or greed were but two roads to possession and enthrallment. For Dom, the meaning of power was control. Control of the physical aspect of the natural world was, in essence, a problem of engineering. Control of Troy-Sterling became a simple matter of mathematics and accounting. However, to control the sweetest prize of all, people of the influential sort, was the apex of his desires. Dom applied a seemingly abundance of money, alcohol, and his mastery of sexual techniques upon the elite of the Republic. If pleasure did not suffice to bring the wealthy, intellectual or political classes to heal, then there was pain. There was always pain.

Fredric Sternz' former receptionist had believed in her heart Dom loved her. Indeed, the now long buried Bolton Masters and red-blond receptionist were some of Dom's earliest conquests. These were nothing compared to his present desire. At the very core of his being, it was because Beatrice was the CEO's only living heir, niece, and second most powerful person within STERNZCO that Dom lusted for her. With Beatrice, he could control not only the Firm, but also eventually the Senate and the Republic.

Beatrice knew nothing of Dom's greater desires for her, but was well aware of his lust for her body, subtly inflaming him with flirtatious hints of yet un-realized passionate liaisons. In her later years, she said it was her pride and long experience in wrapping men around her fingers that led her foolish participation in Dom's power plays. Her uncle's memoirs certainly indicate a strong suspicion of something else. A thing more crooked and undesirable that had resided deep inside of her in her younger years put her on the path of perdition.

Smiling demurely at her uncle, Beatrice slightly nodded her head and gracefully stood up from the table. Before proceeding, she carefully scanned the cafeteria's other occupants. Upon sighting Nils, she sauntered toward him, ensuring her stroll had just the right amount of sashay in it to keep Dom's and all but the CEO's eyes clued to her backside. As she glided away, the CEO leaned over the now empty chair sitting next to Dom and whispered, "Still teaching my Beatrice, I see."

Dom softly replied, affecting the accent of an Ivy League don, "She is my most promising student."

The cafeteria was in hushed suspense when Beatrice reached Nils. Before she could speak, Dom loudly commanded, "Come over here. We are anxious to hear what you've found out."

Beatrice elegantly offered her hand to Nils. This small gesture, in itself, was the fodder of much of the gossip that twittered for many days among STERNZCO's rank and file. Noidz, Dom and the rest of the STERNZCO elite called them. The nerdy technicians and corporate underlings Dom and the other executives ordered about like robots. Beatrice often noticed, in spite of the disdain and abuse heaped on them, just how many of the Noidz seemed to be in an almost puppy-like state when responding to Dom. Not so with Nils, for in spite of his not so sober habits and the ability to genuflect like the rest of the Noidz, Nils, she knew from the first day she had met him, was altogether different.

Nils, looked up at Beatrice's outstretched hand, and leaving the remains of his sparse lunch, he stood up. He took her hand and walked with her to the end of Dom's table. As he did so, the wiggle of the increasing paunch that hung over his belt revealed him as one grown fat from a diet of booze and a lifestyle rather short on exercise. Seeing this and noticing a familiar bulge growing in his trousers, Dom wondered, *Beatrice, that is something to get excited about!*

When he arrived at the table, Nils quickly glanced at Dom, slightly tipped his head in a small gesture of respect toward the retired Marine, and then looked squarely into the CEO's grey eyes.

Nils reported, "Sir. As you may have noticed, there are some, um potential risks with the DENVER project."

Dom hurriedly interjected, "These risks are more in the nature of sequencing than the acquisition itself."

Nils continued, "Yes. They are in the current sequencing plan, rather than future operations."

The CEO asked slowly, "A synchronized approach? Just how long do you expect me keep the Bourse off my neck while all of this takes place? Mr....?"

Beatrice replied, "Sicharis. Nilsson Sicharis, sir."

The CEO sharply interjected, "Well, Mr. Sicharis. Dom makes it clear we need DENVER now. I do not want this thing to drag on until who knows when. What do you propose?"

Nils replied, "We need to make good use of every moment."

Dom slapped the table and chortled, "Need I remind anyone here of CAMP-CO's haste to acquire us? That led to an unmitigated disaster. They went down in flames."

Laconically, the CEO continued, "One hell of a choice. If we do not proceed apace, we face ruin. If not DENVER, then what else is there?"

Dom responded, "The Bourse financiers do not need our answer today. Send a small, select team off-site, perhaps to Raffertys on the lakeshore. Have them comb through the data and report the options they recommend."

The CEO slowly said, "So we wait a bit longer. Mr. Sicharis, you seem to suggest a more, um rapid response."

Colonel Clark had not returned Nils acknowledgement but now gently nudged his young son in the ribs as a sign to pay close attention. Nils nervously glanced over to his boss and read the desired response on Dom's face. Then he looked at his fingers and stammered, "I, ah yes. It would be better to wait."

The CEO sat for a moment and considered Nil's response. He then stood and perfunctorily stated to the group, "Time for the Bourse analysts' meeting. I do not want those sharks to get nervous and start sniffing our blood in the water. Dom, Beatrice, ladies and gentlemen, thank you."

Then turning to the Marine veteran who with his boy now stood, Fredric Sternz smiled as if to a brother and said, "My good friend and to your fine son, I regret we can not spend more time together today. Perhaps I'll see more of you when I am able to visit you in Jackson Hole?"

The veteran smiled and nodded. He then whispered into the CEO's ear, and extended his hand. After firmly shaking Fredric Sternz' hand, he left the cafeteria with his young son in tow, saying, "Come, Ran."

The CEO, Dom and the corporate courtiers soon walked out after the pair. As they left the cafeteria, the CEO hesitated, letting the others pass him by. Once Dom and his entourage were well down the corridor and out of earshot, the CEO looked at Beatrice who had remained behind at the table standing silently next to Nils. The old man motioned her to accompany him spoke softly, "Beatrice, a word please."

Beatrice, without answering, left the table and Nils behind. She strode rapidly to catch up with the CEO as he had turned and was now briskly walking away from the cafeteria and down a long hallway. He slightly slowed his pace to allow her to reach him. Once at his side, Beatrice picked up the rhythm of his steady pace. As she walked at his side toward the closed double doors of one of the many STERNZCO conference rooms, he said to her, "I want that DENVER team put together and out of here by 4 p.m. today."

She asked, "Dom in the lead?"

He firmly responded to his niece, "What did you expect? Dom's smart, aggressive, and clever enough to make it work."

She nearly hissed, as she whispered her response, "He is also very ambitious."

The CEO smiled and responded, "Niece, why do you fret over Dom? He is your teacher and mentor here, nothing more."

"He is..." Beatrice let the sentence die before finishing.

The CEO interrupted, "He is a very long way from your spot in the boardroom, which I can assure you of. You are also well beyond the age of me advising you upon the rashness of playing with someone under the bed sheets. Now for this team of his, put that Sicharis fellow on it as well."

She disgustingly answered, "That drunk? You saw how he folded back there. He's weak, indecisive and has no backbone, like the rest of the Noidz."

The CEO smiled gently and softly responded, "Perhaps he is, and perhaps he is not. Recall Beatrice, I do not lightly disregard the opinion of someone like Randal Clark."

Upon reaching the conference room, they stopped walking and Beatrice opened the door. She looked lovingly into her uncle's eyes and said, "By the way I'm not worried about my place. I'm worried about yours."

The CEO eyes crinkled in love at her as he silently nodded as they entered the conference room and greeted the assembled Bourse analysts with wide, confident smiles.

Raffertys is well known among the Republic's business elite. Its conference center and spacious workrooms full of the latest technology and finest furnishings, was the envy of the other hotels along the lakefront. Raffertys' management knew this and charged a high premium for the services they rendered to their guests. Despite the exorbitant cost, firms that could not clearly afford its price tag gladly paid anyway. Everyone vied to be seen in Raffertys, and talked about by his or her peers. Indeed, there was rumor the financial analysts had 'people' in the place to take note of who was doing and talking within the opulent confines of the swank hotel. Prior to going to Rafferty's, Nils had spent his last night in Iskago in a small back room at Klingers holding a tall glass partially filled with vodka.

He had ceased his drinking when the old man with the sharp blue eyes and silver-grey hair and eyebrows had come in and sat down before him. Fredrick Sternz spoke to Nils in the soft voice of authority that demanded Nil's attention.

"There was a time when you rendered Beatrice a great service. Do you recall it?" the STERNZCO CEO asked.

A flash of hidden pain crossed Nils' eyes, causing him to close his gaze into the twin cobalt wells that seemed to cleave Nils' soul. Eons seemed to pass as Nils recalled the history that resulted in his enlistment into the Legions. He had just reached age sixteen, and was still be-pimpled and clumsy. It had been a sweltering hot afternoon at the country club when Beatrice and Nils first met. It was near the end of the day and closing time as the sun lay low in the sky. Neatly dressed employees busily gathered up the dirty dishes, silver wear, glasses and silk napkins from the umbrella adorned tables on the sun decks. Others carried heavy golf bags burgeoning with drivers and irons to waiting hover-carts. Small parties of golfers gathered near the clubhouse and shared drinks and the small details of the last round. A tennis match had finished, the sweat gleaming on the players exposed skin. A last group of laughing swimmers left the pool, their barely clothed bodies' slick with water and suntan lotion as the pool boys and girls hurried over to dry the glowing skin with long Turkish bath towels.

He remembered the young, tow-headed girl of perhaps eleven years, Beatrice standing in front of the club's gazebo. She wore a large straw hat and a bright green sun suit, posing for a photographer. The camera flashed many times, and after the pictures taken, she wrapped herself in one of the large, sumptuous Turkish bath towels, got an ice cream from a nearby kiosk, and walked to a wide bench in front of a neatly trimmed hedge. Here, she sat alone slowly enjoying her ice cream. The bath towel covered her one-piece sun suit and her pre-pubescent, but still skinny hips. The sun flashed and glinted in her rough yellow hair.

As he awkwardly swept the cobbled walkway, his eye glasses would glide down to the end of his nose on the sheen of sweat as he hunched over to gather debris into a dustbin. With one hand, he unconsciously pushed the old-fashioned glasses up tightly against his face as while continuing his work with the other. The monotonous and robotic movements of his gangly form made her laugh. She flashed a tiny smile and he thought to himself, she must be thinking, *What a funny boy. How poor he must be to have to wear glasses?*

Her childish grin quickly faded as a small group of older boys skated furiously past Nils. Many bumped him and sneered as they carelessly passed. One lanky, long-boned, dirty-hair youth, the gang's rude leader, stopped suddenly in front of the young Beatrice. His companions, nearly running into and over each other, hastily stopped as well. Dirt and small pieces of sharp stone kicked up into her ice cream. Beatrice scolded the young ruffians, "Don't do that."

The lanky boy scoffed at the young girl, "Why not, skinny butt?"

Noticing the new game their leader had maliciously invented, the other boys chanted, "Hey skinny, skinny, skinny butt."

Beatrice, faced with this vile, verbal attack, sobbed out, "You're a beast!"

The lanky youth taunted with his retort, "What's the matter, cry baby?"

Then the lanky youth viciously grabbed the ice cream from her hand, threw it to the ground and jeered, "So? What you gonna do about it? Huh, miss skinny butt?"

Beatrice, having had enough of his bullying gathered her small tears, jumped up and with one of her small fists quickly struck the lanky youth in the nose. Bright red blood spurted out one of his nostrils. Shocked by the sudden attack, the lanky tough stumbled back from her attack and fell down, hissing, "I'll get you for that."

Nil's memory became hazy and raced beyond the next vile events, settling itself on the scene inside the grounds keeper's office. His father sat behind a bent and rusted metal desk covered in grease and thick dust. They were ensconced in an office crowded with buckets of unopened fertilizer, and an untold number of shovels, rakes, and hoes scattered on the bags of grass seed that filled and defined the place. His father reeked of alcohol, even though he had not had a drink since just before work that morning. He was a pale shriveled up prune of a man who had never wanted Nils. However, his Moorish mother insisted on keeping the brat. Now, here stood the snot in front him. Once again, the so-called son of his had found a way to make the old drunk's life harder than he thought it should be. He looked over Nils with blood-shot eyes and grunted, "God, I need a drink."

Nils stood in the small office, saying nothing as he waited for the bombast to explode. He silently inhaled the stench of the mix of sweat and booze that oozed out of his father. Then the old man acidly accused him, asking, "Didn't you think?"

Nils responded, "Sir, they were about to…"

Nils never finished the sentence as his father sharply cut him off shouting, "About to do what, exactly?"

Nils began again, "They were going to…"

Again, his father abruptly cut off Nils' reply, "Enough. You attacked one of the members' children. It is enough Mr. Avery will allow me stay on at reduced wages. Give me your keys. Get out. You're finished here."

Nils reached into one of the pockets of his faded and much patched blue jeans, took out a set of keys, and placed them on the desk in front of the old man. As he left the grimy office, his father stated, "Don't come back. And don't let me find you at the place either crying to your bitch momma."

With those, last words, the only man Nil's knew as father dismissed him from his life as he had done with his wife and so many people before. No regrets. No second thoughts. Nils turned away, walked out the door and disappeared in the night. It was the last time the man would ever see his son. Weeks later found Nils cold, dirty and hungry, standing in front of a painted storefront window. His gaze fixed on the picture of the young man in the dark blue of Legionnaire's dress uniform, Nils muttered, "Well, It beats starving."

Nils resolutely pushed open the door, and walked up to the middle-aged Legionnaire sergeant stoically drinking coffee. Nils put out his right hand and introduced himself, saying, "Nilsson Sicharis."

The recruiter put his coffee down, stood from his desk, shook Nils' hand, and replied, "Welcome to the Marines."

The CEO made a slight cough that broke Nils' reflections, and now with eyes wide open, Nils set the unfinished booze on the small table and said, "Yes, I remember it…all too well.

A tear trickled down the CEO's cheek, and his voice trembled, "Then I humbly seek of you a great and terrible boon. Will you once again place yourself between her and the Coven? Before you answer, carefully consider your reply as regardless of what may occur there shall be consequences. I fear more terrible than those of your past."

The demon began to rise, but something else in Nils, perhaps the memory of the old gunny came forward and he stamped it out of his thoughts. Without hesitation, Nils reached out, grasped the CEOs right hand and said, "Upon my word."

Now Nils silently sat in a corner in the video teleconference room while the presentation wound its course. Dom, Beatrice and the remainder of the team sat around a table facing a large video screen. A microphone stood in front of each person. The CEO's image filled the large screen to their front. Various reports, charts and graphs flickered on and off as he and Dom had spoken over the last hour. As the meeting progressed, Nils recalled his earlier life in the legion when he was SOMEBODY and thought to himself, *So after Seti Four, here I am.*

The cartoon show, as Nils called it, continued as Dom reported to the CEO, "As you can see, this particular sequencing can add 28 percent net revenue to the acquisition by the end of the second quarter. At fiscal year end, we project a 33 percent increase in net."

The CEO smiled broadly and said, "Good job, Dom, team. Some of these cost projections still concern me."

Dom replied, "We still have the option to accelerate the personnel reductions."

The CEO brusquely cut off Dom, "Keep a tight grip on any more of those. Legal says the current lawsuits will be finished by next week. We do not need another one now. Now to the point, Dom, I will need a strong hand on the wheel as we move ahead. Is there any reason why your name should not go up to the Senior Vice President nominating committee in charge of our new subsidiary?"

Dom's eyes gleamed, as he replied, "None, sir."

"Good. Keep at it, team."

The screen abruptly went blank, and all but Dom and Beatrice filled out of the conference room.

Nils did not enjoy any of the complimentary gifts Raffertys lavished on their premium guests. He was, after all, a Noidz. His workspace, although well equipped, was similar to that of his at The Tower, only smaller. A cramped windowless corner near the Tele-conference room was the realm where he had spent his days working the DENVER project. After the Tele-conference, he now sat hunched over at the workstation, his attention fixed on the data displayed on the computer screen before him. Dom burst into the tiny space. His hands trembled at his sides and his face was in a vile grimace of wild rage as he shouted and spat, "You idiot! The old man is all over my ass on these cost estimates!"

Nils stopped his work, sat up, faced Dom and calmly replied, "Wasn't he pleased with the revenue projections. I thought my notes on the sequencing would have been sufficient."

Dom fumed, "You thought. He is not interested in your thoughts of project management. He wants results. That is what he is going to get. I want these costs taken care of. Do not force me to do your job. Understand?"

Nils continued in the same calm tone, "Yes."

Dom's sentences came out in a rapid staccato as he said, "Those bozos at corporate may have stuck me with you. Never mind. Get the revived estimates for my personal review tonight!"

Nils again calmly replied, "Yes."

Dom commanded, "Yes what?"

In the professional tone of an old soldier, Nils responded, "Yes, sir."

Dom turned to take Beatrice's arm. As they began to leave, he sarcastically said, "Remember, old boy, no one else can see these. They are for my personal review alone."

It was now past 9 pm, a good six hours since Dom had given his orders. In spite of the late hour and the vision of Seti Four again perched at the fore front of his mind, Nils walked past the darkened cubicles within the conference center's executive office suite. He carefully carried a file in his hands as he moved toward a door framed in the pale glimmer of incandescent light. Dom demanded strict adherence to his rules. Noidz were to bring in the work, set it before him, and stand in silence waiting upon the master as he meticulously completed his review. Dom's standing orders were, "Don't wait until later." If you think it's done, then get it to me."

Nils did not hesitate nor knock on the door as he turned the handle and walked in. Startled by the sight of the intertwined nude forms of Dom and Beatrice thrusting together on Dom's desktop, Nils quickly turned his face and said, "Here is the...Oh... Excuse me. Miss Beatrice?"

Beatrice's face flashed red shame, as she quickly rolled out from under Dom. She hit the floor and hurriedly covered her naked breasts and pubis with her arms and hands, and sprinted to a corner of the office. There she found her crumpled dress, knelt down and pulled it over herself.

Dom rose from the desktop, turned and glassy eyed, faced Beatrice. He took a long pull from a nearby champagne bottle. The fine bubbly dripped from his lips, and he pushed his hips forward and slurred, "Don't you want anymore of this?"

Dom's brazen actions stupefied Beatrice, and she was unable to accept Nils finding her with Dom. After what seemed to be an eternity, she gained control of her muscles and stumbled out of the office. Tears ran down her face, and her head shook as she passed Nils. She sobbed a great, "Not again, not this way."

Dom watched her finely shaped rump disappear, and shouted, "Get out, you idiot!"

Nils simply turned from the abhorrent scene. As he left the office, Nils whispered, "Indeed."

Within the hour, downstairs a crowd of people pressed against Raffertys' reception desk. The desk clerk spoke animatedly into a telephone, "Yes, we heard a gun shot. No, only one shot. Our staff has secured the area. Yes, we'll stand by until you get here."

The desk clerk hung up the telephone and faced the anxious crowd. Slowly and meticulously clearing his throat, he said, "The gendarme will be here shortly. Now, please ladies and gentlemen, I know you wish to return to your rooms. The bar and restaurant shall remain open at our expense. Please wait in one of them until this dreadful affair is over."

When he finished, the crowd slowly dispersed from the reception desk. Nils had come out from the bar still holding the latest of the many tall vodkas neat in is hand. He swallowed it desolately and watched as the Med-Techs pushed a gurney holding an unconscious Beatrice toward the door. A police detective asked in his best dry monotone, "Anyone in the hotel know who she is?"

Nils sadly offered, "I do. I know her."

The detective looked at Nils with a set of milky eyes and directed in a short staccato of words, "Then you best come with me."

Nils replied, "Of course."

Later that evening, at the end of a dimly lit hospital hallway, Nils held an ancient portable telephone to his head and reported, "They have done all that they can. The best surgeons at hand have attended to her. You will need to come here for her. Yes sir, I understand."

Nils, having made his report to the CEO, closed up the portable phone and placed it in his jacket pocket. He walked down the hallway and looked through the glass widow that separated him from Beatrice lying on a hospital bed. Tubes and wires seemed to sprout from her still unconscious yet breathing form. Hot tears ran down his face as he sobbed, "I'm so, so sorry."

While Nils was calling Beatrice's uncle that evening, Dam sat in a small, smoke-filled bar. He was not in Raffertys. In fact, it was in the part of the city that few ventured into unless on the type of business most familiar to thugs, mercenaries, and whores. At the rear of the bar, safely tucked away from prying eyes, Dom sat in the corner of a dark booth. Smoke from the long, thick cigar he held by his gleaming teeth wafted around his face, partially hiding his features. A sensuous, raven-haired beauty sat opposite him. She was the Archana, Lady Lis-Yan. Her pale, white face and full, burgundy lips highlighted the striking features of her blue eyes and high cheekbones.

Her words were in the sharp and low guttural accent of the Faerevolder. They came out like churning gravel in a metal can as she said, "Tak robatan horsh, Dominare." (A job well-done Dominare.)

In the same harsh language, Dom replied, "Nitchan dol-an. Firme ne ryuk veran. Evo durako." (It was nothing. The firm will be in our hands. The old man is a fool.)

The Lady Lis-Yan asked, "Ah, schta-dan Beatrice?" (What of Beatrice?)

Dom evilly smiled and said, "Eva, ne difkul-an." (She is no problem.)

The Archana looked long into Dom's face and locking his eyes with hers asked, "Dominare, gotov robot veervhre?" (Dom, are you ready for your next task?)

Dom replied smugly, "Ya-dah, kon-ech." (Yes, of course.)

In another part of town at a different bar sat Nils. It was now past 12 am and he sat in a familiar situation, drunk and alone. At the bartender's rough urging, Nils fished some money from his trousers, paid for his latest drink and stumbled out into the street. He pulled his raincoat closer over himself as the evening clouds covered a full moon. The night sky darkened and it began to rain. Nils got into a cab and shakily handed the cab driver a card from Raffertys hotel. As the cab traveled through the dark and wet streets, the glare of oncoming cars and streetlights danced and flickered through the rain-splattered windows in front of Nils' half-closed and intoxicated eyes. Upon arrival at Raffertys, Nils paid the cabby, shakily exited the taxi, and staggered into the hotel lobby.

Upstairs, in the hotel's executive suite hallway, Dom and Lady Lis-Yan entered his rooms. They slowly stripped off their clothes, embraced, and walked confidently hand-in-hand toward the room's large window. The shades and blinds had been pulled aside, revealing the rain soaked skies. They both bowed deeply to the figure with gleaming red eyes that stood in a dark corner.

A few minutes later, Nils stood in front of his room's door. His fellow Noidz believed Nils to have scored some major coup to be staying in one of the plush executive suites on the penthouse level. Nils felt it a curse, as Dom had often summoned him from the adjoining suite at odd hours to tend to some menial task related to DENVER. Nils clumsily worked the plastic key card into the lock, opened the door and staggered inside the room. The door closed silently behind him.

Nils did not register the firm click of its lock. Instead, he gazed at his disheveled and rancid reflection in a mirror. Snorting, he removed the data disk marked "C O N F I D E N T I A L Mr. Avery's EYES ONLY" from his coat and threw it on the night stand next to the bed. He then stripped off his clothes and fell haphazardly onto the top of the bed's covers. Nils passed out as he slurred, "God, I'm a mess."

Later, a constant chanting emanated from the adjoining room, waking Nils. Nils rolled over on his bed and before again passing out mumbled, "What is Dom up to now? Lucky bastard is probably screwing some hard bodies. Why can't I be like him?"

Outside of Raffertys, an intense storm raged. Nils lay asleep; his tortured visions of Seti Four faded into a new nightmare with visions of a great evil creature resembling a half-man/half-bird creature walking up-right in the dark. It wielded sharp cruel claws with a face full of shark's teeth. Blood dripped from its rancid maw and its brilliant red eyes pierced the utter darkness surrounding its vile form.

As Nils' new nightmare continued, the chanting flowed stronger from Dom's room interspersed with the great booms of thunder and flashes of crackling red lightning from the storm. The chanting became louder and cacophonous as the storm grew in its intensity. Nils now dreamt of a young woman, like in face and form to Beatrice, yet altogether different and younger. The dark creature extended its claws and bared its fangs at the maiden as she screamed. A sharp crack of lightning and a cannon boom of thunder outside Nil's window suddenly awoke him. Nils jolted upright, his face streaming sweat.

He got off the bed in a daze, stumbled into the bathroom, and urinated. The thunder and lightning continued to duel at his window as Nils returned to the bed. A sudden flash illuminated the night sky. He looked out the window. Huge lighting bolts of white and red danced and cracked across the night sky. His eyes widened as one great lightning bolt fiercely struck the hotel, blasting a huge smoking hole into the side of what had been Dom's rooms next door. The violet burst knocked Nils to his back and shattered the adjoining door to Dom's suite. He could still hear Gunny O'Conner's Gallic brogue in his mind, saying, *Save who you can, or bring their bodies home. Tey'd do it fer you."*

A lesson drilled into Nils when he was just six months in the Legion and under a Gunny's firm training. Stumbling to his feet, Nils made his way to where he believed Dom must now be in need of aid. For although he despised the man, the years of his Legionnaires' training now emerged and drove him past all personal concern to attempt to save Dom.

Once in Dom's room Nils noted the room's windows and walls had disappeared. Acrid blue smoke mixed with cold rain filled the place, now blasted open to the storm's fury. Nils stopped, frozen by the sight in front of his eyes. Yes, Nils knew he was drunk, but no amount of rotgut liquor could explain what he was witnessing. Three people, all nude, had simply walked slowly thorough the thick, blue cloud that had filled Dom's room, and stepped out into the empty sky. First had gone a tall, dark haired beauty that disappeared, and then the figure of a large man with what appeared to be red eyes followed her to the opening, and last Dom.

Before they left Nils shouted, "Don't!"

Before exiting, the large man-shaped figure turned and sharply asked Dom, "Who is that?"

With a mix of disgust and joy on his face, Dom replied, "No one of consequence Master. He is a future play-toy with whom I shall deal with immediately upon my return."

As Dom and his companion similarly followed the dark haired woman into the sky the thought flashed through Nils mind, *Was that a man with Dom?*

The blue cloud slowly began to dissipate from Dom's room; allowing harsh, cold rain to pelt Nils' naked body. Still drunk, he stumbled forward into the blue cloud and dizzily leaned forward to put his hands where the room's walls and window should have been. He watched in silent horror as his arms, torso, and then legs tumbled out of the hotel room and into the trail of the blue cloud. As he tumbled downward, the hotel walls disappeared. Before everything went black, he thought, *How odd.*

THE GREAT AERKAN DESERT

Nils sat among his contubern, the small group of ten Marines all positioned on their rears with knees crossed, listening and watching most attentively as Gunny O'Connor described and demonstrated the basic motions of the ancient sword fighting technique. With a well-honed and short sword in his left hand, the old Non-Comm intoned, "One!" And he snapped the sword in a flash from his side, across his body and above his forehead. The gleaming blade now extended horizontally from his outstretched arm across a short distance from the Gunny's short gray hair, firmly set with the blade side outwards and the Non-Comm's piercing blue eyes boring into his student's rapt faces from beneath the sword's fuller and back.

"This protects the head and shoulders from the downward thrust. Remember it well."

"Two and Three!" He barked and he turned the sword into a vertical position with the blade facing outwards, and flashed the razor from his right to left. ""This protects the face."

And so it went as he demonstrated the positions to protect the torso and legs. Then he barked, "On your feet!"

As one, Nils and his companions leapt up. They grasped their wasters, the short wooden practice swords issued to the tioviates-the novice recruits now a few short weeks from their final mustering as privates to their respective Legions. They followed the grizzled veteran in unison, mirroring Gunny

O'Connor's movements; the old Non-Comm shouting out corrections to each of their tiniest mistakes in form, timing and position.

Later, during the individual instruction Nils found himself in front of the Gunny's flashing spatha; receiving many small pinpricks from its sharp point, and thumps from its flats. It seemed as if he had been at the sword drill for hours. His arms ached, his breath came in rapid, small gasps of hot air, and the sweat poured down his face in rivers. Finally, with the wooden sword trembling in his exhausted grip, Nils sank to his knees.

"Get up! The Gunny perfunctorily ordered.

Nils gasped out, "Sir, I cannot."

Again he commanded, "Get up! Else believe me upon my word I'll run you through."

With no other word or warning, the Gunny ran toward Nils, his sword pointed straight at the young Marine's chest.

Nils' tired muscles somehow understood that without action, their owner would soon be dead. This information shot through his body, and Nils found himself on his feet, his sword's hilt firmly struck against the brass quillian of the Gunny's weapon.

"That's the ticket." The old Non-Com growled.

Nils breathed out, "I don't believe it."

The Gunny grinned a sly smile. He then said, "Ya gotta have faith."

Then with his free hand, the old vet with short silver hair knocked Nils into unconsciousness.

It was sunrise on the Great Aerkan Desert. Nils lay nude, facedown, as the sun beat restlessly on his bare backside. Fine grains of sand blew softly over his arms and legs while a curious beetle cautiously extended one of its hoary legs into Nils' mouth. He slowly opened his eyes from the dream of his early days in the Legions, sat up and dropped his head into his hands. Having lost its perch on Nils' check, the beetle scurried down his chin, dropped off and hurriedly buried itself in the sand. Nils moaned, "Oh, my head. Good God, why did I drink so much? It's hot, must be late in the day. Late, I am late. Aw crap, Dom is going to have my backside over that report!"

Nils continued to complain to himself as he stumbled up and with wobbly legs and quivering arms, reached out into the clear morning air. Quickly losing his balance, he fell heavily onto his knees and drove his hands into the hot sand. After catching his breath, and waiting for the world to stop spinning, Nils wobbled shakily back to his feet. His eyes opened wide in shock and fear as he surveyed the harsh, blinding landscape. Not for the first time during his sojourn in the Faerevold did Nils ask, "What is this place?"

As he stood on the hot sandy desert floor, thunder sounded in the near distance, threatening rainfall. Of its own accord, a lone tear traced its way from his eye and along his face as he stated the obvious to the bright expanse before him, "This is just great. I'm naked. I'll be wet. And, I am definitely not in my hotel room."

Lightning cracked from above his head as the skies above him opened, and a torrent of rain mixed with hail the size of hand grenades began to pelt Nils. The lighting struck repeatedly very near to Nils. It smashed into the sand, gashing huge, smoldering rents in the desert floor and throwing dirt and debris in all directions like shrapnel. No former Marine Legionnaire's training or habits came to his aid, and fear seized Nils as he began to run from place to place on the barren sand to avoid the lighting that seemed to be actively seeking him out for destruction. After the events of Seti Four, Nils had long ceased to be the dauntless Marine Legionnaire Captain. Indeed, had it not been for influence of the Regimental Deputy Commander, Major Ran Clark, Nils would have faced court martial. Instead, to save face, the Marine High Command gave Nils a medal for valor and promoted him.

On the floor of the Great Aerkan Desert and in the midst of dodging the fierce lighting bolts, Nils ran about in blind panic in wild circles for his life. In this state, he cried out for help. His desperate cries died amidst the lightning, thunder, hail and rain as he sobbed out over and over, "Help! Anyone, help! Anyone at all!"

Nils fell to his knees and rolled into a fetal position. In his moment of need, he recalled fragments of an inscription above his grandmother's kitchen stove. She had lived on one of the more distant systems where the ancient sect had survived. As he felt the nearing embrace of his own dying, he stammered, "Our father…heaven… hollowed name…will not fear, fear…evil."

A great flash of lightning rent the darkened sky. As the thunder crashed and boomed, Nils whispered, "Help…me."

Again, Nils succumbed to unconsciousness, and laid face down on the dessert's sandy ground. After a time, the devastating lightning with the storm's harsh rain and hail stopped, and the storm clouds drifted far away into the sky. The twin suns of Faerevold rose and resumed their harsh and relentless command of the Aerkan Desert.

The fear-induced adrenaline had run its course, and Nils was left exhausted in the once again blazing heat. He realized he was alive and regained control of himself. Drained from the mad rush of the hormone coursing through his system he slowly surveyed the desert's horizon in a 360-degree arc. He then desolately watched as the small rivulets of new rainwater ran down the cracks and crevasses of the desert floor. Nils murmured, "I never did like sitting around waiting. Here is the choice. I stay here. Where and whatever here is, and, I will likely die. I walk out in which direction towards what or where to, and I'll likely die. Since either way, I'm dead. Downhill is good."

Finding a small bit of faith within him and with the first order of business resolved, Nils put his back to the rising suns and began to walk along the moist but still cracked desert floor. He followed the rivulets as they flowed into creeks, then the creeks, as they became a stream. Without warning, the stream disappeared into one of the many crevasses in the stream's rocky bed. With no other good options before him, Nils continued along the now dry stream bed.

In this way, he traveled untold days across the Aerkan Desert, resting at night under a sky packed with foreign stars and strange three sister moons. During the day, the unforgiving suns, sand and wind scarred his face with raw blisters and open sores. A trail of blood followed his bleeding feet. At the last, utterly spent, Nils struggled forward, fell, forced himself up and toddled a few small steps ahead. Finally, nearly dead he collapsed near a small rock outcropping.

He lay face down on the desert floor and dreamt of himself floating on his back upon a river. The warm water tenderly caressed him in its embrace as it carried him gently along. He floated along green banks filled with festival tents. Each one brightly colored and covered in endless tables filled to infinity with drink and food. Gunny O'Connor stood amongst the tents and food, the present wry smile etched on his face. Nils walked with the Gunny among the fest tents, and as he inhaled many aromas, he could not help but salivate. Yet, when he began to sense the taste of the rich food, Gunny O'Connor's face faded and shifted to the blurry form of a kindly, round woman saying something he could not hear. As he struggled to listen and understand the woman, the rough curse of a course tongue jarred his dream state and something cold and very wet hit his face.

Nils woke within the Faerevolder caravan. His tongue eagerly licked at the water streaming over his sun-cracked face. He easily recognized the form of Garm as familiar to the tough veterans in the Legions. Garm was a large, ebony skinned, well-muscled man who rudely pushed his bearded and scared face into Nil's view. His rich black, braided hair specked with gray. His eyes were hard and dark. He wore brightly burnished armor. A sword and stout ax hung from his belted waist. Garm's harsh, guttural voice sounded to Nils like gravel mixed with mud as he spoke, "Kan er no lebtan vomaner? Yada, er komt lebt. Na vasseer er komt lebt." (Woman, does he not live? Yes, the water makes him alive.)

An old woman with gray hair, deep blue eyes, and with the face of grandmotherly kindness silently offered Nils more water. A young, silver blond maiden with sparkling blue eyes approached. Nils was struck by Ka-Tayana's resemblance to Beatrice. In spite of the near platinum color of her hair, Ka-Tayana could have been easily mistaken as the identical twin to Beatrice in her early youth. In a flash of recognition, Nils placed her as the maiden of his latest nightmares. Feeling revived, Nils attempted to raise himself only to find that his legs and arms were tightly bound to the rough-hewn timbers of a wagon bed. Ka-Tayana asked Garm, "Er Wilder-kindt, du rekan?" (Do you think he is one of the Wilder-kind?)

The gnarled soldier snarled, "Ben er ester odern no, Die Archan mochtan sprakt. Du fineran, und er hilfen na no leban. (I know not if he is one. The Archan must judge. You found him, and without your help, he would be dead.)

Ka-Tayana's voice shook with uncertainty, "Und mich, die Archan nikte sprakt krankan na." (And for me, the Archan may judge my acts as ill-taken.)

Garm's voice softened as he gently replied, "Du krankan? Nikte so du tinkts die lienan. Faedervoldern sprekter, Herst im leiban gebtan mack na leiban. Und, Vilder-Zerk nikt kan lieban." (You commit evil? Do not think so, little one. As the Faedervolder say, the heart that gives love brings love. And, the Vilder-Zerk does not love.)

The days slowly passed into weeks as Nils' wagon, intermingled with a long caravan of pack animals, heavily laden wagons, and strangely dressed people moved steadily westward. A team of two large horses pulled the wagon containing Nils' sleeping form along a winding track in the endless and vast Aerkan Desert. Ka-Tayana, as Ambassador to the court of the Grand Fizir of the Aerkan tribes, was returning from the Archana's commission to establish trade with the nomadic desert tribes known as Aerkenern that inhabited the wide and distant spaces of the Great Aerkan Desert.

The Grand Fizir of the Aerkenern, a solemn man of equal portions of caution and conniving, fat and taste for fine wines, and wisdom, and gentleness soon perceived beyond the mere girl's blossoming beauty that the pale Archana had sent him an offer that promised peace and prosperity to both their peoples. For over the ages, the two had cruelly spilled much blood along the caravan routes. Now, at long last, this little one had come alone and unafraid. On the behalf of her sovereign, she had given the blood oath drawn. Without hesitation, she cut her tiny palm by the simple dagger she wore at the side of her bodice. Thus was made the promise that allowed the Faerevolder and Aerkenern cavalry to ride side by side along the length of the trade routes. Soon the merchants would once again exchange the vast grain and herds of livestock of the Faerevolder for the fine silk and rare jewel-stones of the Aerkenern.

As the caravan made its slow trudge across the desert floor, the maiden Ka-Tayana rode in a silk covered kar-el sitting atop a camel. The colors and symbol of her house, a dark green standard with a running red lion at its center, snapped high above her in the wind. Mounted riders dressed in armor similar to Garm's, and carrying stout spears flanked the rumbling mass. Among them rode many Aerkenern warriors on camels, wearing the long, flowing robes and turbans of the desert people, and carrying long lances and broad scimitars.

Upon a long and hot day, Nils woke to the clang of steel and the cries of wounded men and animals. Startled from his slumber, Nils turned his head to see the caravan's women, children and old men huddled together, the wagons having formed a defensive circle around them. Horses and men screamed as cruel, black arrows pierced their flesh. A few surviving Aerkenern mounted troops struggled valiantly against a horde of chalky-white-skinned warriors.

They resembled animals more than humans. Each had large and heavily knotted muscles, flat foreheads, unkempt long white hair, and wide and splayed noses. Fang-filled mouths and small, red, pig eyes outlined the cruel faces of the Vilder-Zerk. The Vilder-Zerk wore no armor over their dirty tunics and tattered loincloths. Some carried rusted pieces of dented shields and brandished blood-soaked rusty cleavers and scimitars. Others wielded swords or spears. All were on foot. Nils watched as one Vilder-Zerk killed two of the Grand Fizir's soldiers with its fangs and bare hands after it had received its death wound.

Such was Nils' introduction to the feared Vilder-Zerk. Bred tough, merciless fighters in the far eastern clefts of the Iron Mountains, the Vilder-Zerk would continue to kill as long as there was any living among its designated enemy or prey. As Nils would soon learn, with their blood lust satiated, they would feed.

Arrows struck the horses hitched to his wagon. Screaming as one, the two horses wildly rushed the wagon out of the melee and into the open desert. Nils was trapped in the now driverless wagon, unable to free himself and helpless to the pitiless deluge of blood and gore spilling onto the desert's floor. The two horses madly raced away from the ensuing massacre. Nils watched from the back of the wagon in horror as the horde of Vilder-Zerk swarmed over the caravan. They butchered everything in their path, cutting human and animal through flesh and bone.

The pain-maddened horses ran away from the carnage, and across the sand, the wagon thrashing from side to side behind them. As they coursed along the edge of a ravine, a dark arrow pierced one of the horses in its neck. Blinded by its pain, the dying horse careened over the gully's edge, taking its mate, the wagon and Nils to its doom. The wagon twisted and turned in the air as it tumbled end over end and crashed into the gully, crushing the two horses in the wake of its destruction. The remains of the wreck came to rest on the gully's rocky bottom, and the sounds of the battle faded away.

In the jumbled wreck, what was left of the horses lay in their harness and trappings, covered with vultures. The squawking carrion birds fought with each other as they feasted on the dead animals' flesh. One of Nil's arms extended outward from within the wreckage. One old bird, pushed from a dead horse by its kin, hopped on the rock supporting Nil's blood encrusted hand, and curiously began to peck at it. Nils' hand grabbed the bird's neck, and then strangled the buzzard. Using the rock for advantage, Nils slowly emerged from the wreckage, his legs and one arm free. The other arm remained bound to a broken piece of wagon. Nils staggered to his feet, stood in the wagon's debris and threw the disgusting creature's carcass away from him. As soon as its corpse hit the ground, its companions pounced on it and began to tear it apart with their ravenous beaks.

Nils worked his free hand around the cord holding his other arm to the wrecked wagon's timber. He eventually loosened the knots of his bound arm. Then, after vigorously rubbing life back into it, he used both hands to liberate himself from the wreckage. After his legs were free and he was able to move, he stood up, turned away from the seething mass of vultures undulating over the horses' remains, and struggled up the gully wall. At each small step up or new finger hold, he rested and gathered his strength. More than once, Nils nearly lost his grip in the loose shale. He was near unconscious with exhaustion when he finally crawled over the top where he long lay on his back with his legs dangling over the cliff's edge.

At the top of the gully's edge, after finally managing to regain his strength and get his legs under him, Nils scanned the horizon. Spotting a smudge hanging in the horizon, he limped toward the column of greasy smoke rising in the distant sky. With halting steps, he slowly walked across the open space between the ledge and the desert. When he and entered the remains of the smoking caravan he found many of the wagons still smoldering from their recent burning. Others lay broken, the contents of their boxes and barrels scattered over the desert floor.

Burned and partially burned bodies of people and animals were mixed where they fell within the debris. His roving eyes saw the many broken spears and scimitars of the dead Aerkenern and Faerevolder mounted troops, but nothing of the Vilder-Zerk. In one pile of smoky debris, he found a sword shard broken past the hilt. Under a pile of torn cloth, he dug out a small and still un-broken water cask. Using the sword shard, Nils cracked opened the cask and drank deeply from its contents.

Later, as the twin suns were riding low in the desert sky, Nils sat by a small fire, finishing a meal cooked over the open heat. He looked over the wreckage, and rising, went to the broken containers and began to sort through the various contents of the shattered caravan. He found a simple linen tunic, breeches, boots and a broad rimmed felt hat. He covered himself with these, and then renewed his search within the debris for usable goods. Eventually he built a small pile of a knife, hatchet, some food and a backpack. Finding a shovel and pick, he walked a short space from the caravan and began to dig. With the moons high in the star filled sky, Nils climbed out of the last large grave. He gently gathered a quilt around a dead form. In the fading light, he tenderly arranged the old woman's blood en-crusted silver hair, closed her dead eyes and covered her face with the quilt. Nils placed the old woman's body in the grave among the many others, and shoveled dirt over the still forms.

Dawn the next day found Nils again eating a meal beside the small fire within the caravan's wreck. As he sat, brisk whirling sand devils danced along the desert floor. Amidst its cavorting, a small sand devil caught a stray piece of hanging canvas from a broken and burnt wagon. Spun by the sand devil's machinations, the cloth flipped a small pebble into Nil's pile of tools and food. Nils picked the small projectile from his meal and darted to the side as the flopping canvas and its mates sharply flipped pebbles his direction. Nils moved away from the fire to a distance safe from the snapping of sharp projectiles. He watched the wind snapped cloth zip small missiles into wooded crates and shatter clay vases, and formed an idea.

After a time, the wind died down and Nils returned to his fire where he cut some material from his poncho and formed a rough sling. He carefully searched the caravan and gathered smooth stones of the same size and weight, all fitting into the palm of his hand. Once he felt he had gathered enough, Nils arranged some of the debris into simple targets and clumsily began to practice with his sling. At first, he more often than not managed to hit himself in the back of a leg, or flip a stone straight up into the sky. Once he even hit himself in the side of the head with the rudimentary sling.

After this event, Nils rubbed the bruised limbs and bumps on his head, and began again. By noon, he could keep the rocks going in the same direction. By nightfall, Nils was splitting and knocking over the crude targets. The next day, the suns rode high through the clear sky as Nils continued to practice with the sling. With each successive try, his accuracy improved. By dusk that day, Nils hit a rabbit scampering in the sagebrush. He gathered the dead creature and returned to his small camp. After a dinner of roasted rabbit, Nils settled into a makeshift bedroll and began to consider his options.

In the morning, Nils stamped out the remains of his fire. He belted his poncho around his waist, and holstered the ax and several knives. He shouldered a heavy water bladder and the now full pack. Nils drew the wide brimmed hat over his eyes, wrapped a large silk kerchief of brilliant red and yellow around his neck, and walked onto the wagon tracks. Without looking back at the broken caravan, he put his back to the twin suns and strode toward the west. On this day, and for the first time since arriving in the Aerkan desert, Nils surprisingly began to feel hope.

Many days and nights passed as Nils trudged along the wagon tracks, now going in a more southerly direction. Eventually, the trail led him to the edge of a shallow stream. Here, Nils stopped, knelt down and filled his empty water bladder. Before him, and beginning on the opposite bank, a narrow strand of sagebrush and scrub grass separated the desert from a line of tall trees standing in the distance. Here, at the desert's edge, the wagon trail led across the strand and into the forest. Nils waded across the stream, adjusted his gear and the now nearly empty pack, and strode along the trail and into the thick forest.

INTO THE
ROHDERNVALD FOREST

The Rohdernvald Forest was filled with tall pines and what looked to Nils as large and very old Oak, Birch, and Aspen trees. Nils had been in the forest for nearly two weeks, surviving on wild berries and roots. An occasional rabbit or squirrel would cross his path, but he had yet to perfect his hunting skills in the deep woods, and all had eluded his shots. Now, Nils stood frozen and hidden among the wide, tall trees and thick underbrush. His intense gaze was fixed on a rabbit. The animal carefully hopped and chewed, its ears perked and body poised to bolt at the slightest danger. Zip-crack! The rabbit fell instantly dead.

Nils nearly surprised himself with the shot. He left his hiding placed and walked to the dead rabbit. He reached down and recovered the stone from the rabbit's head. With a wolfish smile, Nils began to skin the dead animal. That night in the Rohdernvald, a rabbit's carcass roasted on a stick suspended over a small fire. Nils stretched its hide over the branches of a wooden rack. He had gotten two of the unsuspecting creatures that day, and now he slowly wiped the filthy grease of the first one from his dirty beard. With a satisfied sigh, Nils pushed back his long, bedraggled hair.

The next morning, Nils awoke as small snow flakes brushed against his heavily bearded face. When he rose up, he noticed the slight cover of an early snow laying on the bushes and tree limbs. To Nils, the scene reminded him of the mid-winter's Christmas display at STERNZCO. Nils gathered his gear and weapons. He chewed the remains of the second rabbit while he walked along a freezing stream. Nils muttered as his breath puffed into the cold air, "Great, first I burn in the desert, now I can freeze."

Ahead in the forest Ka-Tayana ran steadily along a stream, her long silver blond hair splayed across her sweating brow and streamed behind her. She easily sucked in the cold morning air in measured beats as her bare feet kicked small twigs and other pieces of the forest's debris as she made her way. In the distance behind her, heavy shod boots splashed in the mud, covering her small foot prints weaving between the stream's icy edges.

Many miles behind her Ma-ughk, a large and particularly ugly Vilder-Zerk stopped to survey the trail. He bent down, put one calloused finger in a tiny footprint and carefully traced its pattern. He gathered some of the mud, sat back on his haunches, sniffed the dripping mess, and then slowly licked his finger clean. His harsh speech was inflected with the sound of grinding steel as he said to his companions in the guttural Faerevolder tongue, "Karm cheo-verk. Na less fain cheo." (This way. She is trapped in the forest.)

Without any further words, Ma-ughk and four other Vilder-Zerk jogged after Ka-Tayana. Like their kin at the caravan, they were heavily armed, carrying a mix of cruelly notched rusty axes and swords, and pikes. Their red, pig eyes blazed within their pale, chalky faces nearly hidden beneath their rusty helms. Like dogs on the hunt, the Vilder-Zerk stayed on Ka-Tayana's elusive trail. Every now and then, Ma-ughk would lose the scent. But after a few moments of scouting and back-tracking, he would adjust the freshly cloven head of the young Aerkenern tied by its black hair to the broad belt at his waist. Then once again, he leapt upon the girls' trail. With a hoarse grunt, would begin anew the chase.

Long they pursued her through the forest's trees and meadows, swiftly passing small caves and outcroppings of brush. At the entrance to a tight arbor, Ma-ughk stopped so suddenly his companions nearly ran into him. Ma-ughk held up a mailed fist, signifying he had caught up with his prey. Taken by the unexpected halt, one follower slipped and fell in the wet grass behind their leader.

Ma-ughk bared his broken teeth and fangs in a satisfied smile as he spied what lay trapped before him. Far into the rear of the arbor, Ka-Tayana crouched against the thick brush and trees. Her once luxurious silk clothing was ripped and torn. Tears ran down her dirty face as she silently cried. Ma-ughk and his band faced her; their eyes gleaming with lust. Ka-Tayana sobbed, "Ya tockter Zanderfells, strategor Regant-al. Liebel ma, eo dengani k'namis." (I am the daughter of Zanderfells, the Regent's general. Let me live, and you shall be richly rewarded.)

Garm had saved her during the attack on the caravan. Along with a few surviving nomadic Aerkenern he managed, make their escape from the massacre. For many weeks, they had managed to elude the pursuing Vilder-Zerk, often having to fight free once cornered. Once in the Rohdernvald and three days ago, the party had been reduced to three. Garm had gone ahead that morning to seek out her father and his troops whom he thought might be nearby. The lone Aerkenern had died that morning, killing three of the Vilder-Zerk and giving Ka-Tayana a chance at a desperate escape to succor. But now, rather than seeing the open arms of her father's warm embrace, Ka-Tayana watched in dread as Ma-ughk stretched a mailed fist toward her disheveled hair. This while the other Vilder-Zerk drooled and chortled their rude grunts. So eager and intent was the band on the notion of despoiling her, none of the Vilder-Zerk noticed the slight sound of rustled grass behind them as Ma-ughk strode to her and replied, "Yada nu lieban. Polce sportan." (Yes, you will live, after I have my sport!)

The mad scurrying of deer in the forest had alerted Nils to the Vilder-Zerk's presence that morning. He did not desire to engage them in battle, but he had met their kind after the caravan's destruction. Coupled with the fact the splayed tracks of their hobnailed feet lay directly before him were his memories of those encounters as well what he had witnessed before careening over the gully's edge. He grimly adjusted his blades and hatchet that rode at the small of his back and set out for his prey.

The huge beast that loomed over Ka-Tayana was preparing to rape her. When he came up behind them, Nils did not see the maiden. Rather he saw Beatrice. She had retreated into the brushes by the clubhouse, and now stood over their leader. Nils witnessed her smack the boy in the nose, causing him to fall backwards to the ground. Jumping to his feet, and with one dirty hand, the boy wiped the flowing blood from his nose and in a flash of movement, grabbed Beatrice by one arm and pulled her into the hedges. Tightly gripping her in one hand, he ripped off the towel from her slight frame with the other. Without turning around, he said, "Let's have some fun. Me first, guys."

A rapid series of sharp cracking noises distracted him from pulling Beatrice's swimsuit off her slim body. Angrily he shouted, "What the?"

As he turned his head away from Beatrice, the boy saw a silhouetted figure standing above him. He heard a crack, and then blacked out.

Without realizing his actions, Nils took a stone from it pouch, and with his sling, rocketed it forward. Zip-crack! A stone the size of a child's fist hit one of the Vilder-Zerk in the small of its neck, instantly breaking its spine and killing it. Its corpse fell heavily to the ground. Zip-crack! A second Vilder-Zerk fell dead into the remaining bystanding Vilder-Zerk. Unbalanced, the two startled but very much still alive, stumbled and jostled into Ma-ughk's back as he was busily disrobing Ka-Tayana. Ma-ughk shouted, "K'to sport v'so?" (Who spoils my fun?)

Jumping away from Ka-Tayana, Ma-ughk drew his long, evil scimitar from its sheath, and in one swift stroke, decapitated the nearest stumbling Vilder-Zerk. He turned on his remaining companion and raised his dripping, bloody blade to cut him down. To the amazement of the Vilder-Zerk, Ma-ughk's stroke never came. Instead, Ma-ughk's nostrils flared as his red eyes flashed in hate. He was staring at Nils who stood in a small opening in the brush.

Ma-ughk ordered, "Guman. Varg eo." (A human. Kill him.)

Ma-ughk's companion grabbed his pike and, with a wild and hoary growl, charged Nils. Nils had mastered the martial arts of ancient combat before picking up his first auto-blaster. Now standing once again before a charging Vilder-Zerk, Nils calmly reached into his side-satchel, but his seeking fingers found no stones for his sling. He dropped the sling as the Vilder-Zerk's long legs closed rapidly on him. The enraged Vilder-Zerk plunged the pike toward Nil's chest. Stepping back and away in one swift move, Nils avoided the Vilder-Zerk's charge. Surprised his attack with the pike did not run home, the Vilder-Zerk attempted to halt its progress. Now off-balance, it slid on the slushy ground, dropping its pike as it attempted to regain control of its hoary feet. Before it could recover, Nils grabbed his hatchet from its place at the small of his back, and in a swift movement up and down, struck deep into the Vilder-Zerk's exposed neck. Blood sprayed Nils as the decapitated Vilder-Zerk fell at his feet, its legs and arms twitching in the final throes of death.

Ma-ughk, holding his scimitar in both hands strode toward Nils. Nils, sensing that Ma-ughk would not needlessly expose himself, crouched away from the huge Vilder-Zerk's advance. Seeing the fallen pike, Nils dropped his hatchet and quickly bent down to pick it up. Ma-ughk, believing Nils to have given him an advantage, jumped into a quick run, swinging the scimitar down onto Nils. Nils deftly placed the pike's butt by his foot and swiftly raised its pointed blade. Ma-ughk's maw sprouted fresh blood as the scimitar fell from his mailed fists. Frothy blood gurgled past his fangs and over his chin. Ma-ughk's hands opened and clenched as his body struggled against the pike that impaled him through the gut and out the back. Nils stood, drew a knife from its sheath, and slit the huge Vilder-Zerk's throat.

After wiping the blade clean on the moist grass and sheathing it, Nils retrieved his hatchet and carefully walked to Ka-Tayana. She cried as she lay on the soggy ground. She sobbed and huddled uncontrollably in a small ball, attempting to cover her nakedness with her arms and hands. Nils gathered the remains of her torn cloak and covered her with the muddy and shredded garment. He cooed softly into her ear, "Shush, shush Beatrice. It's all right. Let's wipe that face. Maybe a few bruises, nothing more. Let's have look."

Turning her tear-streaked face, Ka-Tayana eyes opened wide in shock and fear upon seeing Nil's bearded and filthy visage. Hearing his foreign speech and thinking he was her attacker returned, she screamed, jumped up, and scratched Nils with her flailing hands. Surprised by her violent response, Nils rapidly stepped back. Now standing, Ka-Tayana clutched the remains of her cloak around herself and bolted past Nils. Quick as a deer, she jumped over the dead Vilder-Zerk and sprinted through the small opening and into the forest brush.

He quickly pursued the young maiden, but her slim figure wove in and out of the trees as she disappeared before him. Nils abruptly stopped running and turned his head about listening to the faint blast of horns ringing in the distance. Hearing the sound of many horses galloping through the brush, Nils rushed to the spot he last saw Ka-Tayana. As he ran after her along a narrow track, he shouted, "Wait."

Even though Nils could no longer see Ka-Tayana, he continued to run along the track through the forest until it opened onto a broad, green meadow. Before him stood Ka-Tayana, exhausted at the lush meadow's edge. Nils, upon reaching her, looked past her shoulder and viewed the shear drop of a tall cliff. A narrow valley filled with tall trees that stretched from its bottom to the cliff's edge was outlined behind and just below Ka-Tayana.

Zip-thunk! An arrow impaled itself on a tree trunk near Nils' head. He spun around, placing Ka-Tayana behind him. Just as the Vilder-Zerk did not note his approach, Nils had not paid attention to the heavy tromp of the horses that now stood behind him. A large group of tall and mounted Faeder-Ganger Faerevolder riders in polished and gleaming mail sat silently upon their mounts in the opposite tree line. The Faeder-Ganger wore bright helms, and carried emblazoned bucklers, sharp axes, javelins and swords. Many held short recurved bows with arrows strung and pointed at Nils. He noticed many of these mounted Faeder-Gangers were like Garm, ebony of color, with eyes of dark brown, high cheeks, and proud, bearded chins. Others were blonde or dark haired with blue or green eyes.

As Nils watched, the Faeder-Ganger broke into three groups. The center group moved slowly forward, while the other two closed on Nils and Ka-Tayana from the left and right flanks. Nils' fixed his gaze on one Faeder-Ganger in dark mail at the front of the center group. This one opened his helm's visor, revealing Dom's face. Garm, his mail dirty and dented, sat next to Dom. Garm drew an arrow to his bow. Nils said to himself, "Strange, yet not surprising."

Unlike Nils, Dom had long been in the Faerevold. Like a wisp of morning fog, Nils had faded from Dom's thoughts upon his arrival with the Lady Lis-Yan on the docks of Leak-Mor those many decades of Annands ago. Dom sat on his steed and considered the man standing between the young maiden and the armed host, evidently ready to fight and die if need be. Dom looked upon Nils and a vision of Nils standing in brilliant glory flashed before his helmeted eyes.

A spasm of fear ripped through Dom as he recognized the dire meaning of Nils in the Faerevold. Yet none among the Faeder-Ganger noticed these things. The vision passed and Dom dissembled his thoughts at seeing his doom appear before him. He now closely noted Nils' rags, disheveled hair and beard. His voice n firm control, Dom nonchalantly spoke to Nils, "Hear me, if you understand. There is no place left for you to run."

Nils began, "How, where?"

Nils had barely spoken the question when Dom responded and completed it, "Where are you? How did you come here? What is this place?"

Before Nils could respond, the zip-thunk sound again registered in Nils' ears as another arrow seemed to sprout from his left shoulder, spinning him to the ground. Nils fell, then raised on all fours, and crawling past Ka-Tayana, slid over the cliff's edge. As he fell Nils hit wide branches that jutted from the tall trees, breaking his fall. Upon reaching the large branches at the trees' trunks, Nils dropped into the cover of the low cover and climbed down to the valley floor. Stumbling to his feet, he swiftly disappeared into the foliage. When Nils fell, Garm rode to the cliff's edge and dismounted next to Ka-Tayana. Reaching the spot where Nil's had fallen, he drew another arrow to his bow and scanned the tree-filled valley below.

Ka-Tayana, oblivious to Garm's presence, gathered her torn cloak about her body and shivered near Garm's mailed legs. It was at this moment when Lord Zander-Fells, leader of these Faeder-Gangers rode upon the scene. He was taller and more brilliantly armed than the other riders were. Had Nils been there, he would have been amazed how much a twin of Fredric Sternz this warrior was. His blue eyes flashed in anger and his grey hair streamed behind him as he spurred his steed away from his escort and out of the forest, reining in next to Garm. His green standard snapped in the breeze as his escort galloped in behind him. Lord Zander-Fells ordered, "Garm. Kazal nostral, eo leiban." (Garm. Hold your bow. I want him alive.)

Dom rode toward Garm and Zander-Fells, saying, "Remember the speak shifters and the Val-Kiren my Lord."

Garm retorted, "My mind is indeed darkened by the evil made among us, my Lord."

Zander-Fells flatly stated, "Again you speak truth, Lord Dom. It appears Garm followed his heart."

Dom replied, "Yes, it is so, Lord Zander-fells of the Faeder-Ganger."

Zander-Fells turned in his saddle and directed his words to Dom, "Yet, he did not follow my orders."

Dom did not hesitate in expressing his displeasure at the Faeder-Hander's words exclaiming, "Lord Zander-fells!"

Lord Zander-Fells cut off Dom with one quickly raised mailed hand, "Nay say me in council, if you will, Lord Dom; I hold command here, not you. What say you Garm?"

Garm stood at attention and responded, "I wait upon my Lord's judgment."

Lord Zander-Fells replied, "I give it now. Return to your troop Faeder-Ganger. Serve me well and perhaps you may once again ride as Serzian Domo. Escort the maiden to the Keep at Geldenherm."

Garm rode away as Dom sneered, "A quick and decisive judgment befitting a high lord and Hander of the Faeder-Ganger. I would have chosen a harsher punishment to keep these others in line."

Zander-Fells firmly said to Dom, "I expect nothing less from you. Garm is a good soldier and faithful servant to my household."

Dom hissed, "You question my counsel? I can assure you, the Lady Lis-Yan does not."

Zander-Fells intoned flatly, "What counsel the Archana accepts is the Archana's business. How I command my troop is mine. Now, where is my daughter?"

Garm carried Ka-Tayana away from the meadow's edge in front of him on his horse. His massive arms held her firmly over the large fur coat in which she was now ensconced. He resolutely passed through the flanking Faeder-Ganger, neither looking at any of his former subordinates. Spurring his horse, he galloped out of sight. Zander-Fells said to no one in particular, "There. Good man Garm has her. Ride swift and sure, Faeder-Ganger."

Lord Zander-Fells then sat silently in his saddle as the sound of horns blasted and the clash of bitter steel echoed in the distance. Then, in a voice loud enough for all to hear he shouted, "Mai-Yanna's troops! There is Vilder-Zerk this side of the river!"

Dom made a short bow from his saddle, saying, "I shall take my leave of you now. An escort if you please."

Zander-Fells perfunctorily ordered, "An escort, two riders."

Dom sniffed, "Only two. How now you propose these will be enough to secure my passage to Geldenherm?"

Two riders, one with long blond hair flowing from under his helm and another dark-haired and with narrowed squinting eyes, rode forward towards the two antagonists. Without looking at Dom, Zander-Fells replied, "It is more than I have given to my daughter. One, whose life I hold much dearer than yours. Take them or go on your own."

As Dom and the escort rode away, Dom sneered, "Each to his duty, Faeder-Hander."

Within the Rohdernvald forest, Mai-Yanna, a tall, raven-haired, shapely figured Faeder-Hander strode through the detritus of Nils' recent battle with the Vilder-Zerk. Her long dark hair streamed from under her helm and framed her determined face. It trailed over the rank badge at her neck, a single, wide strip of gold with three evenly spaced red bars running perpendicular in its center. Her sleek movements were not hindered by the weight of the armor now dented and stained with dirt and blood. She stopped her pacing and she stooped to examine the Vilder-Zerk Nils had killed earlier.

Without any flourish of rank or protocol, Lord Zander-Fells rode in and dismounted. He walked to Mai-Yanna, and holding his sword arm across his chest, saluted her. "Hail and well met Faeder-Hander."

Mai-Yanna did not remove her searching eyes from the ground as she grunted, "Well met."

Pointing at the fresh corpses, Zander-Fells asked, "Which of your Hand slew these?"

Mai-Yanna stood up from her inspection and said, "None of mine, or yours 'tis clear. See, this pike was driven through this one from below. As if its prey was trapped and found the lance in desperation."

Zander-Fells asked, "And of Ka-Tayana?"

Mai-Yanna noted the hint of anguish that played upon Zander-Fell's face. Then she replied calmly, "Over there. I will lay odds this big one tried for a bit of sport with her first. But he got interrupted before he could accomplish much. She was not despoiled that is clear. That one in the brush got it from the big one's scimitar. It probably got too close for its own good. As for these other ones, I don't know."

The relief of knowing his daughter had not been raped washed over Zander-Fells. He said, "So they quarreled over her, and she made her escape. The overlord killed them, but not before one made sure he would not live. Her footprints lead off into the woods here. I see no Vilder-Zerk followed."

Mai-Yanna asked, "And Ka-Tayana yet lives?"

With a firm smile, Zander-Fells said, "Aye, in the care and strong arms of Garm."

Mai-Yanna advised, "Then you should be off, my Lord."

He gently asked her, "And you, Faeder-Hander?"

She flashed him a wolf grin and said, "There is other Vilder-Zerk in the wood this day. I think I'll stay and hunt a bit more."

Zander-Fells looked her full in the face then said, "Consider carefully the suns and the ford at Westernfalls. I intend to hold the far side. Do not tarry long in the wood before nightfall."

Making her first note of Nils, Mai-Yanna asked, "And this other thing that was here? What of it?"

Zander-Fells answered, "I am not sure. Dom was speaking with it when I rode up. Then Garm's arrow."

She stated more than asked, "Then it is dead?"

Zander-Fells muttered, "Garm kills what he aims for. This one fell into the trees."

Mai-Yanna now asked in startled surprise, "Then it still lives?"

Zander-Fells answered her, "Perhaps, Garm saw it disappear under the trees. Alive or dead, we will find it."

With this piece of disturbing news in hand, Mai-Yanna turned and began to walk toward her mount. She stopped and ordered her troops, "We are done here. I shall not hunt but gather our strength at Westernfalls Ford."

Mai-Yanna mounted her horse, and saluting Zander-Fells said, "Until then, Faeder-Hander."

Zander-Fells said in a loud voice more for the assembled Faeder-Ganger of Mai-Yanna's command than Mai-Yanna herself, "I shall see you at the falls, Faeder-Hander. It will not be well with any human found this side of the ford this night."

Mai-Yanna saluted him, and Lord Zander-Fells mounted his horse. He then signaled his escort to follow as he rode out of the glen. Once out of his sight, Mai-Yanna signaled a Faeder-Ganger who spurred his mount and rode to Mai-Yanna's side. She ordered, "Stack and burn these vermin. Be fast about it."

GELDENHERM

It was dusk when a Nils disturbed a crane from its lone hunting of the tasty frogs and small fish that inhabited the river's shallows. Like an old man disturbed from his nap, the gangly bird ruffled its feathers and took flight for more quiet places. The crane had fully disappeared into the darkening sky when Nils crawled out of a pile of leaves and brush near the river's edge. Garm's broken arrow shaft painfully protruded from his shoulder, encircled by the smear of half dried blood on the left side of Nil's poncho. Across from him, Nils saw another stand of trees waited silently next to the slow moving water.

Throughout the remainder of the day, he had managed to elude the Faeder-Ganger riding through the forest searching for him. Repeatedly he had slipped from their sight in the midst of the thick trees and brush of the valley. Yet a scarce two hours hence, he had been forced to take cover deep within the brush and concealing leaves pushed into piles by the river's urgent motions. Here he had lain while not one but three of the heavily mailed riders had ridden near his hide-away with one steed stepping gingerly over his prone form buried in the bracken. After stopping to water their mounts, and unable to find their quarry, the riders turned and, following a deer path, disappeared around the river's bend.

Nils had waited the last two hours, ensuring the riders could neither hear nor sense him in any way before he dared risk leaving the cover of the leaves and brushwood. In the meanwhile, the crane arrived and began its slow and steady search, stopping every so often to espy its prey—fat and lazy—that it neatly impaled with its long, sharp beak. Now it was near dark, and Nils let out a heavy sigh and entered the cold stream. Due to the wound caused by the arrow's bolt, he hesitatingly swam with the river's current toward the far bank. Often his head would disappear under the water, and then quickly it would re-appear in a spurt of coughing and gasping. Near exhaustion, Nils reached the far side and using his right arm and legs, crawled up a muddy and shallow bank. Once up on his feet, he stumbled into the woods.

Night fell and he lurched his way about in the now dark woods going in no certain direction. He simply followed the path of least resistance as he lumbered over exposed tree trunks and pushed his away under low hanging branches. After a time, a distant light appeared before him in the trees. It seemed to beckon to him out of the deepening darkness. The sight of the light warmed Nils, and without a thought, he moved one heavy step in front of the other through the woods and toward the light.

>~~~<

At Westernfalls Ford, Mai-Yanna and Lord Zander-Fells stood next to each other waiting with their assembled Faeder-Ganger. Although they much preferred to fight mounted, the troops stood in silent and disciplined ranks of spearmen, men-at-arms, and in the last rank—archers. The flicker of torches in the night reflected on their armor and weapons.

As they patiently waited, the clash and screams of battle echoed from beyond the ford. A group of five riders galloped toward them across the ford. One rode an exhausted horse flecked with foam. To his front, he held a slumped form. With a sigh of relief Mai-Yanna announced, "Garm."

Once safe on the Eastern side of the ford, Garm halted his blown horse. His four companions slipped behind the ranks of their fellows. Before Garm could dismount, several of the Faeder-Ganger ran to his side and gently took an unconscious Ka-Tayana from him. He then dismounted, saluted and reported, "Lady Faeder Hander, we must get her to the surgeons quickly."

The Faeder-Ganger carried Ka-Tayana behind the lines of waiting troops. Garm then saluted Zander-Fells and continued, "Beg pardon sir. Since finding her in the meadow, I have ridden many kloms avoiding the Vilder-Zerk. The wood is thick with them and it took me sometime to make my way. I made better time once I met up her ladyship's troops."

Mai-Yanna interjected, "Well done, Ka-Tayana lives. Are there any others behind you, Faeder-Domo?"

The exhausted warrior replied, "No, we are the last. A few formed a rear guard some half klom behind."

No other response or information was required. Lady Mai-Yanna had grown up in the Ganger first as a mere page, then rose to the ranks to become Faeder-Ganger in her own right. She had led her troops enough times against the Vilder-Zerk to know that the fading sounds of battle in the distant wood were those of Faeder-Ganger who had willing decided to fight and die in order to give Garm and his precious cargo a change to cross the Westernfalls Ford.

Mai-Yanna announced what everyone in the assembled mass already knew, "Very well. The Vilder-Zerk will be here soon."

Garm continued, "I am only Faeder-Ganger now. Where do I report?"

Zander-Fells replied with a wide smile on his face, "Here, by my side, Serzian-Domo."

Deep in the part of the Rohdernvald called the Vintern Wood, far from the battle brewing at the Westernfalls ford, the sage Anadan sat rocking back and forth silently in a rough chair. He and the rocking chair were perched most precariously on the front edge of the porch that fronted his small cottage of rough-hewn stone and logs. His unkempt hair was long and gray. Wisdom etched his tired and wrinkled face as he gently picked an ancient scroll from the small pile on his lap. With his free hand, Anadan quietly drew a long sword from beneath his robes.

He stopped rocking, and stood as a crash sounded from the woods. Not taking notice of the scrolls as they spilled onto the porch, the old sage stepped quietly into the cottage, and silently closed and barred the door. For a long time the he stood behind the door, his sword at the ready. Then, moving silently like a mouse, Anadan pushed aside wide and heavy curtains and peered out a window. On the ground mid-way between the dark forest and Anadan's cottage, Nils lay sprawled face down. In a hushed tone, Anadan said to himself, "Not one of the dark ones. Not at all from on this side of the river either."

Taking a lamp, Anadan unlatched and opened the cottage door. He slid his sword into its scabbard within his flowing robes, and carefully walked to Nils. Then, furtively looking left and right, he grabbed Nils by the feet and hastily drug the wounded man into the cottage faster than one could say beans and taters.

><~><

Dawn at the Westernfalls Ford found Mai-Yanna surveying the piles of dead Vilder-Zerk lining the far shore. With steady purpose, she mounted her horse. Then surveying the remains her troops, she announced, "Our Lord Zander-Fells is well ahead by now. There will be no more Vilder-Zerk this season. Serzian-Domo, form the Hand."

A surly veteran in blood soaked armor saluted her commander, and curtly asked, "An wha be you doing yout ere in the cold?"

A fine snow began to fall on the bloody ground, covering the dead Faeder-Ganger and Vilder-Zerk with a thin layer of white. Mai-Yanna sat on her steed for a moment and then ordered, "Honor our dead, then escort the wounded to the citadel at Geldenherm."

Serzian-Domo Liz-Tana cocked her silver encrusted head, as through the falling snow the howling wolves could be heard in the far distance deep within the Rohdernvald. Pointing to the dead Vilder-Zerk, Mai-Yanna directed, "Leave those to the wolves. They sound hungry. I will meet you at the citadel."

With this last brief command, Mai-Yanna and two of her Faeder-Ganger galloped through the ranks and along the snow filled road. They rode throughout the day until they reached a small fork in the forest. Here, they stopped to allow the horses a rest as the sun began to descend in the western sky. The main trail led straight on, the faint outline of citadel Geldenherm in the foggy distance. The smaller route turned and led deeper into the forest toward the Vintern Wood. Mai-Yanna sat quietly and looked at the citadel's outline before her. Then without a sound, she reined her horse over and into the thin line of trail leading away from the citadel.

At dusk, Mai-Yanna and her escort halted at Anadan's cottage. The three mud spattered riders dismounted while Anadan met them at his doorstep. The old sage made a short bow in Mai-Yanna's direction asking, "What brings the gallant Faeder-Hander Mai-Yanna to my door this day?"

She curtly replied, "War, and to seek counsel."

Then to her escorts ordered, "Tend to our mounts and stand watch."

The two Faeder-Gangers led the horses to a trough. Once the horses began to drink, Anadan noticed how quickly they drew their dented swords as he kindly said to Mai-Yanna, "Then come in. Let us see what an old man can tell a warrior about war, or what counsel he may give."

Once within Anadan's cottage, the old man began to scurry about finding cups and some biscuits. He placed a steaming tea pot on a rough, but well worn table. Anadan asked Mai-Yanna in a grandfatherly tone, "Some hot tea or fresh biscuits?"

Mai-Yanna came directly to her point and abruptly asked the wizened man, "Would you find it odd to find Vilder-Zerk in the Rohdernvald so near the on-set of winter?"

Anadan replied, "Odd? Yes, but not unheard of."

Mai-Yanna pressed, "Even to the far side of Westernfalls Ford?"

Anadan sat quietly digesting this news for some time. Then, remembering his guest, he proffered her a cup of tea. As he waited for her to take the tea, Anadan sat at the small table and sipped from a steaming clay cup. The warrior who sat opposite him was short on time and temper and demanded answers to her questions. Impatiently she responded to his polite gestures, "I have little time to sit at tea with you, old man. I and Lord Zander-Fells out-fought three times our number in Vilder-Zerk last night at the Westernfalls. What do you make of it?"

Finally, he sighed and said, "The Vilder-Zerk is simple, cruel, and fierce. They follow their instincts for food and mates. In spring and summer, they fatten themselves. Come harvest time, they gather in dens to breed. Winter finds them asleep under the snow."

As when she sat as his student, Mai-Yanna sensed the old man had more to tell her. So she sat opposite him and held a cup of tea between her hands. For long minutes, Anadan was silent, again lost in his thoughts. When he spoke next, it surprised both himself and Mai-Yanna, "To come so far from the Iron Mountains means their need, or their fear, must have been very great. Very great indeed."

Mai-Yanna nibbled at a nearby biscuit and finally sipped her tea. Anadan continued, "A need and fear so great and terrible it burns the base at whatever souls they possess."

Mai-Yanna asked in a hushed tone, "Is it as the old ones sing about? The end of light and life? The Dark Wars?"

He replied firmly, "Who knows such things? I believe an ancient wickedness is gathering in the Faerevold."

Her tone changed and she demanded, "Old granny's tales are for children. What proofs do you have?"

At this, Anadan stood and drew back a curtain, revealing Nils unconscious form lying under a thick cover. "I? I have no proofs other than the one who comes from afar. Look, yourself at the sign of these darkening days."

Mai-Yanna gasped, "Who is this?"

Anadan answered, "His name, I do not yet know. But he is neither Vilder-Zerk nor Faerevolder."

Astonished to find Nils in Anadan's cottage, Mai-Yanna asked, "You took an arrow from him?"

The old sage replied, "Of course."

Quickly standing from the table, Mai-Yanna held out her hand and commanded, "Let me see it."

Without a word, Anadan produced the broken arrow. Mai-Yanna slowly turned it over and carefully examined the broken shaft. Keeping the arrow, she swiftly turned on her heel and strode to the door. Opening it, she barked at the escorts, "You two come in here."

The two Faeder-Gangers left the horses and entered the cottage. She instructed them, "Bind that thing. Find a wagon suitable to hold it for tomorrow's journey. Till then cage it and set a guard."

Anadan softly asked her, "You fear what you do not know?"

She spat out, "I fear no man or beast. That thing laid its dirty hands on my family, and it shall answer for it."

Anadan rose from his chair and his form seemed to tower over Mai-Yanna and her escorts as he said in a deep voice, "You will not make your judgment in my house."

Mai-Yanna unperturbed by Anadan's display coldly replied, "I do not intend to. I will take this matter to the Archana. She sits on the Dais at Geldenherm Citadel.

In an instant, the old man's form withered, and Anadan said, "Then this old man shall accompany you."

The Faeder-Ganger tied Nils' feet and arms tightly about him. No more words were exchanged as Mai-Yanna and her escort went about the business of putting Nils in the back of a wagon. Once the watch was set, Anadan retrieved some heavy blankets and robes from his cottage. He gave three robes to the Faeder-Ganger, and after placing one of the heavy blankets over Nils, retired to his home. Long into the night and into the next morning the Faeder-Ganger watched both the dark forest surrounding them and the lamp light-silhouetted figure of Anadan reading scrolls.

Geldenherm Citadel was an ancient keep that lay next to the river. The keep itself was tall and broad, and surrounded by three ring walls. Each wall contained arrow towers, and fronted by a dry moat with gatehouse and bridge. Upon the outermost ring wall, the Archana, Lady Lis-Yan, stood on a high parapet. Her hard cold eyes pierced the snow covered and wind swept plain. Dom stood warmly covered in rich robes next to her. Far below them, Lord Zander-Fells led a slow column of muddy and battle weary Faeder-Ganger along the mucky road and through the citadel's gate. Lady Lis-Yan spat to Dom, "I will be Archana now and forever, Lord Dom. How much longer shall I have to suffer these simple fools?"

Dom pointed toward the weary column and coolly replied, "Everything in its season, my lady. Do you see that wagon near Lord Zander-Fells? It carries a very precious cargo."

Lis-Yan eagerly asked, "What sort of treasure? I know of none our great Faeder-Hander would lightly risk his or his troops' lives for."

Dom sneered, "His daughter, Ka-Tayana. That is a cargo more precious to the great Ganger Hander than all the jewels of the Faerevold. Nay, a treasure more valuable than his life lies hurt in that wagon."

She cackled as she and Dom turned from the parapet and entered the citadel, "See that she is brought into my chambers. Fool that he is! He brings her here to me, to me."

Within Citadel Geldenherm's hallways, Lady Lis-Yan strode majestically, Dom ever at her side and one very small step behind. A bevy of maidens, guards, and other courtiers and members of her retinue followed them at some distance, but within hailing of the two. Lady Lis-Yan commanded, "See that she is placed in the care of the best surgeons and my personal nurses."

Dom slyly asked, "In a private chamber close to yours?"

With an equally sly smile, she answered, "Of course."

Later that day, an ever-changing group of aides, courtiers and guards surrounded the Lady Lis-Yan and Dom within the Regent's council room. A guard announced, "The Lord Zander-Fells."

Turning from her court, the Lady Lis-Yan remarked, "My lords, see there is a man who in the midst of a great victory has now nearly lost all that is most dear to him."

Zander-Fells bowed, saluted, and then as he stood at attention asked, "Lady Archana. It seems you have no need of my report of our actions at the Westernfalls. What are your commands and my commission?"

Lis-Yan responded nonchalantly "Only that you continue to serve me and Our Landkreiser. I am told not to concern myself with the Vilder-Zerk you fought so far away from their dens."

Zander-Fells answered his liege, "It is now an early winter. Your advisers are correct. The Vilder-Zerk should not trouble us this season."

With venom in her voice, she spat, "They came as far as the ford. Our Lord Dom's foresight in sending Mai-Yanna and her Hand into the forest stopped them from crossing."

The accusation of disloyalty and incompetence did not go unnoticed by the retinue. Zander-Fells responded flatly, his position of attention hiding his wrath, "As you know, I and my Faeder-Ganger were there as well."

Lis-Yan stated coldly, "Yes, you were. Yet, not on any mission of ours."

Zander-Fells, undaunted by the Archana's ire replied, "You knew of my need. Even now she needs rest to regain her strength."

Dom sneered, "It seems your soldiers' surgeons are not up to such a vital task."

Dom's insult to Zander-Fells also did not go unnoticed. More than a few of the courtiers moved discretely from his side of the council room and toward Dom's. Zander-Fells bowed toward the dais and said "I thank our Archana for the great kindness she shows to my daughter."

Lis-Yan asked curtly, "What of Mai-Yanna? I am told her regiment is billeted here in the citadel. Yet, she has not come to show us any courtesy."

Zander-Fells responded, "She is yet in the field my lady."

Dom hissed at Zander-Fells, "Our Archana knows full well your failure to capture the thing your impertinence let loose."

Zander-Fells fists clenched in their mailed gauntlets as he replied, "Mai-Yanna is on the road escorting the creature here. It lays wounded by Garm's arrow."

"Lis-Yan shouted at the two fuming roosters before her, "Enough of this! Lord Zander-Fells, I require persons of great skill and courage. You seem to have abundance of both. Can you give me your loyalty as well?"

Surprised at the turn of events, certain courtiers found themselves stranded in the gap between Dom's and Zander-Fells' factions. Zander-Fells solemnly replied, "As these here are my witness, Lady Regent, I do."

Dom took close note of those who now scurried to Zander-Fells' side of the room. Lis-Yan placed a vermillion baton with caps of gold in Zander-Fells' mailed hands. The assembled courtiers bowed as she announced, "Hear me. We give Zander-Fells appointment to serve as Strategon from Gelde to the edge of the Iron Mountains."

She placed a gilded chapeau on Dom's head and continued, "To our Lord Dom, I place the Fyrd Gelde in his care, naming him Landkreiser. This is his keep to command and hold. To him I provide our Strategon Zander-Fells the Citadel Geldenherm's garrison of Kaeder Ganger and those Faeder now in the Fyrd."

Dom ordered, "Right. Strategon, here are your orders. Make haste and relieve Mai-Yanna of her captive. Bring it here and place it under the care of the dungeon warders."

Zander-Fells saluted and said, "I will see to it."

As he strode out of the council chamber, the courtiers also made to exit the room as many felt as if Dom's gaze pierced their very minds and souls.

That evening outside of the citadel, Mai-Yanna and Zander-Fells stood alone. The spoke to each other in hushed whispers, the fog of their breathing hung over their close heads in the cold, pale air.

Mai-Yanna whispered, "So, Dom holds all the strings."

Zander-Fells blurted out in dismay, "It is as we feared. She is blind with the lust of it. To think to be Archana while there is yet life in Ka-Tayana. Long has it been when as a young page I attended her first sitting on the Dais. The Huskarl has spoken; Ka-Tayana is to be our next liege."

Mai-Yanna coolly said, "Hold your tongue. Like it or no, we must obey. For now, your agreement with the current state of affairs is all that stands between Dom and all of our lives."

Zander-fells quietly sighed, "Wise words, little one. Dom knows he can keep me busy in the field here while he continues to hoist Lis-Yan on the Dais at Raffer-Moor."

Mai-Yanna whispered in his ear, "Take heart, dear one. He can order our bodies but not our souls. Besides, there are others with whom he still must contend."

Under the triple moons, their hands gently touched, and without words, they parted.

Within the Lady Lis-Yan's chambers, an old Strategon's rheumy eyes were held in rapt attention by Lis-Yan as he knelt before her. She coyly asked the ancient warrior, "Strategon, how does one know if a blade be true or false?"

Throatily he replied, "One would test it, my lady."

Completely disregarding the old Strategon, now stuck to the floor, she asked, ""Dom, what sort of trial may we make for this thing Mai-Yanna brought to us?"

Anadan offered as he came into the area from behind a plush curtain, "One brought by the offended to the Dais."

Dom turned his attention away from the prostrate Strategon and slyly asked, "Did my ears fail me? Or, were the guards incompetent in announcing you?"

Anadan replied, "Neither, Lord Dom. Your ears are in good order. I have no need for any announcement, or of guards."

Dom hissed, "Indeed!"

Beyond the curtains, a guard cried out, "My Regent, Mai-Yanna wishes the Archana's favor."

Lis-Yan directed, "Let her approach. And you as well, Anadan."

Mai-Yanna entered the area and curtsied to Lis-Yan. If Dom had been paying attention, he would have noted that it was from behind the same curtain that Anadan had come from. Nor did Dom note that with a gentle tug at the elbow, Anadan pulled the old Strategon up from his knees. Whereupon, the old man realizing that Lis-Yan had long ago ceased needing his person offered a silent salute and retreated from the room.

Deep inside the citadel, Ka-Tayana lay within a rich chamber. She slept restlessly under layers of rich bed covers. A nurse silently and dutifully wiped droplets of sweat from Ka-Tayana's brow as she fitfully slept. Lord Zander-Fells stood beside her bed. He had the appearance of any weary father who had spent much of his time pacing and worrying the surgeons rather than taking the sleep his disheveled and ragged appearance revealed. He huskily inquired of the nurse at Ka-Tayana's side, "What new of the lass?"

The nurse stoically replied, "A fortnight and three days she has lain thus. The wounds to the flesh are healed. But some other hurt lies deep within her."

Zander-Fells began, "I am overly long in the field and weary from my travels."

His words were interrupted by a guard's voice from the hallway, "My Lord, our Archana demands your presence and report."

Zander-Fells sighed, "The Archana demands much of me. I shall return when I may."

He and the nurse left the chamber. As they came out of the door, Zander-fells spied Anadan walking toward them in the hallway. Hurriedly he took the sage by the hand and pleaded, "Ah, Anadan. I must leave her and make my report. Nurse, give the sage what assistance he requests."

Zander-Fells and the guard made their way down the hallway. After entering the chamber and with a gaze at Ka-Tayana, Anadan walked to the bedside and placed his hand on the maiden's sweating forehead. He smoothly commanded the nurse, "Let us see to this sick girl of ours, shall we? Bring me some fresh steamed water."

The nurse curtly replied, "As you wish."

Anadan noted the not so subtle contempt in the nurses' voice as she left the chamber. Once sure she was out of the room, Anadan picked up the bowl of water at Ka-Tayana's bedside. He gingerly smelled its contents and grimaced in disgust. Taking the foul brew in his hands, he strode to an open window and unceremoniously tossed out the bowl's contents. With a happy sigh, he returned to Ka-Tayana and took her hand. Then, in low voice he began to speak to her, cooing, "Yes. You are sore hurt, wandering lost in the wood. Ka-Tayana, Ka-Tay, Ka-Tay."

Ka-Tay, Ka-Tay. The name curled over and over just outside of her consciousness. She sat in raptured Bliss, for how long Ka-Tayana did not know. She did know with whom else she sat, yet all there understood the import of the Maker's Golden words. She had learned of her doom, and was loath to leave the Great Presence of Infinite Glory. Silently she begged, *Please, I would stay with you for all time.*

The True Lord of All Things with the Great Voice that rang said, *This I know little one. But I and others have need of you elsewhere Ka-Tay.*

She then left the Great Throne. As she passed, a grim man with short silver hair and wearing a pale blue uniform moved forward to sit before the Great Maker. As she returned to the mortal lands, she said to herself, *So much like the Ganger.*

Anadan became silent at the sounds of footsteps in the hallway. The nurse had returned with a bowl of steaming water. He took the bowl from her outstretched hands and placed it on a nearby low table. He removed some non-descript leaves from within his cloak and crushed them into the basin. He systematically dipped a cloth into the mixture, removed it and gently squeezed a small amount on Ka-Tayana's lips, saying, "There you are."

Ka-Tayana softly sighed, and her eyelashes fluttered.

The old sage said to the nurse, "I believe she will now mend quickly."

The nurse asked, "Will you fetch the Lord Zander-Fells?"

Anadan replied, "No. I think I shall stay here for a bit."

Later, in a secluded and darkened hallway within the citadel, the nurse and Dom were huddled together. She whispered to him, "I cannot keep that old peddler from my nursery."

Dom answered lowly, "Then watch and report all that you see and hear."

From within inside his cloak he produced a bag of coins. Before disappearing in the dark, he furtively passed it to her saying, "Payment in advance."

⊱⊰

Like many an ancient keep, deep within the bowels of Citadel Geldenherm were the cells. It was in this collection of dark, stinky, and filthy chambers Nils laid bound and gagged. Outside of Nils' cell stood Galen, a young Faeder-Ganger in full battle armor. His mailed fists gently, but firmly grasped the handle of a battle ax. Its broad and sharp head rested firmly on the stone floor at his mailed feet. Galen's eyes pierced the faint darkness and his head turned at the slightest sound. At one such tiny scratch on the stones, Galen commanded, "Hold. None may enter save on the Archana's orders."

Dom's voice echoed, "I speak for the Archana."

Galen snapped to attention and saluted as Dom came forward and produced a key. With this, Dom unlocked Nils' cell and entered, leaving Galen with his salute frozen in place. Nils was sitting up and instantly recognized Dom's form silhouetted before him. Carefully, Nils intoned, "Dom."

Reaching a hand inside his robes, Dom brought forth several small, white pills in his palm. The vile man locked his eyes with Nils and said, "I know the nature of that which haunts you. These and many more will calm the monster that inhabits your soul"

Nils replied, "You know nothing. As for my soul, I believe I have already found its cure. "

Like a distant thunderstorm, Dom's voice then lowly rumbled, "Swear fealty to me and you shall feast on the finest foods, sleep in the thickest feather bed, and enjoy the company of more than one accommodating wench. These are the smallest of tokens I shall give you. Prove faithful, and riches and glory beyond reckoning are yours."

Sweat ran down Nils' face as he considered Dom's offer. Truly, he desired all that Dom offered. Yet something he could not explain had happened to him in the midst of the storm. Some how he was different, and as in the aftermath of Seti Four when Major Lewis slid the resignation papers in lieu of court martial across the stainless steel desk aboard the *Sergeant York,* he could not accept. Nils' chest heaved and his voice cracked as he passed the words through his choked throat and split lips, "What, and give up the dry bread, this cot of rushes, and the company of the occasional rat?"

Dom's back arched at Nils' refusal and he shouted, "Then you shall know pain and suffering no other man has endured. Understand I alone have the power over you while in this realm!"

Nils scoffed at the man who could have given him his heart's desire, "You have no power over me than what I may grant you. I give you none."

Dom snapped his fingers and a bolt of incandescent blue light shot across the cell, hitting Nils square in the forehead. Nils body was slammed against the cell's walls and he collapsed onto the cot. As he laid there, his mind drifting into unconsciousness, he heard Dom's fading voice say, "That was a mere flicker of the touch you will receive when you stand in the rendering chamber."

Within his chamber, Dom placed his seal into the hot wax sitting atop a rolled piece of parchment. This he gave to the tall golden-haired Faeder-Ganger who had accompanied him from the ford at Westernfalls.

"Take this and ride to the Iron Mountains. Do not concern yourself with the Vilder-Zerk. Our Master has seen to it."

Later, Pa-Val had met the squint eyed Gim Bayz at the fords some miles east of Geldenherm. The large blond rode uneasily next to his short and swarthy companion. When the two men reached their Master, Pa-Val delivered Dom's message as directed. Later, while they sat at the feast surrounded by delicacies and buxom lovelies, Pa-Val and Gim Bayz drank the rich wine and raised the jeweled encrusted golden goblet in a toast to Dom.

Little did he consider the weight of his decision to serve Dom. Perhaps if he knew the contents of the message he had delivered he may have chosen a different path. If he had been able to see Dom's twisted and mal-formed desire for usurpation that lay very deeply buried, he may have cast his lot elsewhere. Far, far in the darkness of Dom's heart, and well hidden out of sight of his Dark Lord it lay. However, Pa-Val saw none of this, only the reward of lands and a title, and soon the ability to be able to grant favor to his own thralls.

THE RENDERING

Within the dungeon, Galen's eyes were again attempting to pierce the darkness around him when he felt a nearby presence. Again, Galen gruffly commanded, "Hold. None may enter save on the Archana's orders."

Anadan softly answered the challenge, "The Archana's orders you say? How can that be, young Galen, when Our Lady yet holds court in chambers? Do you not know me?

Galen did not want Anadan, or whomever it was in the dark claiming to be the sage, to think anyone could sneak up on him unaware in the dark. It had been bad enough when earlier Dom had seemingly done so with ease, and the young guard replied proudly, "Our Lord Dom commanded me in the Archan's name. I did not see you, Anadan. But your heavy feet gave you away some minutes ago while you were still on the steps."

Anadan lit a small lantern and said, "Yes, you did hear steps, those of Lord Zander-Fells. I have been here since before you took your place at guard. Now be so kind as to let us pass."

The light from Anadan's lantern flickered across the new stubble of a beard beginning to show on the young Faeder-Ganger's face. Galen forcefully replied, "I have sworn by my ax. None but those on the Archana's orders may enter."

Anadan gently asked the young man, "Orders? Yes, we heard you. Who do you think goes about these worrisome days in the name of the Archana? You may not have heard while on duty in the cells. Ka-Tayana lives."

Doubt shot through Galen's eyes, and he tightened his grip on the ax handle. At this, Zander-Fells reached for his sword. Anadan ordered, "Hold, Zander-Fells. See, it has begun. 'Tis true, Galen. As long as Ka-Tayana lives, Lord Dom must wait to elevate the Lady Lis-Yan permanently to the Dais.

Anadan leaned close to the Faeder-Ganger and commanded, "Awake Galen."

As one startled from deep dream, Galen shook himself and said, "My lords forgive me. I must have fallen asleep at my post. No. I was awake when I heard, when we all heard Lord Dom's words at watch change."

Zander-fells said hotly, "Dom. Again I find his name attached to too many things. Galen, Let us pass. Anadan must speak with this prisoner."

Anadan said soothingly, "Do not fear, Galen. These passages can be deceiving. Often it is said one may not discern a man's step from that of a rat's."

The puzzled guard asked, "Yet you are here before me. How came this to be?"

Anadan moved past Galen and standing before the cell's locked door said, "Rest your mind Galen. I shall tell you another day. In the meantime, keep a close watch. I mean to keep my inquiry private."

Zander-Fells observed, "The wisdom of the simple truth clears the crooked paths of a maze of lies."

"So it does." Anadan replied.

Galen then stood aside and unlocked the cell door. Anadan gave Zander-Fells the small lamp as they walked past Galen and entered Nils' cell. Once within the small space, Zander-Fells held up his lamp high above his head. Upon seeing Nils, he asked the sage, What thing is this? He is so similar, yet different."

Anadan replied, "This is no thing, but a man to be put on trial. He is not some strange beast. A man as sure as my staff, somewhat dirty and in need of a good hot bath to be sure."

Nils opened his eyes. He could make out the dim forms of Anadan and Zander-fells as they stood above his bound form. Anadan asked in the Faerevolder tongue, "Tak namen?" (What is your name?)

Surprised to hear someone asking him a direct question, Nils asked, "Who are you? What is this place?"

Zander-fells asked Anadan, "Sch-to sprakern?" (What does he say?),

The old man replied, "He is one of the younger people. I have read the ancient text but did not begin to think, to believe I should speak to one in my time."

Amazed, Zander-Fells asked, "Tis true, the old prophecies?"

With a brusque wave to Zander-Fells, Anadan turned to Nils and spoke in the heavy accent of the Faerevolder, "I am Anadan and this is Lord Zander-Fells. He does not speak your tongue. You, my young friend, are deep in the cells of Geldenherm citadel. The present keep of our Lord Dom, High Councilor of Faerevold."

Stunned to hear the name, Nils hurriedly asked, "Dominare Avery is here? In the meadow! I saw him there, then that arrow. I thought it was my imagination, then he was here not log before you two."

Anadan turned to Lord Zander-Fells and said, "Lord Zander-Fells, trust me now as you have never before. Make all haste. Go and secure as many Faeder-Ganger that remain un-sullied by Dom. Be at the Dais at morrow's dawn."

Zander-Fells asked, "What did you say to him?

The sage ignored the question and commanded, "I must leave you now. There is much to discuss between he and us. Tomorrow, after the trial. Now go."

Without further discourse, Lord Zander-fells gave Anadan the lantern and exited Nils' cell. Nils looked deeply into Anadan's face and said firmly, "My name is Nils. Nils Sicharis. Call me Nils."

It was now Anadan's turn to be surprised as he said, "Nils. You may find this hard to understand, for you are our great hope and doom. Believe me you must for, you, we all, are in great perilr. There is no time to explain. Know you this, be you of Taerevold, the younger kint. Moreover, you have declared yourself Sicharis to me. Now sleep."

With these words, Anadan placed his hand on Nils' forehead. Nils immediately fell back onto the rough cot and slipped into a deep sleep. After watching Nils for a brief moment, Anadan turned and hastened out of the cell and passed a glassy eyed Galen.

⸎

Like most seats of government, Citadel Geldenherm had a council hall used for the conduct of the Archana's affairs of state. On a raised Dais at the one end of the long hall sat Lis-Yan. Dom stood imperiously at her right side. Two rows of guards in battle dress lined each side of the hall. High upon the council chamber's huge, exposed rafters, hung the colors of the Landkrieser and the various battle flags and banners of the Faeder-Ganger regiments. Courtiers whispered and twittered among themselves behind the guards as Lord Zander-Fells, wearing a wide green sash, strode toward the Dais. A few feet in front of it at its edge, he stopped and bowed.

The Lady Lis-Yan yawned as one bored and asked lazily, "Our Lord Zander-Fells, I see you appear before us as spokested for your house. What judgment for cause do you wish from us today?"

"For sorcery upon our house," was his laconic reply.

Stifling another yawn, she commanded, "Bring forth the prisoner."

Guards led Nils bound in a long chain along the hall and to the Dais. There they forced him to kneel. Lady Lis-Yan stood up before the prisoner and in a loud voice of command addressed the assembly within the hall, "What say you now? How does it happen that such a heap as this finds its way to our court? Does it not have a tongue? Or perhaps, as a rude beast that grunts in the field, it cannot speak?"

Nils lifted his eyes to Lady Lis-Yan and stared into her dark orbs. For a moment that seemed an eternity, their eyes locked onto each other. With a shudder, Lady Lis-Yan finally broke the trance and weakly sat back on the thick cushions. She turned to Dom and said, "Lord Dom, all here know you have great skill and the understanding of many things; what say you? Can you speak for this thing?"

With a sneer, Dom replied, "As you command."

Dom stepped down from his place on the Dais and stood over Nils. In a sweet hiss, Dom asked him, "Do you know where you are? How did you come to be here? Speak wisely, your fate hangs by a thread. Speak carefully. Do you know me?"

Nils knelt silently and did not reply.

Frustrated at Nils' behavior, Dom stood erect and shouted in disgust, "Bahg. This thing is mute or chooses silence to its doom."

He returned to his place on the Dias and angrily inquired of the courtiers, "Who may stand at court and speak for this trash?"

Regaining her composure and command of her voice, Lis-Yan pointed to Zander-Fells and asked, "House Zander-Fells, set forth your plea."

Zander-Fells quickly replied, "Aye, and gladly."

He turned to the courtiers and asked, "But does not the law require that even one such as this accused of vile sorcery toward the maiden Ka-Tayana have someone to speak in its defense?"

Lady Lis-Yan grabbed the opportunity to regain control of the situation. She rose from her place and left the Dais, stood next to Lord Zander-Fells and said, "Wisely spoken and point well taken. We have all seen how our Lord Dom's words found no purchase for its behalf."

The courtiers all nodded and whispered in agreement. Seeing the court's reaction to this move, Lady Lis-Yan continued, "Can any here speak for it? I think not. We at court recognize the law. Yet, how can we follow the law when none is here to fulfill it?"

In reply, Dom hissed slowly, each word laced with venom "A summary judgment, if House Zander-Fells were to request it."

For many heartbeats, it seemed Zander-Fells stood silently before the Archana and her court. Carefully considering the course Dom lay out before him. Then, looking Dom full in the face, Zander-Fells replied, "In times past such a judgment as you now propose would seem adequate."

Zander-Fells then turned and walked slowly among the courtiers, and inquired, "I put it forth to you. To judge in summary fashion now at our simple conveniences may be in haste. For upon the morrow, cannot, perhaps, a spokesperson for this one be found? Can we, upon the morrow, find that this one has a voice that we may hear? Can we in future days trust the needs of our narrow passions? Are there none that can stand and speak in its defense?"

A long silence filled the hall as none spoke. Not even the sound of the air passing by could be heard within the court. As Dom began to open his mouth, Anadan's voice came from within the crowd, "I may, my lord. Nay, nay hold your words my lords and ladies."

Dom, now fully aware of his challengers' presence, hissed and coldly proclaimed. "Who is this come in rags and dust unannounced to this court?"

Anadan walked out from the huddled courtiers, and staff in hand strode from the end of the hall toward the Dais. Once there, he stopped, made a slight bow and said, "A good morn to you, Lady Lis-Yan."

She signed her recognition of him, and responded, "A good morn it may be to you as well sage."

Straightening himself, Anadan turned and faced both Dom and the assembled courtiers. With a heavy sigh of regret he said, "We find ourselves in judgment, so it seems."

Dom spit out the words along with a stream of drool from his mouth, "How dare you?"

Looking square at Zander-Fells, Anadan replied calmly, "How dare I not? House Zander-Fells, if this one may speak through me, shall you find me an acceptable spokesman for its defense?"

Lady Lis-Yan responded, "What is your business here today? We sit in capital judgment and have little patience for your meddling."

Anadan turned to her and replied, "May it please this court. Did not the injured party call for a defense?"

Directing her stare at Zander-Fells, Lady Lis-Yan coldly asked, "What says House Zander-Fells?"

With a slight smile of satisfaction, Zander-Fells responded to her curtly, "I accept and submit the sage Anadan as worthy defense and counter to my charges. I pray, Archana, proceed and be quick about it."

Now it was Our Lady Lis-Yan's turn to sigh in relief as she pointed at Nils and commanded, "Very well. We know your complaint. Anadan, what are its words?"

Anadan walked over to Nils, bent over, and whispered in his ear. In kind, Nils also responded in whispers. As they furtively conversed in this manner, no one in the hall could make out their words. Not even Lords Dom and Zander-Fells, who were very close, knew what transpired between the two figures. Eventually, they finished their secret discourse and Anadan stood erect. He gazed at the Regent on the Dais with Dom at her side, and then he turned himself full circle, as his eyes flickered over every courtier and guard in the hall. Finally, he looked long at Zander-Fells and said, "Archana, as is the law, House Zander brings cause before you. But in this matter, I deem it right that Lord Dom, Landkrieser Fyrd Gelde and Keep Holder of Geldenherm, judge this for us. This one calls himself Nils. In his tongue, he pleads innocence toward the House of Zander-Fells."

Without hesitation, Dom answered, "The rendering." My Lady and court, waste no more time here. The noon hour is close upon us."

Lis-Yan stood and proclaimed, "We accept."

Zander-Fells exclaimed, "Who shall stand for the Archana?"

The suddenness of Zander-Fells' reply led more than one courtier to suspect that somehow Dom, Zander-fells, and Anadan were in league to quickly resolve the matter before the court. In latter days, it came as a bit of surprise to more than a few to learn that their suspicions had been, if slightly incorrect, well founded.

The Lady Lis-Yan stood up and proclaimed, "As the law proscribes, I name the resident Keep Holder and our High Councilor, Lord Dom. Guards, lead the prisoner. I summon this court to witness judgment in the matters concerning House Zander-Fells and this Nils."

With these last words, she came down the Dais and strode out of the council hall, followed first by Dom, and then Zander-fells. The courtiers and Fader-Ganger followed behind. Nils and Anadan followed last surrounded by guards in the trail.

Row upon row of high balconies surrounded the walls of the rotunda that formed the Judgment Chamber. Each balcony filled with the various members of the court and Faeder-Ganger. A hollow well topped by an iron fence and gate sat in the center of the ancient rotunda. A closed reticule sat in the rotunda's ceiling. It was into this grim place that Dom, the guards, and Anadan accompanied Nils. They entered into the well where the guards unceremoniously secured Nils to a post in its center. Anadan then turned and silently left the well. Dom stood before Nils, lifted his hands and arms toward the assembled court in the balconies, and cried out in victory, "What say you? I declare judgment. I declare the rendering."

With one loud voice came the court's reply, "Aye!"

In one balcony overlooking the view below, stood Lady Lis-Yan and Lord Zander-Fells. Lady Lis-Yan raised her voice and proclaimed, "All of you here stand in witness. I have named our Lord Dom to take the Archana's place. Is this just?"

With one solemn voice the courtiers, Faeder-Ganger and guards replied, "Aye."

She then turned to Zander-Fells and said, "House Zander-Fells, I sat upon the Dais and heard your cause and now stand ready to bring about doom. What say you now?"

Zander-Fells, stony faced, answered her in a full voice that echoed of the chamber walls, "Fulfill the law. They shall stand together."

Then bending to her ear, he said softly, "Well played my Lady."

With a wicked smile at him she commanded, "Lord Dom, take our place, for we shall have our justice."

"Aye, aye, aye" the crowd echoed off the walls as the guards held Dom and bound him next to Nils.

Once done, they left the well and closed the gate. As the tumult of the crowd faded away, the reticule opened above Dom and Nils. Lady Lis-Yan recited the oath of judgment, "Of long ago, pure light rendered the justice, as it shall now."

The reticule opened wide, revealing a large diamond held in a band of thick bronze set within the rotunda's stone ceiling. A bright, searing burst from the diamond and brilliant light filled the well. The courtiers hid their eyes from the bright stream that flashed into the well. Lord Zander-Fells and Lady Lis-Yan covered their eyes as cries of pain and anguish began to follow the oily smoke that soon billowed up from the well.

Flatly, Lady Lis-Yan said, "So shall evil be rendered from among our houses"

"Its true nature revealed," Zander-Fells responded.

"Aye." This was all Lady Lis-Yan could muster the energy to say as the reticule closed. Many of the court coughed as slowly the oily smoke began to fade and then clear from the well. The entire assembly gasped at one time as Dom's blackened, clawed hand opened the gate.

Dismay and disgust filled Lady Lis-Yan as she cried out, "No. It cannot be!"

The remains of Dom's burnt features looked at her with what had been the hint of a smile now quickly transferred into a frown. He opened his charred maw to speak. Horns blared and cries of alarm echoed throughout the citadel, and the croak that emanated from him was drowned out. A winded guardsman rushed into the rotunda, looked up at Lady Lis-Yan and shouted, "Vilder-Zerk are here! We are under attack!"

SIEGE!

Outside Citadel Geldenherm's granite walls, a vast army of armed and mailed Vilder-zerk marched across the wind swept plain. As one, the tens of thousands massed Vilder-Zerk marched resolutely toward the high and thick walls of the ancient Citadel. As they stepped in time to the beat of war drums, several Vilder-zerk carried the severed heads of Faeder-Ganger, riders of Zander-Fells and Mai-Yanna's troops.

Unopposed they reached the curtain walls and overtook the outer gatehouse. Those Faeder-Ganger and Faerevolder stationed at the entrance perished under the flash of swords, spears and scimitars. Seeing the perimeter walls lost, Mai-Yanna led the surviving Gangers in a fighting retreat across the moat and into the inner walls. With Vilder-Zerk streaming through the open gatehouse, and close behind, she ordered the inner gate closed, and the large bridge that spanned the moat to be raised behind them. The ancient oaken bridge was thick as the length of a man's arm, and covered on its surface with a mesh of broad steel bands. A barrage of dark arrows pierced the exposed portion of the bridge's wooden exterior as it sealed the remaining entry into the citadel.

Within the Judgment Well, Zander-Fells hotly interrogated the messenger, "Is there word of Mai-Yanna?"

The Guard replied hoarsely, "She retained her colors and yours within the inner walls. The outer wall is lost and the enemy holds the field."

Zander-Fells grasped the Faeder-Ganger by his mailed sleeve, and firmly stated, "All is not yet lost while we live. Guards, do your duty and escort the Archana safely to the docks."

Turning to the still disbelieving Lis-Yan, he commanded her, "Lady Archana, you and your court must leave now. Board the first boats you find and hasten to the Raffer-moor."

Stupefied, she huddled among her guards as Dom climbed out of the smoky well. She gazed long at his horribly burnt and disfigured form while upon her face played a mix of disgust and lust. She sobbed with tears running down her face, and cried out to him, "You are no more? How am I to claim the Dais without my councilor, my love?"

Dom's raspy voice gurgled, "Insect. You are not fit to sit at my master's chamber pot."

In response, several Faeder-Ganger arrows glanced off Dom's blacked shell of a body, bursting into flame at his sides. With a crisp command to the archers Anadan said, "Hold. Save your arrows."

Then in a firm voice, he commanded Dom, "Leave us and go to your master."

Dom replied, "Bagh, hiss! Not yet."

At these words, portions of the rotunda exploded outward, rending a great gash in its stonewall. The rotunda sagged and its roof and reticule shattered, scattering flame and debris down into the balconies and well. Like some disjointed insect, Dom scrambled out of the well and up the sheer side of the broken rotunda, making his escape through the shattered remains of its walls. Zander-Fells stretched out his cape, covered Lis-Yan, and shouted, "Leave this place now, while you can."

He pushed her toward a solid staircase as falling stone crushed many of the courtiers and guardsmen who were struggling to escape the ruined balconies and alcoves.

Dusk at Citadel Geldenherm found Mai-Yanna, Anadan, Zander-Fells, and Garm standing on the inner walls overlooking the massive Vilder-Zerk camp that lay in the fields that surrounded the citadel. Mai-Yanna's face was flushed with hot passion as she said, "We let her flee unharmed. We may pay dearly for that decision."

Softly, Anadan replied, "What other option was there?"

"None", Mai-Yanna stated flatly.

Continuing she inquired, "What of this Nils? Truth be told, I would have killed him outright had I found him in the wood and not in your cottage."

Agreeing with her, Garm growled, "As would I."

Anadan sighed, "Aye. But, you did not."

Zander-Fells, turned away from his view of the Vilder-Zerk camp and said, "Nils rests and asks for Anadan. As for those out there, I make it near one thousand campfires, say an easy ten thousand or more Vilder-Zerk. I did not know there could be so many this close to winter."

Anadan spoke firmly to his companions on the wall, "I fear this is long made and laid up for these days. Consider they are in a field of snow in front of these gates. So far from the Iron Mountains they have come."

The four of them stood overlooking their enemies below for some time as darkness fell. Then, Garm, Mai-Yanna and Zander-Fells retired into the relatively warmer interior of the Citadel. Lastly, Anadan muttered alone to the cold darkness, "How long may they stay outside of the shelter of these walls and without the rations laid up in the storehouses?"

Nils had long been in conversation with Anadan, as he lay awake in a bedchamber within Citadel Geldenherm. He was ensconced in linen undergarments and covered by warm blankets. For the first time since his arrival in the dessert so long ago, he was bathed clean and shaven. He gazed silently at the merry fire burning in the hearth. Anadan rocked forward in his chair toward Nils and said, "So you came by way of the desert after they took the caravan. Then it was through the forest to me. Yet, how is it you came from the Kunkern-kint of Taerevold to our lands?

Not recognizing the place the old man had stated, Nils asked, "From where?"

Anadan's eyebrows rose and his eyes twinkled as he remarked, "Taerevold, your home world."

Nils removed his gaze from the happy fire and said flatly, "I fell, from a tall building. Dom was in the room next to mine."

With a look of amazement, Anadan exclaimed, "Dom is come from your lands the same as you? How can this be? He has been among us many, many years. And you have only arrived this summer last."

Looking at the old man's shocked face, Nils answered, "I do not know the answer to your questions." Then, taking a deep breath he asked, "Perhaps you can answer mine?"

Stunned by Nils' response Anadan sat unmoving and silent in the rocking chair. Then with a shake of his head, he came out of his stupor and replied, "What is it?"

Cautiously, Nils continued, "When you were in my cell, you said something about my name. What did you mean?"

In a hushed tone, Anadan answered, "An ancient doom, prophesy some say. Na Sicharis tak no, durt am naktern Peridon blitz. The searcher will come as friend in the time of the evening emerald."

Nils asked, "You mean now, in winter?

"No.", Anadan crisply stated.

Confused at Anadan's curt reply, Nils asked, "Then what does this prophecy mean to me?"

Anadan rocked to and fro in his chair as he began, "It is an old legend of our two worlds. Once, long ago, the Great Maker formed the Faerevold and her twin, the Taerevold. This is Faerevold, the land of the Alten-kint. You are of the Kunkern-kint, a searcher from Taerevold."

Anadan stopped his rocking and continued, "Long ago the Great Maker made a vast garden, the Mitvold, and filled it with plants and animals of all kinds. Some of these inhabited the sky and sea, while others covered the land. Although pleasing to him in every sense, he was lonely. He brought forth the Val-Kiren, the first companions. The one among the Val-Kiren we do not name was first in Mitvold and to it, the Great Maker revealed much of his mind and desires. To this Val-Kiren was given great measure of power for creation and knowledge, sharing in the Great Maker's endeavors. Yet, the Great Maker desired other companions, and hence, became us. Some say we were formed from within his mind, others from the very stuff of the garden.

"When we were brought forth, it perceived our place in the Great Maker's heart and grew jealous. For it did not wish to give up its exalted placed in Mitvold. Desiring power over all things, it rose in rebellion against its master. Great and terrible was the rebellion, for it deceived many of the Val-Kiren to eagerly rise up and make war in Mitvold. These rebels were utterly defeated by the Faithful, driven out of Mitvold, and their leader was cast into the dark abyss."

Anadan, got up out of his chair and began to pace around the small room. As he quietly moved about, he continued, "We, the Alten-kint lived in his presence. We were not as the other creatures, and he desired others like unto us. Hence, became you, of Taerevold."

Anadan sat back down in the rocking chair and Nils asked, "This garden and its Great Maker, where are they now?"

Anadan resumed his rocking and replied, "We know not. I will tell you this. Upon a time, a great tempter came to us, a servant of the mightiest of the fallen Val-Kiren. In its rebellion, it had learned to gather power by devouring the souls of its fellow Val-Kiren. This was a great crime against the Maker and the Faithful unrelentingly pursued it.

As it fled the Great Maker's wrath, it and others stumbled onto one of the secret paths between the volds, disappearing into the maze that lies under and between them. Here the Faithful contained them, sealing the way back to the garden. Cursed by a never ending thirst, it fell upon its companions lost in the maze, ravaging its own kind. Eventually, it grew strong and powerful enough to reign supreme. It spent its time hunting and swallowing the tortured souls trapped in the maze beneath the volds.

However, upon a time it had no longer quarry, and now alone with its lust, it began to seek out others to devour. In time, it found us and we eagerly drank its wine and joined with it, reveling with it in our lust. So great was our thirst, only the blood of many seemed to slack it."

It was quiet in the room for a long while before Nils asked his next question, "What happened then?"

A tear slowly traced a path down one of Anadan's cheeks as he answered, "We near had destroyed all life in the Faerevold, feeding on our own flesh when the Great Maker found us. Terrible was his wrath. Some say he took a great hammer in his hands to destroy us. But, seeing that we were his own creation, he took mercy and held his blow."

Like a young child, Nils asked in a gulp of air, "What then?"

The old man replied, "The Great Maker stood in the middle of Mitvold and called all the beings of Faerevold to him. Birds, animals, the Val-Kiren, and the peoples. Once assembled, he bade each stand before him. As they did so, he searched out his or her heart and one by one, each creature took its place on the Maker's left or right. To the vast host on his left, he gave the lands east of the Iron Mountains. Of these came the Vilder-Zerk."

"Seeing what evil had transpired in Faerevold, he desired to keep Taerevold hidden from the tempter. He separated the two volds, Taere from Faere so the tempter may not have dominion in each. After he rendered our lands with each kint to its vold and each vold to its kint, he made a small part of the garden as a joining between the two. For at times he would walk this pathway between the two Volds, Faere and Taere."

Nils asked himself as much as he put his next question to Anadan, "So I came here by this pathway?"

Anadan, smiled widely and said, "No, I think not. None have ever found its gates. Or finding them, once having entered has returned."

Nils asked, "This tempter, what of it?"

Anadan answered, "Fled, to where, none know nor speak of it."

Nils said softly, "Yet, here I am."

Anadan continued, "Some say there are other ways between the volds. This is how many believe the tempter was able to escape the great maze and travel between the volds, gaining entrance into Taere and polluting both. Once the volds became despoiled, the Great Maker shut himself in the garden. Yet, some believe, as I do, the Great Maker desires redemption of all of his people and a re-joining of the volds."

Smiling, Nils said, "So I came through one of those other paths."

Anadan heavily replied, "As it seems Dom did as well."

Nils continued, "Dominare Avery. That is his full name. Where is he now?"

Anadan pointed in the direction of the window in Nil's room and said, "Out there with that army you have heard so much loose talk of the last few days. Now rest."

GELDENHERM FALLS

Within the Vilder-Zerk camp that night, the conversations were more brutish and sharp than that of Nils' and Anadan's. Huge Vilder-Zerk overlords knelt as Dom, his words guttural and broken commanded, "Then crash it in, and hammer it down! You will find no shelter or fodder here. The plain and high passes are filled with snow. Succeed or perish."

One Vilder-Zerk Overlord replied disrespectfully, "Ach-Bagh. Easy words from a g'uman. One that desires much that yet remains out of his reach."

Dom's hand moved toward the scimitar at his side and rested it on the blade's hilt as he said sweetly, "My desire is not mine alone. Fail this season, and I will return with another host to finish what you could not. Succeed, and who knows what rewards may await you."

Many days had passed with the Vilder-Zerk attacking the Citadel's walls, and its defenders repelling them. Terrible were the losses of the dead and wounded Vilder-Zerk. Yet, with each casualty he suffered, Dom supplied a never-ending stream of replacements. For the beleaguered Faeder-Ganger, the re-supply boats had stopped arriving soon after Lis-Yan's departure.

The Citadel had been designed and built to hold a great supply of food, water, and weapons. Warriors were the problem as for each Faeder-Ganger lost to death or injury, there were no replacements. Soon, very soon the mass of Vilder-Zerk would simply overwhelm the defenders. These grim thoughts were foremost in Nils' mind as he sparred with a bruised and very tired Faeder-Ganger in the Citadel's training area.

When Nils took a position upon the ramparts, the two types of Faerevolder soldiers, the Kaeder-Ganger that made up the garrison's foot, and the Faeder-Ganger remnants of Zander-Fells and Lis-Yan's mounted troops, ignored him. These warriors gave him little heed as he dispatched one Vilder-Zerk after the other with his hatchet. Nevertheless, others similarly trapped in the citadel gave great thought to the strange man who did not speak their language and knew not of their customs. These were of those who did not man the ramparts, yet fed and drank at the common mess. The members of the merchants and guilds, and the courtly folk who had not found passage downstream often hotly debated the presence of the foreigner who seemed to be held in high regard by Anadan and Lord Zander-Fells. It was of these Nils learned of his social status in the Faerevolder lands.

Not every day was there strife upon the citadel's walls. Indeed, the Vilder-Zerk would at times abandon their attack for weeks on end to seek game or burn and pillage within the outlying lands of Gelde. During these days of respite, Nils often took lessons in the ways and tongue of the Faerevolder from Anadan. Long and difficult was this schooling for Nils, yet he persevered and began to grasp the meaning of what he heard spoke. After one of Anadan's droning lectures on the finer points of Faerevolder society, Nils sat in one of the Ale houses. As he quaffed the last of the lightly alcoholic hard cider in his tankard, Nils could make out the gist of discourse that lowly rumbled around him.

At one table, groups of men were discussing the state of their cattle herds. Nils heard one say, "T'aint long afore my Steward runs the herd to the pens at Weslon."

"Aye, and what weight of coin?" was the terse question from one of his companions.

At the far end of the bar, a middle aged woman with grey beginning to streak her hair, and wearing the uniform of a Kaeder-Ganger was bemoaning the loss of some heirlooms, sobbing to the bar maiden, "It was the last of my dowry, and your master now has it in his hoard."

"Now, now dear." The bar maiden consoled her customer while wondering, *Now how will she make do for herself and the children? Too old to bawd when she is no longer good for fighting?*

Nils gazed into his empty tankard and began to consider the odd chances Dom's machinations had dealt this soldier and himself when a rough voice grumbled, "An ta look at 'im. Dumber an me ox, yet drink'n and eat'n wid decent folk."

Disturbed from his reverie, Nils looked up and spotted the Alehouse's owner staring directly his way. The innkeeper was a well-muscled, dark haired and squint-eyed man, his face well scarred. Nils instantly did not like the look of the man, nor of his companions. The squint-eyed Alehouse owner turned his gaze and said to bar maiden, "Unless you want to offer yourself or your house for her quits, then it is done."

The bar maiden patted the soldier's hand and said, "I can not do it."

Another man waited until she was well pst the door, then nodded toward Nils and grunted, "Aye, an' we uns can 'spect no less for a for-faet. Dat one has 'is Lord Zander-Fells a holden the markers for 'is board."

Forfeit! The thought shot through Nils as he realized his place among these people was no more than as serf. *Self-sold to gain a meager portion of porridge!*

Nils thought to speak and explain his situation. He held his own on the walls because he was a legionnaire and knew his duty in a hard fight. He fought to show his gratitude as a mere guest of Anadan in the Faerevold. However, before he could speak to do so, the bar maiden returned with the female Kaeder-Ganger, and they approached her squint-eyed employer. The three moved to a remote corner, and began to whisper. Then covering her face with her soiled apron, she scurried away. The Kaeder-Ganger spit in her palm and then shook hands with the Alehouse owner. She then turned, squared her shoulders and left the place. At this, Nils got up from his table and with a wry smile, a wink and a nod toward his detractors, left the Alehouse.

On one of the citadel's cobbled streets, a young lad had just finished making his blood oath. A Faeder-Ganger Serzian with the Zander-Fells house colors held tight to his cuirass by a wide belt grunted, "Now, make yer mark on ta parchment."

A lad not much more than the 16 I was when I first enlisted. Thought Nils.

The perfunctory scratching of the quill pen finished, the youth moved ahead and joined the small group of volunteers standing together in two loose rows. Nils advanced and slit his left palm with his hatchet, which he pressed on the parchment. The Non-com gave him a long slow look up and down, sizing Nils' temperament and judging his muscle tone. When he was finished, he and Nils locked eyes for a brief moment. Nevertheless, in that silent eternity where veterans meet they shared a common understanding.

"Welcome to the fight."

"As long as there are enemies to slay."

"Aye, and well met."

"Well met indeed." Said Nils, as he signed his name with a flourish on the enrollment parchment.

Awestruck at his display, the young recruits did not respond when Nils joined them. After the non-com had signed up a few more, he turned to Nils and said, "By your leave, please escort these Gangers to our barracks."

Nils nodded to the non-com. He then looked his fellow recruits over with a professional eye and said, "Now then, we are off to soldier together, and I know not your reasons for being here, nor do you know mine."

Then with the old voice of command returned to him, he intoned, "Face to your RIGHT!'

After a short pause, Nils said, "Now, lets try and at least look like soldiers. Now with the left foot first."

He paused again, and then commanded, "MARCH!"

A week later, Nils and his contubern stood in the Alehouse. When they had finished their drinks, they slapped their tankards on the rough bar top. He then reached into his pouch and threw a handful of gold and silver coins at the bar-maiden, saying, "Note this to the master of the house and his mates. I pay my own way."

His fellows mimicked his actions. Then Nils led them unceremoniously out of the one Alehouse in Geldenherm that never again saw their coin.

⤞⤚⤝

Targets, shields, and wooden waster practice swords stood in rows on the edge of the snow covered ground within an old corral. Near the shields, the exhausted Faeder-Ganger recruiter held his knees as he gasped for air. Nils, seeing his session was at an end walked to a water barrel. Using the pommel of the wooden waster, he broke the barrel's cover of ice. He laid the waster against the barrel and plunged his head quickly in and out of the icy water.

Not since his early days in the Legions, had Nils felt so physically fit and invigorated. It was as if the past years simply fell from him. Grinning like a young schoolchild, he scooped out more water from the barrel and rinsed the sweat from his bare chest. Training once again with the ancient weapons of war was much more fun than the hours Nils spent under Anadan's tutelage learning the Faerevolder language, history and customs.

Nils continued to drink from the barrel as Lord Zander-Fells and Anadan entered the training area. Seeing they had not come to simply observe his exercises, Nils wiped the water from himself with his bare hands and walked to them. Zander-Fells looked at Nils with a professional eye that made Nils think of a horse trader silently considering the various aspects of a new acquisition to his stable. The warrior said, "Anadan, it seems, was right to vouch for you. Very well, I declare you Freiholder, Nils of the Taerevold. Do you accept?"

Nils replied in the Faerevolder language with a thick accent he could not seem to shake, "I do."

Reaching out his bare right arm, Zander-Fells said, "Take my hand as man to man. You have well earned my favor for what you did for Ka-Tayana."

Nils grasped Zander-fells arm with his own right hand. Zander-Fells winked and continued, "It will not be so easy to earn the favor of others."

Releasing Nils, Zander-Fells turned and greeted Garm and Mai-Yanna, "Garm, Mai-Yanna, well met."

Garm saluted Zander-Fells and said, "Well met, Faeder-Hander. Is he ready?"

Zander-Fells replied, "He may speak for himself in due course. Mai-Yanna, did you find a more suitable instructor?"

Mai-Yanna smiled mischievously and answered, "Not I, rather old Garm did. I think his Suze-Li should be more than able. I am to the Raffer-moor this morning."

Nils shifted his gaze beyond Zander-Fells. His jaw dropped as he watched the form of a Faeder-Ganger, as brown as she was well muscled, walk confidently toward the training arena. She strode toward him as if she owned each tiny bit of real estate her booted feet stepped upon. Nils thought to himself, *If God created a Nubian Valkyrie, she would be the one.*

She was younger than Nils and carried the short javelins of the Faeder-Ganger in one hand. A short bow and full quiver rode over her shoulder. On her back was a broad shield. A scimitar, smaller than that of a Vilder-Zerk, rode easily on her left hip. The shining gleam of her armor helped to hide its several dents. Pride rode upon her helmeted face. Two jade-jeweled silver pins held back her braided black hair. Upon reaching the training arena, she stopped, looked Zander-Fells straight in the face, saluted and said, "My lord, at your service."

With a grin toward Nils, Garm said, "Be not gentle with him, daughter."

She dropped her salute, gave her father the shy smile of a little girl and said coyly, "Since when have I ever been so?"

Another day and another battle had passed. Within the Citadel's surgery wounded Faeder-Ganger lay on rough made cots while blood pooled into the rushes strewn by their beds. Zander-Fells and Garm watched as orderlies carried out the dead and the surgeons and nurses applied stitches and bandages to a sea of hurt warriors. A weary surgeon, upon finishing the gruesome task of removing a terribly mangled leg, rose from his patient. He managed to keep the exhaustion from his voice as he addressed Zander-Fells, "Yes, I know you can hold on as long as you have life. But these, and any other that are willing, must be sent downriver."

Zander-Fells tore his eyes from the now disembodied limb lying on a growing pile and said, "Very well. But know this, when the last boat departs, I will remain."

Garm held back the growing bile in his mouth and said, "He is right my lord. We have held here long days and can remain longer still. But…"

"We cannot hold forever.", Zander-Fells finished Garm's sentence.

He then commanded to the Serzian-Domo, "Prepare the old tower, when all is ready, we'll give him the inner walls. Surgeon."

"Yes, Lord." the surgeon replied.

Zander-Fells' head lay on his chest as he said, "Make your desire so. Garm will relay your offer for those that wish to go with you."

"And what of the dead?" asked the surgeon.

Raising his head and in a cold voice, Zander-Fells said, "I will attend to them."

At the training arena, Nils and Suze-Li thrust and parried at each other with the wooden waster swords. Nils was finding out it was one thing to fall in love with this warrior. However, quite another to keep her from inflicting bruises on him as if he were a clumsy boy. When he finally managed to block one of her strikes aimed at his head she chided him, "Better. Now thrust. No, you idiot, stay on your feet. Watch me. When you go in, eyes on the body, keep your balance. Then slide under his blade and into the gizzards."

Seeing a small advantage, Nils shifted his feet and deftly closed his body next to Suze-Li's. Their eyes were locked and lips almost touching as he said, "Like this, and then this, and this."

"Yes. Very good. But not too close. You must watch for the counter with the other hand," as she slapped Nils on the face.

"We are done here today." She continued as she broke contact with Nils. When she turned about abruptly, a sly smile crossed her blushing face. Nils' eyes followed her as she strode out of the arena, a wide wolf grin plastered across his face from ear to ear.

Within the many chambers of Citadel Geldenherm, one in particular was receiving the close attention of Zander-Fells and Garm. It was neither overly spacious nor narrowly tiny. One could say it was an altogether ordinary room except for two significant features, which made it the most extraordinary chamber of all. One of these was its close proximity to the bedchamber of the Archana; its passageway hidden by the clever use of false panels hidden within the chamber's library. The other, that it had been Dom's.

The place was in a state of disarray due to the presence of the jumble of stone that had recently formed one of its walls lying scattered about. Indeed, it had been the collapse of this certain portion of the citadel that now exposed the chamber to the Faeder-Ganger sent to secure the Archana's quarters. In the chamber's center, maps, and wooden models of war machines covered a large table. Drawings and sketches spilled from smaller tables onto the floor. Lord Zander-Fells was intently examining one of the maps in the light of an open window when Garm poked his head through the opening and said, "The keep is ready."

"Our wounded?" replied Zander-Fells.

Garm stepped into the chamber and looked about at the disordered mess, grunted to him and reported, "The last full boat left two hours ago. Messy bastard, eh?"

Zander-Fells, still looking at the map replied, "Yes, but a clever one to be sure."

Garm picked up one of the miniature ladders that lay against the model of a keep. He pointed at the model trebuchets and catapults, and holding the tiny ladder up to Zander-Fells, said, "I can understand these little ladders. He means to scale us. But what do you make of these contraptions?"

Zander-Fells dropped the map, looked at the models, and said, "I do not know. I hear Suze-Li's instruction is going well."

With a short snort, Garm replied, "Well enough."

Anadan stepped through the remains of the secret passage and exclaimed, "Here she is, and her pupil. Let's see what our new warrior can make of it all."

Behind him came Suze-Li and Nils. With a curt sigh of impatience, she said, "Ladders and towers on wheels. Sure to get over the walls. These?"

Nils looked over her shoulder and answered, "These are catapults and trebuchets. Machines designed to throw heavy stones to break down the walls bit by bit. Eventually, the walls fall leaving huge gaps for the assault troops to storm through."

Nils carefully picked up a model and continued, "This is a battering ram to burst open gates and strong doors. It carries a span underneath. This way they can bridge the moat as well."

Going to the window, Suze-Li directed her gaze outward and said, "The mess is awash with wild stories of the Vilder-Zerk building something beyond their camp."

Garm tossed the tiny ladder onto the table, pointed at the model trebuchets and catapults and asked, ""How do we fight such things from inside the keep?"

Nils responded, "You do not. They must be destroyed before they can inflict significant harm."

"How?" Anadan asked.

The next day the Vilder-Zerk managed to press the battering ram with its portable bridge up to the moat surrounding Geldenherm's inner walls. Once they spanned the moat, the creatures spent the next day exercising the battering ram, and hammered a breach into inner wall. Upon the walls and within the breach, the Faeder-Ganger fought hard and bravely. For every warrior that fell that day, ten Vilder-Zerk went into the void. They could not hold and eventually gave way in a rout as mounted Vilder-Zerk crashed through the narrow opening and attacked the defenders from every corner and flank within the inner ring.

High upon a parapet, Nils and Anadan watched in silence as the Vilder-Zerk pushed their advantage further into the Citadel's interior. Soon, they would be at the innermost wall, the citadel's final defense. Looking over the carnage, Nils spotted some abandoned wagons in an outlying alley below. Nearby a group of confused and panicked Kaeder-Ganger from the garrison was attempting to flee from the on-rushing cavalry. Turning to Anadan he asked, "How long do you think it will be before they reach us?"

Pointing to the assembled mass of Vilder-Zerk cavalry pressing the advantage, Anadan answered, "Not long. See there, Dom has committed his horse to the chase. The quicker with to secure his victory."

Nils smiled at him and said, "Dom always was an impetuous man."

Then he leapt past Anadan and sprinted quickly down the stairs. As he passed out of sight, the sage cried, "And what do you think you are going to do?"

Nils' faint reply drifted back, "To deal with those horses."

Then a fainter echo came to Anadan as Nils neared the parapet's bottom, "And perhaps buy us another day."

In the cobbled stone ways, Nils ran past panicked Kaeder-Ganger fleeing from the oncoming Vilder-Zerk. As he continued on, he noticed how one then, two and then more of the garrison troops slowed their pace, then stopped their retreat and fell in behind him. Without looking back or saying a word, Nils continued to run toward the enemy. He could hear the steady stomp, stomp of the small company of Kaeder-Ganger that followed him at the double. Reaching the place where he had spotted the wagons, Nils stopped. He quickly surveyed the area, then turned and asked, "This lane we are on, is it the only one that leads into the inner keep?"

One old Kaeder-Ganger Serzian replied in a guttural brogue, "Aye. Tis so an you gona mete out our end'n 'ere so's we's won't ne counted as co'ards in the telling o these times?"

Nils replied, "Counted as cowards, I'd say not. Moreover, as for endings, I do not intend for it to be for us this day. Now, then who among you will give a stranger a hand?"

"An' do what?" asked a voice from within the company.

Nils walked over to one of the wagons, reached down and lifted its tongue. Then, he bent his back and pulled the wagon out of the alley and into the lane, saying, "This!"

Catching his meaning the Serzian ordered, "Aw right you louts! The man 'as showed ya wa' he wants. Now git to it!"

With that, the Kaeder-Ganger broke into small groups. Each found a wagon, and pushed it likewise into the lane. Once in position, Nils ordered, "Over with them!"

The warriors pushed and pulled the wagons onto their sides, each one crashing into the other. Soon they were all down, forming a stout barrier. Nils found the sergeant and said, "Spears, man. Find as many as you can. Place them so the points face outward. You archers, line yourselves up back there behind the wagons."

About ten Kaeder-Ganger sprinted into the side alleys and soon re-appeared in a ragged line behind the wagons.

Nils asked, "Serzian, do you have a Kapral with you?"

From one group, appeared the stout female Kaeder-Ganger Nils recognized from the alehouse. With her graying hair in a tight bun, she stepped through the bustling Ganger, saluted Nils and said, "Kapral Smythe, at your service."

Nils looked at the two Non-comms long and hard, then said, "Split these Gangers into three. One of archers standing behind the wagons, and the other two evenly divided between you. Hide yourselves in the alleys. One group goes on the right the other in the left. When they get here, charge out and give them all you've got."

Kapral Smythe asked, "Aye, but how's ya gona git dem bag-tards here?"

With a grim smile, Nils set his face forward and said, "You leave that up to me."

Nils then ran down the cobbled lane toward the oncoming Vilder-Zerk cavalry. The Kapral and many Kaeder-Gangers stood, drop-jawed as they watched Nils disappear down the lane. With a rough smack on the Kapral's cuirass, the old Serzian said, "Hey ya no seen a rabbit run the hounds? Now git to yer posts!"

With that rough rejoinder, the two groups split and faded into the recesses of their respective alleys. Meanwhile, Nils regretted his decision as soon as he left the small company of Kaeder-ganger saying to himself, *Much better to have not done this at all.*

Then, with a quick start, he slid to a halt. Before him, came the Vilder-Zerk cavalry. Nils spun on his heel and sprinted back toward his colleagues, shouting, "No, you should not have done this!"

At the sound of Nils' voice, the large Vilder-Zerk in the lead spotted Nils and spurred his mount after the fleeing human. It was indeed a close race, as the Vilder-Zerk charged closer and closer on Nils' considerable head start. They did not hesitate when Nils darted aside and disappeared in the cobbled lane. Beating their lathered steeds, the Vilder-Zerk charged full tilt after Nils as he slid and disappeared underneath a turned over wagon, shouting, "Loose!"

A small shower of arrows arched from behind the wagons and felled several of the oncoming riders. A second volley of arrows quickly followed the first, then Nils commanded, "Here, get behind a spear"

Each archer grabbed a spear and thrust it forward as the Vilder-Zerk crashed into the makeshift barrier. Above the screams of the dying horses and last grunts of dead Vilder-Zerk, Nils shouted, "Now! Now!"

With a great "Ha-zah!" the two groups of Kaeder-Ganger poured out of the alleys and into the confused mass of Vilder-zerk cavalry. They chopped and slashed through horse and beast, pulling many of the Vilder-Zerk off their mounts, hacking off arms, hands, and legs.

Those Vilder-Zerk that could, jumped off their horses and onto the Kaeder-Ganger, preferring to fight it out on the ground. The melee ended when Nils led the archers around the wagons and charged the Vilder-Zerk with their spears.

"Ha-zah!, Ha-zah!", the Faeder-Ganger cheered as they charged into the melee.

After the last of the Vilder-Zerk cavalry lay slain on the stone path, Nils wiped fresh blood from his face and commanded, "One more great deed this day, my heroes, to the gate!"

Under the old Serzian's competent hand, the remaining Ganger quickly re-organized. At the double, Nils led the band to the inner gate, leaving the wounded and slain behind. Among them was the still form of Kapral Smythe, her once tightly braided gray hair splayed out on the cobbled stone in a pool of glistening red blood.

Within the Citadel, Zander-Fells busily made his final preparations for battle. Nils' destruction of Dom's cavalry had indeed gained not one, but many precious more days. Zander-Fells, Garm, and Suze-Li huddled alone together as they reviewed their plans. Zander-Fells walked away from his companions. Keeping his back to them he said, "Garm, I need you on the tower parapet. They must see you. Suze-Li see the remaining boats made ready and all able to get aboard to cast off. I'll not have the Vilder-Zerk take any needless trophies."

"What shall become of those too wounded to travel? Suze-Li asked.

Zander-Fells wiped away a tear as it coursed its way down one dirty cheek and said quietly, "Give them weapons. They shall die as warriors."

"And what of Anadan and this Nils?" Garm asked his leader and liege lord.

Zander-Fells straightened his hunched form, turned to his companions and replied, "Let them find their own spot, since it is evident they intend to remain to the end. Hold as long as you can, then to the pier. I shall meet you all at the Raffer-moor."

Citadel Geldenherm's storehouse were crammed full of provisions and weapons. Wall to wall, barrels and bundles were stacked high upon each other from floor to ceiling. Torches illuminated Nils and Suze-Li as they moved among the cramped stores of weapons and provisions. Suze-Li silently looked over one stack after the other. Eventually Suze-Li's gaze settled on dripping olive oil as it leaked from one barrel and trickled into a small, but growing, pool near one stack of dried apples.

Several days passed since Nil's actions at the middle gate, yet Suze-Li had not appeared at their daily routine of weapons practice. Within the mess, she was often found to be in deep conversation with one of the Serzians or her father. Now today they had spent the last hour silently inspecting the various goods within the storehouses. Grown weary at Suze-Li's cold silence, Nils asked, "Why are we down here and not on the walls with Garm?"

Shifting her eyes to Nils, Suze-Li responded, "Because, like it or not, after our Lord's charge there will not be enough of us to hold this keep. He will destroy those machines, as you call them. Few will return to the inner tower. It will not take the Vilder-Zerk long to find this place."

Nils, realizing the importance of Suze-Li's comments said, "The stores, of course! Anadan told me how they desperately need them to survive the winter."

With a wicked smile, Suze-Li moved past Nils and out of the storage room. She turned and stated matter-of-factly, "My Lord does not intend for them to have them."

Within Ka-Tayana's room, the young maiden was engaged in a hot debate with her father, Zander-Fells. "Do not send me away father. I am now hale and should be by your side."

Zander-Fells looked into the eyes of his impetuous daughter and said, "Dear Ka-Tay, daughter. You are the most precious of the vast treasure in these walls. We may lose gold, this pile of rocks, indeed our very lives. It will be nothing if we lose you. The escort is here. Now, to the docks with you."

Within the inner walls of the citadel, near where Nils had repulsed the Vilder-Zerk chargers, Lord Zander-Fells' banner led a Faeder-Ganger host in close formation. It passed the middle barrier and crossed the Vilder-Zerk bridge, and through the remains of the outer gatehouse and onto the plain.

Once on the plain and with silent command, the riders formed into a long, thin line. They carried swords, javelins and blazing torches.

To their front, in the distance were set the trebuchet and catapults. Beyond stood the Vilder-Zerk infantry, massed in dark formations, their spears and halberds glinted red. The banner went up and then down three times. The mounted host drew their weapons and their steeds began to walk, and then trot. Rapidly and remorsefully, the Faeder-Ganger troops closed the distance between themselves and their enemy.

On they came across the frozen plain, the rise and fall of the beating hooves made a steady rhythm as they cut through the snow. The few Vilder-Zerk placed near the war machines formed a line and presented their pikes and spears. Finally, the onrushing Faeder-Ganger let loose the energy of their eager warhorses and broke into a charge that hit and collapsed the Vilder-Zerk lines.

In an instant, the surviving Vilder-Zerk panicked and scattered out of the way of the onrushing host. The retreat soon turned into a rout that left the several trebuchets and catapults exposed to the galloping Faeder-Ganger. Mercilessly, the Faeder-Ganger cut down the Vilder-Zerk. They then followed the Zander-Fells banner as it moved through the machines. Many of the Faeder-Ganger threw their flaming torches into the works of the wooden machines. Soon, Dom's prized toys burst into flame.

Dom and a Vilder-Zerk overlord stood near a mass of on-looking Vilder-Zerk. He watched impassively as the Faeder-Ganger chopped his troops to pieces and set his contraptions aflame. His troops seethed in anger and frustration as their nostrils flared open at the smell of the burning flesh and wood. The Overlord growled, "Wait for the command. Wait I say."

Peevishly, Dom said, "Oh, you may proceed at your convenience."

The Vilder-Zerk Overlord's voice roared over the cacophonous grunts and growls of his impatient troops, "You hear him. Take their heads! The banner is mine!"

Emerging from Zander-Fells standard's flanks, two large formations of Vilder-Zerk charged into the mounted Faeder-Ganger. Within moments, the Faeder-Ganger and Vilder-Zerk were embroiled with each other in a wild melee. Back and forth, they fought as they hacked at each other with mutual hate, lust and abandon. The Zander-Fells standard moved through the intertwined groups. Wherever it went, the Faeder-Ganger formed ranks and fought with energy beyond men, killing two, three, or more Vilder-Zerk for each of their number. Yet, their ranks diminished as more and more Vilder-Zerk poured into the battle.

At one desperate point, the Vilder-Zerk surrounded a group of struggling Faeder-Ganger, the Zander-Fells standard stood flying in their center. One by one, the Faeder-Ganger fell as they slew the pressing Vilder-Zerk. Heedless of any danger, the Vilder-Zerk clambered over each other as the bright green standard with its golden lion fluttered and fell. Just as the standard collapsed, a group of mounted Faeder-Ganger charged over the angry mass. The hated enemy fell in heaps as the riders slew them. One rider leaned over his saddle, reached down and pulled the bloody and dirt- stained standard from the dead hand of the Vilder-Zerk overlord.

"To the citadel!" the rider commanded and spurred his steed over the dead and toward the Geldenherm Citadel. The remaining Faeder-Ganger rushed from the battle, across the field and through the gate. As they disappeared into the citadel's walls, they were too few to raise the moat and close the gate. The mass of Vilder-Zerk followed close behind the retreating Fader-Ganger.

As the horde reached the citadel's outer perimeter walls, one Faeder-Ganger raised Zander-Fells' standard high on the inner walls. The Vilder-Zerk killed all they encountered as they surged through the gate. Smoke billowed from the citadel as a portion of the inner tower wall fell. Falling stone, smoke and flame engulfed screaming Faeder-Ganger and Vilder-Zerk alike.

Suze-Li could hear the screams of the dying warriors echo through the walls of the storage room. She knew she had little time and hurried about as she and Nils finished placing candles and wicks among the stores. Once done, Nils moved out of the way as Suze-Li threw her torch onto the now substantial puddle of olive oil. The oil slick exploded into a ball of fire; its heat forced them to hurry from the storeroom. As they moved away from the rapidly growing conflagration and turned into a stone passageway, Suze-Li grimly said, "Now to make my Lord Zander-Fells' victory complete."

><:~--><:

Within the citadel, Anadan and Garm escorted Ka-Tayana along a long hall toward the docks. Faeder-Ganger lined the docks, waiting to load the already overcrowded boats. As they pushed their way through the crowd, a Vilder-Zerk leapt out of a passage way and attacked Garm. Garm pushed the maiden ahead of him and ordered, "Go! Go now!"

Anadan and Ka-Tayana ran toward the docks. As they did so, Vilder-Zerk poured into the area and overcame Garm. Simultaneously, wounded Faeder-Ganger, Nils and Suze-Li rushed onto crowded the docks and toward the few remaining boats. Vilder-Zerk continued to attack and strike them from behind. The Faeder-Ganger first one at a time, then in small groups, turned and met them sword to scimitar. Within the mad melee, Suze-Li lifted a stoic young girl and a small crying boy into the nearest boat and ordered the Faeder-Ganger closest to her, "Get in the boats. If there is to be another fight we must get in the boats."

With Anadan and Nils in the lead, Faeder-Ganger and Vilder-zerk slew each other as arrows and darts flashed from the walls and boats, lodging into the Faeder-Ganger and Vilder-Zerk alike. At the last boat's edge, a dark, vicious arrow pierced Suze-Li's side. Grasping the bleeding wound, she fell away from the boat and onto the dock. Her blood staining the oaken dock crimson, she lay at the feet of the fleeing mass. Anadan cut his way through the melee, and upon reaching her, he bent and retrieved her slumped form from under the trampling feet of her comrades and enemies.

Nils slew a Vilder-zerk and had begun to sprint with Anadan toward Suze-Li, and then stopped suddenly as a hoary Vilder-zerk captured Ka-Tayana by her hair. The young maiden kicked and screamed as she was pulled into the Vilder-Zerk horde. Nils, seeing he could not help Ka-Tayana, turned again, picked Suze-Li's limp body from Anadan, and pushed her and the sage into the last departing boat. The remaining Faeder-Ganger on the dock leapt onboard as Nils pushed the boat away. Nils looked into Suze-Li's eyes, and then turned to blunt a blow to his head from a dying Vilder-Zerk, his sword shattering into many pieces.

Nils grabbed up two scimitars from the bloody dock, and running toward Ka-Tayana, he killed her captor in one blow. Nils stood by the maiden and slew another Vilder-zerk, and another and another. Finally, a Vilder-Zerk managed to hit Nils in the head with the hilt of its battle-ax. Nils faded into darkness as he fell at Ka-Tayana and Garm's sides.

Ka-Tayana knelt before Dom as the suns rose, hidden by the gray sky. Behind his gilded carriage, Nils and Garm lay bound in chains on the ground. Dom stood regally in front of his carriage as he examined Ka-Tayana's supplicant form. In a gravelly voice, he said, "Is it not a very easy decision? They survive the day, and in return, you accompany me."

Ka-Tayana raised her eyes to Dom and defiantly said, "As your prisoner and slave?"

In the sweetest tone he could muster from his broken visage, Dom replied, "As my most honored and precious guest."

Pointing to some nearby Vilder-Zerk ogling Nils and Dom's prostrate forms he ordered, "You there, make way. These are mine. The rest take as your sport."

Dom reached out a crooked claw from his robes, raised Ka-Tayana from the ground, and walked her to the carriage door. The Vilder-zerk grunted eagerly as they attached Nils and Garm to the back of Dom's carriage.

Dom and Ka-Tayana entered his carriage. Once settled in, the carriage driver snapped a long whip and at a slow but steady pace, the horses trotted ahead. A small mounted escort fell in, and Dom's convoy rode out of the camp. Nils and Garm could only run in a quick jog in an effort to keep up with the carriage as jubilant Vilder-Zerk began to dismember dead and living Faeder-Ganger.

Within the smoking remains of the citadel's storerooms, Vilder-Zerk slew each other as they pillaged and plundered the contents. Great explosions of fire and debris roiled up from the citadel's storerooms and into the sky. In many places, the citadel's ancient walls broke and fell. As Suze-Li had anticipated, the ensuing destruction killed all but a few of the pillaging Vilder-Zerk within the ancient structures. In the wake of her sabotage one could see the jagged outline of what had once been Geldenherm Citadel's walls.

❧

Dusk on the river found the remains of Zander-Fells' army moving toward the Raffer-moor. Through the drifting mist and thick fog, the Faeder-Ganger boats slowly plied their way toward the Raffer-moor's docks. The Raffer-moor palace was, and remains, the largest and most splendid of the

Archana's residences. It has neither high walls nor towers of stone. Its layout and design are for the measured affairs of state, and the genteel recreation of the Archana. It was to this splendid place the remains of the broken Faeder-Ganger made its new home among its vast gardens and out buildings.

Anadan stood on the shore with Mai-Yanna as the boats made landfall and began to disembark their cargo. He asked, "These are the last?"

Mai-Yanna answered him sadly, "There will be no more. I do not see the banner of our house. He is no more."

With a nod of his head toward the palace, Anadan asked, "And what of her?"

Mai-Yanna responded carefully, "She sits alone in her chamber, become foul in her bloated flesh. And dark in word and mind. With Dom separated from her, the ageless mask she wore no longer holds. Old, so old she has become. None but the maidens I command serve her."

Anadan replied hotly, "Yet she remains Archana!"

Mai-Yanna answered in a professional tone, "For now. A select escort from my regiment stands as guard of honor at her doors."

"And of the Huskarl?" Anadan asked.

Mai-Yanna replied, "Those that survived gathered here to this last refuge. Zand Gelde and Zand Rohde are completely in Dom's power. I am unsure of Fyrd Dente. Fyrd Lind remains steadfast and loyal; its Steward, Jens Larzmon, and my spokested for Fyrd Zand are strong bulwarks. Nevertheless, the remainder of the Huskarl debates and discusses. None dare raise another from the Landkreiser in her place for fear of…."

Anadan responded, "Of Him? I should not wonder at it. Those that fell into his deceits will soon depart and follow those that are already his".

A guard approached, saluted, and said, "My Lady. The more sore hurt are overwhelming the surgeons. They beg you come and give some command as to what may be done."

From dawn until dusk at the Raffer-moor, Mai-Yanna directed every detail. From the raising of tents, to feeding the hungry and burying the dead, she provided much needed leadership, counsel and inspiration. In those days, she was grateful for the vast stores long laid at the ancient fortress that overlooked the place.

Some say Faerevold was re-born those long days along the shores of the Raffer-moor, even as Faeder-Ganger and Freiholder alike carried the wounded to the surgeons or placed the dead in the mass graves. Although much was attributed to others in later times, it was Mai-Yanna who organized and assembled the Faeder-Ganger and the Kaeder-Ganger into a force fit to fight during those dark and dangerous days.

Upon the end of one such hard day, and long into the evening, a cloaked man sat quietly in a dark corner in the rear of Mai-Yanna's tent. She strode in, stopped and swiftly drew her sword across the man's throat. She coldly ordered, "Stand and show yourself."

Careful not to slice his arteries against her extended razor, the man stood. He wore only a stained and tattered cloak over his dirty mail. A hood covered his head and face. Looking at her, the man slowly removed the hood. Eyes wide, Mai-Yanna dropped her sword and leapt upon him. They embraced in a long kiss. Pulling away from his tight embrace, Mai-Yanna asked, "All is to your plan?"

Zander-fells smiled and said, "To some degree, yes. The Vilder-Zerk will not be a threat to us this winter. Suze-Li saw to that."

"And Garm, he is not here?" she asked.

Zander-Fells' body shook and he cried sadly, "He fell at the docks protecting her. They took her. In spite of all else, they took her."

Mai-Yanna responded flatly, "Then we are lost. What use is it now to raise a host for battle when he has her?"

Wiping away the tears from his face, Zander-Fells said, "Dom does not know that I am here. That gives us at least one more advantage."

"Another advantage?" Mai-Yanna asked, "What others could there be?"

Zander-Fells replied in the tone he used when giving his subordinate instruction, "The Faere-kint are driven asunder in great dissent. Even in this camp there are those who will go over to him."

"And that is an advantage?" Mai-Yanna asked.

"Yes. Among a few others. Now, what of Anadan?" Zander-fells asked.

She replied, "He is with the court and council now. The Huskarl has made cause for a Tektar and the High Justice is to announce her decision on the morrow's cockcrow. I fear there shall be more than a few that will depart from the Fyrds."

Zander-Fells responded to this news stoically, "Yes, and from among the Ganger as well. We must replace those lost. You sent word?"

Mai-Yanna replied, "Suze-Li has sent riders through the Fyrds to raise recruits. Perhaps we will find a few fit to ride come this spring."

Zander-Fells looked loving at Mai-Yanna and said, "Tomorrow you will find this one. Tonight I wish to enjoy my wife."

Mai-Yanna slipped off her cloak and said, "As you wish, Faeder-Ganger". Then she flashed Zander-Fells a wife's sly smile of love and gently pulled the tattered robe from him.

IN DOM's HOUSE

I t is said among the Bebuznikas (the old grandmothers of the Faerevolder), that after his defeat at the hands of the Great Maker, the tempter retreated and hid itself. Deep it hid within a dark vale in the line of tall, jagged mountains that lay astride the farthest edge of the nethermost region of Faerevold. Indeed, it was in this very same cleft in the Iron Mountains that Nils and Garm found themselves trudging one sore foot after the other, held in the heavy chains that bound them behind Dom's carriage. On each side of them marched lines of heavily armed Vilder-Zerk.

Val Dunkerz is the name of the gray, desolate vale of smoke and drifting ash. Slimy muck oozed through the sparse and vile streams. At the vale's narrow end, a tall, dark tower, the Zat Erzern, protruded from the mountain's sheer rock face. Its thick iron gates rested open on shoulders made of piles of foul rubble and rock. As Dom's carriage entered the gates, harsh blasts sounded from within and echoed of the vale's walls. As they passed through Garm surreptitiously glanced about then poked Nils with an elbow and asked, "What do you notice about these ones?"

Nils did not raise his head when he muttered, "They are Vilder-Zerk. What else is there to notice?"

Garm replied under his breath, "They carry weapons and mail clean and well kept. It has been the same since we entered within the vale. They even march in ordered ranks. These are not your average Vilder-Zerk of the Iron Mountains."

This was met with the butt of a Vilder-Zerk spear applied forcibly to the back of Garm's head as the Vilder-Zerk Overlord growled, "Ach-bagh. No talking among the fodder!"

Had Nils raised his head he would have seen that Garm was indeed correct. The Vilder-Zerk amassed in the vale wore sable cloaks and gleaming hauberks of a single design: Dom's token—a crimson mailed fist holding an ax in the center of each breast plate. Each likewise held a long halberd and had a scimitar riding at the left hip.

Zat Erzern, the place that Dom now called home was made near the beginning of all things within the Faerevold. How it got there and its true name was the subject of much myth and ancient lore. Only few of the wise who had long studied Faerevold's history in the archives of the clerics knew the tempter himself had wrought it out of the cold stone in the hour of his most desperate need. Pol-Temna'k, the hall of darkness, the great evil had named it. For age upon age, the Zat Erzern and Val Dunkerz had remained hidden from human or Vilder-zerk eye by the vile mists that the tempter created to shroud the secret place wherein it long gathered its strength and power.

Ranks of bowing Faerevolder stood assembled on the steps leading up and into the dark maw of the Zat Erzern. Dom had personally culled the most beautiful of those from the herds of fools that had followed him to perdition. Some Dom sent to the dens hidden deep in the many twisted vales of the Iron Mountains to be slaves or brood mates of the Vilder-Zerk. The others disappeared into the caverns of the Zat Erzern as fodder. Of his select supplicants, they greeted Dom and his escort Ka-Tayana with great flourish of music and dance. For Nils and Garm, the Vilder-Zerk roughly hustled them through a narrow portcullis, and deposited them in a dark and moldy cell, still in their chains.

Once seeing Ka-Tayana ensconced in comfort in his personal rooms, Dom made haste with one buxom maiden and offered her as sacrifice to his Master. After the beast was satiated, Dom bowed low and reported all that had transpired at Geldenherm.

"Good" echoed the hollow voice, "And what of our servants, the two you have sent to see to our possessions?"

Dom made his obeisance lower and replied, "One is to take up our seat in the western Fyrd to better contain any that may befriend our enemies. The other attends us within the Huskarl, and surely no action may be done or spoken of without our knowing or influence."

"Then take up your residence and see to your...dinner guests" the voice intoned.

Later, deep within the bowels of his hideous abode, Dom sat nude at the edge of a steaming pool. To regain his human form, he was required to bath in hot Faerevolder blood. As the leathery skin was replaced by pustulant flesh, Dom would retire to a pool fed by the hot waters that passed near the molten lava coursing far beneath the Zat Erzern's foundations. Here he sat and held court.

His disfigured face flushed red with wanton lust as his courtiers, well-proportioned men and women, undulated in a steamy haze. Some mixed heavy red wine and blood in golden flasks. Others drank deeply from the flasks or engorged themselves on raw human flesh. Many copulated with abandon.

As he surveyed his court, Dom slowly caressed the breast of a voluptuous woman sitting next to him. She gently stroked his dark purple erection that was as enormous as it was disfigured. Before Dom stood Ka-Tayana, bathed, perfumed, and dressed in a thin silk garment that revealed the outline of her young breasts. A bejeweled tiara adorned her hair. Heavy gold and silver rings encircled her toes and fingers. Gazing at her, with misty lust in his eyes, Dom offered her a golden goblet and asked, "Shall it be my pleasures that entice you little one? No? Then perhaps something else?"

Standing still as stone and keeping her eyes fixed away from his crippled form, Ka-Tayana replied, "You are a beast. I will not drink from your bitter cup nor eat from this table of horror. Think that I shall easily lay with you in your corruption?"

With a mischievous grin, Dom said, "Others have found themselves doing so, your Lady Archana, for instance. She indulged and fed herself on but a thin portion of my feast. You yourself have seen how she has kept her beauty these long years. Yet, she shared none of what I offer you."

"Never!" came Ka-Tayana's curt response as six Vilder-Zerk escorted Nils and Dom, still in the heavy chains, and knelt them before Dom.

Dom shifted his gaze to his other prisoners and said calmly, "Never can be a very long time, little one. And time is something I have in large store."

To the guards he ordered, "Escort her to her rooms. I tire of this lean and most unrewarding conversation."

Quickly, two of the Vilder-zerk came forward, took Ka-Tayana by the wrists, and led her into a dark passage. She scarcely had time to flash Garm a glance of defiance as they hustled her away. In that brief moment, a clear understanding and firm resolve crossed between the two of them.

Not noticing the silent exchange between Garm and Ka-Tayana, Dom sneered at his prisoners and said, "Ah, the great Faeder-Serzian Garm. And who could this be? Why, none other than my old associate, Nils old boy."

Garm looked at Nils directly in the face, "You know him?"

With one voice Nils and Dom replied, "Yes."

Seeing the confusion on Garm's face Dom began, "Garm, I see your predicament. Whom do you trust now? Lady Lis-Yan is my thrall, Mai-Yanna is missing, and Lord Zander-Fells' body is fodder for my hordes. And, what of Anadan; who commands Garm now?"

Stiffly Garm answered, "I need no one to direct my deeds."

Dom looked long upon Garm with a curious gaze then said, "Bold words do not fool me, Garm. I know you, the brave, courageous man, and the great warrior. Yet, always in the service of Zander-Fells or Anadan. Do not deny it."

The Serzian did not reply and Dom spit out his evident disgust with Garm and ordered, "Guards. Take this Faeder-Ganger. Leave the other one with me."

As the Vilder-Zerk hauled and shoved Garm into an ill-lit side-passage, Garm shouted to Nils, "Beware, man. His offer will turn to dust in your mouth as soon as you taste the hint of it."

With rough grunts, the Vilder-zerk guards unceremoniously drug Garm into a passageway. Dom looked at Nils, much the way a nanny might as she prepared herself to scold an errant child, "Nils. My, my, just what am I to do with you?"

Nils stood erect from the stone floor and looked Dom in the face, "What do you want? I did not ask to be here."

With a heavy sigh and a shake of his head, Dom responded, "No, you did not. Yet, here you are, a mere miscalculation that I can easily correct. But, oh it helped things fall into place so neatly. That asinine court and council was so taken up with the idea of you in their precious Faerevold, they plumb forgot all about little ol' me."

Nils retorted hotly, "Anadan did not!"

Ignoring Nils' outburst, Dom sipped red liquid from a flagon, and then said sweetly, "He, like those of his order, is a fool to strive against powers he so little understands. His reward shall be pain. Not so for you Nils. You want it? I see the lust in your eyes as you look upon me and mine. I can smell the desire in your sweat. Pleasure and wealth immeasurable. All yours. This is what I offer."

Nils had proven himself in combat at Geldenherm and he would fight many great battles during his travels through out the Faere-Vold. He had resisted Dom's deceits at both The Tower and Geldenherm. Yet, no conflicts were as difficult or as dangerous as the one he fought-the silent war within his soul and mind as he stood before the full display of Dom's power and lust.

With intensity greater than the incident in the cell, the lamps ceased to flicker and the light blurred as a cold sweat rose on Nils' brow and dripped down the back of his neck. It seemed the air in Dom's chamber became thick, musty, and hot. Nils licked his lips and his chest heaved as that of a man exhausted after a long, fast-paced foot race. His eyes glazed over as Dom indulged himself with the voluptuous female at his side.

Dom could sense Nils was deep in the trap his Master had set. He motioned with one clawed hand and the two Vilder-Zerk nudged and prodded Nils with their spears toward Dom. Nils' shuffling feet reached the edge of the steaming pool. Nils stood on the precipice; a foot raised to take one, small final step. Then, the lamps flickered and Nils felt a small, quick breeze move slowly, gently and steadily over him.

As one coming awake from a deep sleep, he moved his lifted foot backward, and announced in a low, yet clear tone, "Power. Yes, I can feel it. The pleasure you offer is but pain in a different form. Another holds my marker, and I will never be yours. I will not."

Dom released his grip on the woman's breast, and leapt up out of the steaming pool. His now flaccid penis flapped on one thigh. A cascade of hot water shot off his grotesque form and splashed over his court, scattering the sycophants. Dom's body violently shook and he shouted at the guards, "Avast with that! He rejects my pretties. No matter!"

The Vilder-Zerk stood, bewildered at the turn of events. Dom glared at Nils, and then drained the remains of his flagon. With the red fluid dripping from his lips, he threw the golden chalice at a cowering courtier and ordered, "Take him."

The guards grabbed Nils and pulled him toward the shadowy passageway where Garm and Ka-Tayana had disappeared before. Nils heard Dom's cackling voice fading as he was hustled away, "Go along Nils, old man, and see the rest of my house. I am sure you will not be comfortable."

Their cells lay on each side of a long hallway in the deepest center of his lair. Like everywhere else in the foul place, the cells lay shrouded in darkness. How long Nils and Garm had lain beaten, and unconscious in their reeking cell, neither could say. Upon a time when their tormentors were absent that Ka-Tayana came to them and cried silently as she observed the cold chains that held their severely cut and bruised bodies to the wall. Ka-Tayana stood outside of the cell's bared door holding a torch, its faint light dimly flickering in the dark. She kept her voice to just above a whisper and called, "Protector, awaken."

Garm opened his eyes and in a low groan said, "Ka-Tayana, little one. Flee this place. Leave me."

Young in years she was, but not for nothing had she been singled out to rise to the Dais. Under the teachings of Anadan, she had become old in knowledge. While under the tutelage of the Grand Fizir, she had gained a great store of wisdom. Above these all, while infirm in her sick bed at Geldenherm, she had sat at the High Throne of the Great Maker. In The Everlasting Palace, she had learned the great and terrible secret she and Nils shared. Firmly, the young maiden scolded the grizzled warrior, "I must not. Do not ask me how I know it. Only believe me that it is you two who must flee. I am to remain here awhile longer."

The old veteran knew something of this lass, having been near at her side since her breeching. He had been a constant companion and guide, and had noticed the changes beyond the normal maturing of her body. Unlike other lads and lasses of her age, she had become much like the sage. Even more so after her sojourn among the Aerkenern. In the days at Geldenherm, he had noticed a deeper change, something in her eyes that seemed to look beyond the horizons or the faint sighs as she considered an infant babe in its mother's arms.

After the events in the Rohdernvald she had passed into and out of a darkness Garm did not wholly understand. Yet, he sensed she had returned in a form more wonderful and greater than all the Ganger host assembled. She had become a being more of legend and fable than of the House of Zand. Hence, he took her at her word, did not protest, and only smiled and said, "Rare are the opportunities given us to choose our doom. You have chosen yours. Ours is before us."

Nils, who had regained consciousness, weakly croaked out, "I fail to see how we are to flee anywhere as we are pinned to this wall."

Ka-Tayana raised her other hand and with a slight jingle revealed a thick ring of keys in her tiny grasp. "I have the keys. Dom is satiated with his lust. He and his court sleep, as do the guards."

She then hastened and unlocked the cell door and freed Nils and Garm from their chains. Rubbing his sore wrists, Garm said approvingly, "That's a good lass now where is the way out?"

"Follow me." She replied and began to walk into the long hallway that led to the cells. Garm and Nils stumbled out of the cell, and struggled to get mastery of their legs as they hobbled behind Ka-Tayana's flickering torch into the dark passage.

On and on Ka-Tayana led them at a trot thru the twists and turns of the underbelly of Dom's hideous tower. As they moved along, both men found their legs and balance, and soon were right behind Ka-Tayana as she guided them thru the labyrinth of closed store rooms lining the narrow corridors. The maiden turned into one and going to a slimy wall, searched for a hidden door.

While they waited for her, in the flickering light of her lantern Nils espied the familiar outlines of engineering schematics deeply etched into the stone. He moved to get a closer look but on her command of, "No time! You know what these are and now we must make haste."

She opened the door, revealing another passageway. Into this, they passed and began once again to trot. Unlike the other rooms lining the earlier corridor, these were open. Nils shuddered as he caught a glimpse of the piles of rotting human flesh suddenly revealed by the flicker of light from Ka-Tayana's lantern. It was after passing one of these charnel rooms that Ka-Tayana stopped and pointed at a small door at the end of the hall.

Nils, Garm and Ka-Tayana stood for a moment at the bottom of the long and narrow passage way they had traveled upon. Nils could see stairs off to the side that led upward behind them toward a dull, red glow. Ka-Tayana opened the small door to the starlit night, and Garm stepped through. Ka-Tayana placed her small hand on Nils' arm, "He will have more need of you, I fear, than you of him. Now run as fast you can. This house will soon awaken and you must be far from it."

Nils nodded his understanding and exited the door to stand next to Garm. They looked back at Ka-Tayana framed by the outline of the small door. The maiden took two small steps into the clean, cold night air and stopped. Garm and Nils turned to face her, but before they could enquire as to the nature of her hesitation she said, "Time is your most precious friend, and fiercest enemy this night. My doom had found me long before I reached the age of womanhood. Feel neither despair nor sadness at what I now must do. By my remaining, it shall confuse the not so great and powerful Dom, and his master."

Nils made to speak, to force her by his words to accompany them in their flight. Yet the young maiden pressed a finger to his lips and said, "Naysay me not. I shall lock the door and return to my rooms, and you will have a bit more time on your side."

Garm turned his head and wept, "Until our next meeting, young princess."

Then they placed their backs to her and began to run away from the Zat Erzern. Once they disappeared well out of site, Ka-Tayana closed and locked the door. Neither Garm nor Nils saw her drop her head, slowly turn and sadly bowed, sobbed, "Garm, by either my life or death, I will hold true."

She then began the long, lonely climb toward the dull, red light.

Under the night sky, Nils and Garm ran steadily along a cliff's rocky and narrow ledge. Their heavy strides and slapping feet punctuated quick gasps for air. Garm suddenly gasped out as he grabbed Nils by the sleeve, "Halt man! We need air!"

They slowed their pace and stopped, holding their knees, gasping exhaled fog into the frigid air. Garm, in between gulps of cold air intoned, "The pure heart. Courage in the dark. The evening star, a light for all."

"What is that?" Nils asked as he also sucked in the night air.

"An old song. Prophecy some say. Lay on before your muscles freeze. There is nothing for it but to press on." Garm commanded as clouds passed overhead. Slowly at first, then quicker and quicker, Garm and Nils ran along the cliff's edge.

Evil was Dom's lair, full of his foulness and filth. Yet, within a secret place, that none but Dom knew of sat his lord and master. Dom lay prostrate and convulsing before the dark form; his face pressed against the harsh stone of the chamber floor. In the deep dark, its eyes sparked red and blue flame passed between its knife-like fangs. Its voice hissed and spit foam as it spoke, "Need I remind you by whose power you yet breathe in this place?"

With a cry like an infant's, Dom shakily replied. "No, my master."

The Dark Lord hissed, "Shall I have patience with you, slave? Shall your soul be a morsel in my mouth?"

Splaying his arms forward and pushing his head along the cobbled floor toward the dark form, Dom whimpered, "I am as you wish."

The Dark Lord's form stood and leaned over Dom and growled, "Thou fool of a man. Understand what your weakness has brought forth."

Dom peeked his head up slightly above the level of his outstretched arms toward the towering figure above him, "The two shall not get far. Even now we hunt. Soon you will feast."

"Bagh!" came a disgusted reply from the chamber's ceiling.

"And what of the one that I desire?" it hissed as the Dark Lord took its seat.

Now, daring to look up, Dom raised himself and fully exposed his face to his lord, "She…she remains in the keep, Master."

The Dark Lord leaned back, "She has done this to us and still remains. It is her doom. Win her to me, Dom."

"As you command, Master." Dom now knelt before the blue flame and red flickering eyes.

"Her soul shall be mine," came the hissed reply.

Dom stood and asked, "And those two?"

"If the prey slips your beasts, then let the cold have them." The Dark Lord responded.

Dom stood, bowed deeply toward the red eyes shrouded in darkness, and then backed out of the chamber.

Near the breaking of dawn Nils and Garm found themselves at the edge of a high cliff of rock. The mountainside was strewn with ice, and the wind blew hard snow and tiny splinters of ice into their faces. Far in the distance, the Zat Erzern lay shrouded in the grey morning mist. Far below, boulders of ice crashed into each other as swift water hurled them downstream. Garm was gazing intently back at the track they had followed, and then said, "Dom has surely noticed the small matter of our absence this morn. I'll wager he was on our scent as soon as he awoke."

Nils answered, "Perhaps she has delayed him? Why haven't we seen or heard any pursuit?"

Garm snorted, "His vanity. My Lord Dom loves the hunt. A master hunter he is in his own mind. The greater the challenge, the greater the glory. Simple lust for pride. That's his doom."

Looking about him, Nils chattered out, "Then we must get out of this place."

Noticing Nils' blue, cold pinched face and his own shivering, Garm realized they had taken neither cloaks nor boots. Or anything else to protect them from the bitter winter in which they both found themselves freezing. Not that there had been much time nor opportunity for Ka-Tayana to have gathered all of the necessities for a winter's march. The old Serzian winked at Nils and said, "Aye, and much farther than this if you want to live."

Nils jolted erect as screeching howls echoed faintly in the air. "Hear that?" asked Garm, "He's sent his blood snuffers on us. We have little chance on these icy rocks."

Nils knew he could not continue to run, much less avoid blood-tracking beasts. He put his head in his hands and sighed to himself. Then he pointed at the stream below and said, "Look down there, running water."

Garm looked down at the coursing, ice-filled stream, "So. What of it?"

Nils straightened and grinned, "I do not know about your world, but in mine, water is a great way to throw off a blood sniffing beast."

Exasperated at his companion, Garm growled out, "This is no time for storytelling."

Nils flatly said, "We have no weapons, and I'm blown. I cannot outrun them."

"We've our fists and teeth!" The warrior shouted.

"And something else." Nils pointed to his head, "Our brains."

With a curt grunt, Garm replied, "Brains you say? Let's use 'em while we still can."

"Then follow me.", Nils stated as he led the way forward along the cliff edge.

At the base of the cliff, two black saber toothed wolves, snapped and growled at each other and against their steel leads. Large Vilder-Zerk tightly held the stretched leads in mailed fists as Dom gingerly sniffed he air and said, "Release them. Even I can smell Garm's stink now."

The Vilder-Zerk released the leads. With a jump and a snap forward, the snarling beasts leapt ahead of Dom and his party. It was not long before they had Garm and Nils trapped, the men standing at the edge of the high cliff edge. The small river ran far below. Before Dom's prey stood the two slathering Blood Snuffers. Nils and Garm watched Dom and several mail clad Vilder-Zerk with weapons drawn move from behind the snarling beasts. Garm asked Nils, "If you've got something else, let's have it. A'for we're Vilder-Zerk fodder."

Nils stood behind Garm, and looked into the boiling water. He asked, "Tell me Garm, can you swim?"

Garm knew Nils had lost what remnant of sanity he may have had and cried, "You mean flail about in the water? I'd rather sprout wings and fly."

Nils grinned at the Serzian and with all of his strength, unceremoniously pushed Garm off the ledge shouting, "Fly? I thought you would never ask."

Following him. they fell through the raising mist and hit the coursing stream. Their bodies bobbed in and out of the roiling water as it covered their forms. Dom, the Vilder-zerk and Blood Snuffers ran to the ledge. Together, they gnarled and growled in hate and anger.

⊱━⊱━⊰

Wisps of steam floated up from a boiling chalice as Dom stood bowed at the waist before the form of his master. The flashing red eyes intoned, "Dead you say?"

"See with my eyes, Master." Dom bent and pointed toward the bubbling chalice. Two gnarled black claws shot out and grabbed Dom's head. A trickle of blood oozed from Dom's temples and out between the knobby hooks that served as fingers for the Dark Lord. Dom swooned as from within the floating steam, the image of two human forms floating in the water appeared.

Blue spit drooled from its long fangs as the beast watched the bodies of Garm and Nils roil and disappear under a rush of swift water. It announced, "There, under the ice and cold water. They are gone."

The claws released Dom's temples and from the burning orbs came a slow hiss, "So it is as you have said. Excellent!"

>⟋⟋~⟍⟍⟍

Down, down the two swirled in and out, below and on top of the roiling stream. Eventually, the stream widened and slowed, and the ice blocks became fewer and smaller. Nils and Garm crawled out of the now near-still water. Both shivered uncontrollably as ice began to form on their legs and in their drenched hair.

A thin line of blood trickled out of Garm's blue lips as he stuttered, "Fa-fa-fire mmm-mann. We-nnn-need a fire."

Nils looked at the wounded man. He had seen this type of injury before in the Corps, and knew Garm would live. That is if he could keep the old veteran from freezing to death. Then manage to get him to a surgeon. Their exit from the icy stream was at a wide, sandy beach boarded by a slight slope. Nils looked about, his gaze settling on a pile of bracken left stranded higher up upon the shore's bank. He grabbed Garm by one elbow, and stuttered, "Th ther. We-w-we ggg-go up there."

"Aye." Garm grunted and then coughed up more blood, "Me chest, I've cracked ta' lung."

Up the gentle slope they moved. Together crawling and puling each other along each slow foot of the snow-covered incline. Eventually, and near dead from exhaustion and exposure to the freezing water and cold air, they reached the bracken. Nils rolled and pulled Garm's now near lifeless form into the pile. Once in himself, he cleared an area of broken branches and leaves, revealing a bare spot on the frozen ground. On this he made a small pile of dry tinder and kindling. He gathered together a good store of larger tree limbs which he broke into arm-length pieces and stacked to one side.

Through glazed eyes, Garm mumbled, "Wha-what y-ya doin'?"

Now ready to begin his fire, Nils reached into his left boot and withdrew a small piece of flint and a short steel rod. With quick clicks, He began to strike these together, throwing tiny sparks into the tinder. When the tinder began to smolder, he blew into the small tendril of smoke and replied, "Watch."

Soon a fire blazed within the makeshift shelter of the bracken pile. Nils and Garm dried their cloths and themselves. Once recovered from their grueling journey through the snow fields and ice floes, they gave thought and word to their next needs. Food was the most pressing, but they also needed to make sure of their escape from Zat Erzern.

Garm said, "One day here, maybe two, and then we must move."

"Aye, and far as fast as we can. But to where?"

"To the Rafermor. It remains the only place where we may find succor this side of Steppes."

"The steppes?" asked Nils.

"Aye." replied the grizzled veteran, then he coughed up a thin trickle of blood and passed out.

The sleepy Faeder-Ganger guard had begun the appointed rounds at mid-night and now dawn found him once again at the docks. It was early spring, and a grey mist hung close to the water of the Raffer-moor. The guard stopped his measured pacing and stared intently as a small, makeshift raft floated slowly out of the mist. A man lay bundled in rags of torn animal furs. Another, similarly attired, rhythmically pushed a long pole in and out of the stream, moving the raft forward. The sentry shouted, "Hold and off I say! Sergeant of the guard, a raft comes un-heralded!"

The man made a small adjustment with his pole and the raft turned toward the now alert sentry on the shore. The man shouted, "Ease off of your bows. Fetch a surgeon. Garm is in great need."

Nils said this as he observed more than a few Faeder-Ganger lined along the far bank, bows pulled with long sharp arrows at the ready. The guard ordered, "Slow the pace, man, else death comes quickly."

Lifting his voice, Nils cried out, "Fair said. Here, I'll lay off in the shallows. Do as you fit with me. But see first to Garm!"

He then poled the raft into a shallow area, pulled the long pole up from the stream, and laid it at his side. Several Faeder-Ganger guards waded into the calm water and, taking the raft, moved it to dock. More eager arms and hands reached out as they took Garm and laid him on the bank. After making the raft secure, other guards bound Nils' wrists and led him to a cage. The Serzian said, "Garm it is and greatly hurt. Send word. Into the cage with the other."

The guards thrust Nils into the cage and locked its door. Nils, caught the eyes of the Serzian of the Guard and said "Send for Lord Zander-Fells."

The Serzian of the Guard drew his sword and growled, "Stay your filthy tongue."

Nils sat back on his haunches and hung his head down despondently between his legs. The Serzian of the Guard was impatiently pacing back and forth in front of the cage when Nils heard the unmistakable voice of Mai-Yanna as she was asking, "Serzian, what is all this commotion so early in the morning?"

The Serzian stopped his anxious tramping and pointed at Garm as he lay on the bank and reported, "This hurt one is Garm, long thought dead."

He pointed his mailed fist at Nils and said, "And that one, Tektar, in the cage is the outlaw Nils, I'll wager."

The warrior princess's hand flew to her throat as she exclaimed, "Garm, come from the dead?"

She ran and stooped over the bundled form. Then after looking intently at the heavy gray beard covering his face, she stood erect and proclaimed, "Aye it is so. Make haste and get him to my surgeon's chambers!"

Several Faeder-Gangers gathered up Garm on a stretcher. With as quick a pace as they could manage, for Garm, although thin from his arduous adventures with Nils in the wild, was still a heavy man, carried the Serzian Domo away from the shore and toward the palace. Mai-Yanna gazed over the scarecrow figure of Nils as he sat with his back to the cage. The Serzian asked laconically, "And what of our other guest?"

Quickly turning on her heel away from the sight within the cage and heading after Garm, she ordered, "Let him stay where he is."

Mai-Yanna's chambers as Tektor of the realm within the Rafermor were those befitting an officer of the Faeder-Ganger. That is to say sparse on space, lean of comfort, and lacking the amenities of civilian life. Yet it was abundant in weapons and gear of war. Within were a small field desk and the unique trappings of a mounted warrior. A place served both as her bedchamber and as her command post. In a corner of this Spartan room, lay Garm awake on a cot under thick covers. In spite of the cramped quarters, Lord Zander-Fells, Suze-Li and Anadan stood next to the bed. Zander-Fells asked, "Into the thin air you say?"

The now clean-shaven old warrior answered, "Aye. We fell like two bags of rocks."

Zander-Fells looked at the grey hair, wrinkled and scarred face, and twinkling brown eyes of his most trusted friend, and continued, "And the water? How did you manage to survive?"

"Nils." Garm answered, "It was him that brought me up from the bottom and kept my head above water. Relax he says. Whilst I's a drowning like a fresh kitten. Close to death I was when he finally managed to drag us both out of the drink."

Suze-Li wrapped a deep blue cloak over herself and said in hushed and fearful tone, "So it has dark powers over water."

With a jolt, Garm sat up, spilling the covers on the floor and revealing his broad, a still well muscled, chest, "Ah, no girl! Did you not hear a word I said? He was as wet and near death as I."

He looked around at his amazed companions and pronounced, "Swimming he called it."

Suze-Li could scare believe her father's words. She shook her head and said to him, "Two months in the wild during the dead of winter. Now you expect me to believe that this Nils managed to keep you both alive?"

Garm sat back, placed his arms over his chest in the universal sign of the Faerevolder merchants as they announced their last and final offer and said, "Believe it or no. He hunted and fished. Made us fire with steel and flint when it was safe. He bound these hurts of mine and made that raft with his own bare hands. He got us through on his own. Not by any dark power."

Gently taking her father's hand, Suze-Li implored, "So a hurt man with a dent in his head might say."

Anadan proclaimed from behind her, "And so say I as well, and I have no dent in my head. At least not yet."

Zander-Fells now convinced said firmly, "As do I. I do not yet know much about this Nils. But I do know Garm. There was a day when the word of Garm was good for all to hear."

Dropping Garm's hand, Suze-Li stood at rigid attention and said, "Forgive me, Strategon. Much evil had been done in these past days of high winter. Shadow and cold mist bring us rumors of vast numbers of Vilder-zerk moving in the land."

Anadan moved forward, put his hand on Suze-Li's shoulder, and said, "Garm, these days we see neither full sun nor a clear night. The shadow days are upon us. The age of the Dark War has come."

Garm squinted up at the old man, and with a wry wink at his Suze-Li, said, "So, you thought us enthralled, daughter?"

Garm recognized the shy, little girl's tone she used when Suze-Li answered, "Yes. I…we did. Dom's treacheries are many and have been well made and hidden."

Garm released a heavy, sad sigh as he gazed out the window at some unseen object far away, "The great Dark War foretold. Loath I am to see it in my days. I thought it only was a story to help bring up the little ones in the right way."

Suze-Li uttered the words that would haunt the noble companions throughout the coming arduous days, "Yet, here it is; a bad dream come true in our time."

Silence fell about them as each considered the innermost thoughts and fears that lay deep within their hearts. Long they stood in the small room, none speaking. Seeking to quell the discord within her soul as well as that still hanging in the room, Suze-Li left Garm's side and leaned out of the window. Her gaze moved aimlessly over the camp displayed below her. Faeder-ganger drilled under the watchful eye of the non-coms in the open spaces between the neatly ordered rows of tents, stacked arms and equipment of war. Finally, her keen eye settled on the cage holding Nils and the Archan's banner floating in the breeze nearby. Suze-Li firmly announced, "The Tektor holds council here. I will tell her you may be presented at the Archan's court."

Her words awoke the rest of the group, and Garm spat out in disgust, "Lady Lis-Yan is one of his creatures!"

"Yes, we know. She does not sit on the Dais. Much has changed since you last saw us at Geldenherm, father."

Unlike Geldenherm Citadel, the council hall within the Raffer-Moor was wide and richly appointed. Large archways supported its high ceiling, and light streamed in through the spacious windows that adorned its sides. Courtiers and Faeder-Ganger moved and twittered about the council hall as Mai-Yanna sat on the Archan's Dais hunched over a scroll laid open on her lap. By her right hand side, in the position of High Councilor, stood Anadan. In his arms, he held more scrolls for the Archan's attention. On each side of them and spaced at each alcove, stood heavily armed guards at rigid attention, silent in their bright mail.

A herald, wearing Dom's livery of sable and red had just completed her audience with the Tektar. She had brought an offer of truce, providing peace in exchange for horse, and dominion over the Fyrds Gelde and Rohern. To the first demand, Mai-Yanna agreed; to the second, she flatly refused. While the herald was waiting for the scroll containing Mai-Yanna's reply, Garm and

Suze-Li unceremoniously entered the hall, strode through the crowd, and stopped at the Dais' foot. The guards crossed their spears, blocking the Dais and its occupants from any further progress.

Mai-Yanna, glanced up from her deliberations. With one hand she motioned to Suze-Li to come forward. The guards crisply moved the spears back and stepped aside. Suze-Li brushed past the herald and whispered in Mai-Yanna's ear. After giving the scroll to Anadan, who gave it to the herald, Mai-Yanna raised her head and said, "The devourer. A time of sorrow is indeed upon us."

At this, Dom's representative made a slight bow, and without ceremony, departed the Dais.

Once the herald had left the hall, Suze-Li gave Anadan another scroll and reported, "It sits in its silence and hate, waiting for the evening jewel to come to it."

Anadan placed the scroll Suze-Li had given him in a neat pile at his side and said, "So goes the lay. But now it seems that Dom will not wait, but seeks to swiftly take us in these twilight days."

Mai-Yanna looked down at Garm and asked, "What say you, Garm? Is it back to the sick bed for you, or to horse and war?"

Garm saluted, "I have need of the armory."

Mai-Yanna took another scroll from Anadan, returned his salute, and said curtly, "Take only what a courier will need for defense. You must ride long and hard."

Garm dropped his salute and said in dismay, "You have no need of me in our army?"

Mai-Yanna applied hot sealing wax to the scroll now in her hands, "The greatest need I have for you is to raise an army. Our ranks are not as they once were. Also, the realm has need of Hine Lords and Graef Barons."

She offered a set of scrolls to Garm, "Many went over to Dom."

At these words many of the assembled courtiers hissed in unison and angrily stamped their feet. The Faeder-Ganger guards slapped their armor with weapons and mailed fists. Garm came forward and Mai-Yanna gave him the scrolls she had bound with the Archan's seal. As he took them, she leaned over a spoke softly, "Read this while on the road. I only ask you remember we are in great peril."

Garm put the scroll in his sash, "By my life or death."

Mai-Yanna then stood and left the Dais. Garm turned, took Suze-Li's arm and together they strode out of the council hall. As they disappeared around a corner at the end of the hall, Anadan said softly, "And I fear by many others as well."

Dom's herald moved away from the gathered Gangers, and quietly slipped out of the Raffer-moor. As she spurred her lathered steed across the steppes, her nipples swelled as she anticipated Dom's caresses upon her ample breasts once he heard her news of this day.

Many winter days had passed, and the high noon of one found Anadan, Zander-Fells, and Mai-Yanna looking at Nils as he sat dissolutely in the cage where he had been incarcerated. Mai-Yanna said to him, "Man thing."

Without standing from his place on the frozen ground, he responded sullenly, "It is Nils. My name is Nils."

Mai-Yang placed her arms behind her back and rocked her heels back and forth on the hard packed snow, and politely said, "Nils. See how this evil from your kint has made us a strange and hard people."

Zander-Fells interjected, "You have shown us a true heart and great service. Yet, we fear that Dom may still use you against us. Garm told all what he saw and what was said while you were in the dark keep."

Nils stood and asked, "What else could he have done?"

Mai-Yanna looked him square in the face and said, "Many here wish you dead. It is a sure path to your loyalty. These and others spoke for you, none more than Garm and my Lord Zander-Fells."

Zander-Fells continued for her, "To return you back to the wilds would not guarantee that you would remain out of our affairs."

Anadan broke in, "Since we can neither kill nor banish you, one question remains. What shall it be, him or us?"

Nils looked long and hard at the grim visages before him. Proud and grand they were. A great and strong people standing on the precipice of doom, boldly facing the meter of the Great Maker. Often he would remark that in that moment their noble eyes could not hide a certain sense of desperation that hung about them like a clammy shroud. He said to them, "I knew I faced death the moment I awoke on the desert floor. What of it? Kill or release me. I am not Dom's. Do as you please."

So spoken. I take this one." Anadan in-toned as he clasped Mai-Yanna's arm.

"As do I." she responded and clasped Zander-Fells'.

"And I.", said the Faeder-Hander as he extended an arm to Nils.

Mai-Yanna looked at Nils and asked, "And will you join us?"

"Aye. By my life or death," Nils said as he reached his hands out of the cage and clasped their arms.

HIS LORDSHIP, HINE SKRAPMOND

In the great hall Anadan had called, "Nils of Taerevold brings us cause as to the matter of his station."

Now Nils had stood some half hour before the Dias, wondering what the stern Mai-Yanna was to pronounce. She sat behind a small portable desk, busy with the affairs of state. Nils noticed how she adroitly used the small pot of hot wax and signet before her. Unlike Lis Yan's richly colored dress and bejeweled tiara, Mai-Yanna sat ensconced in plain brown robes and wore no sign of rank, her hair bound behind her in one long ponytail. As he later learned, her plain dress signified her duties as Tektor of the Realm, appointed by the High Justice as steward due to Lis Yan's inability to fulfill her duties of office. For the creature known as Lis Yan lay in her own filth and drool behind the closed and carefully guarded doors of Mai-Yanna's chambers.

Anadan was at her right hand side. Behind him stood orderlies, aides, messengers and valet's in a long line, the retinue of a sovereign. Over Anadan's shoulders was a large bag suspended by a wide strap that ran diagonally from left to right across his chest. From within its depths, he retrieved a variety of scrolls and passed them to Mai-Yanna. Having once approved its contents, she would pour hot wax on the scroll, and then firmly press the signet home. Once the wax cooled, she quickly re-rolled the scroll and returned it to Anadan who in turn passed it to one of the waiting pages. As the pages received the scrolls they quickly and silently tucked them into a valise, carrying the orders, commissions, and messengers to their destinations.

Repeatedly this process continued while Nils stood. To keep himself from falling asleep on his feet, he shifted his attention to the tapestries, hanging banners, and various persons in the Dais chamber. He had seen enough of the Faeder Ganger to know their ranks and functions and quickly passed his glance over them without thought. Others he now began to recognize: a merchant by the full coin bag suspended over an ample belly, a boatman by her billowing trousers, dagger and hair pulled back tight, and the Manor Stewards by the multi-colored badges they wore signifying the arms of their houses.

During the days following his arrival at the Rafermor, Nils had become impressed with the sense that the Faerevolder were a fair and noble people. Indeed, to Nils they seemed an honorable folk compared to his fellows in Taerevold. Yet, one of the Stewards in particular held his attention, for Nils instantly recognized the scarred face and squint eyes of the Alehouse owner.

Why had not this one fled to Dom? Nils asked himself.

He was deeply pondering the answer when he heard Mai-Yanna voice, "Freiholder Nils. I say, man, do you not hear me?"

The low murmurs and twittering of the courtiers instantly ceased as Nils snapped his attention to Mai-Yanna's intent face. The courtiers now tensed uncertainly as they observed how their new Tektar handled the rude stranger before her. To Nils, the air became stuffy and the hall suddenly hot. Sensing the change of mood in the hall, his face flushed a bright red as he found himself trapped in a most embarrassing situation. The hall remained quiet as a tomb as the Tektar long held him in her gaze. Then with a sly smile on her face she asked, "Perhaps he may be forgiven his impertinence, as he is new to our lands and customs?"

As if a window had been opened, the air-cooled. Anadan answered, "Of course he does, Tektar. But I do caution my friend Nils to pay closer attention while before the Dias."

The old man flashed a wide smile. The courtiers relaxed and a small ripple of light chatter once again filtered about the hall; the tension of the moment long dissipated by Mai-Yanna's and Anadan's words. Nils realized his moment of embarrassment before the Dias passed and saluted Mai-Yanna saying, "What will you have of me, Archana?"

"Tektar! Not Archana." Anadan sharply intoned, "She sits in the Sovereign's stead. But you did not know that, and no harm was meant."

"Truly." Nils said. "What will the Tektar have of me?"

Anadan reached in the pouch at his side and withdrew two scrolls, and handed them to Mai-Yanna. She reviewed their contents and said, "Many have those been that betrayed us. Their lands and titles are forfeit. Certain Landkrieser and Barons plead I confirm offices upon such persons as they see fit." She poured the wax, pressed the signet and after rolling the scroll, held them out to Nils saying, "A sted is both your source of wealth and power. This Hine is in need of a Lord."

Nils took the scrolls from her, wondering how he was to carry the things, as he had no valise. Mai-Yanna continued as she produced a golden ribbon with thin red borders and three red roundels aligned on its center, "Also, The Faeder Hander Suze Li begs you be commissioned Faeder Letnat."

Hearing these words, the grim looking Steward began to step forward. The Tektar shot him a fierce glare, stopping the man in mid stride. Mai-Yanna then finished saying, "Since none have come forward in objection, we see no reason to deny her petition."

Nils took the ribbon and bowed at the waist. Anadan whispered, "You may leave now."

Nils, embarrassed at his continued lack of proper courtesy, again blushed. However, he managed to turn and leave the Dias without tripping over himself. In the hall, he quickly passed into a small crowd of Faeder-Ganger that eagerly congratulated him by hard blows to his shoulders and chest crying, "A few wee quaffs o the Mistress' ale is in order!"

This proposal was eagerly seconded and in moments, they pressed Nils away from the hall. As they were departing, Nils heard Anadan call the next petitioner before the Dias, "Steward Gim Bayz brings us cause in the matter of the debts of one Kapral Smythe."

Had it not been for her familiarity with Faeder Ganger and the banker's advance of coin on behalf of His Lordship's new land holdings, the mistress would not have allowed the past night's fête. Long into the night the Ganger celebrated Nils' promotion with singing and wild dancing, for truth be told none of the revelers had been shy with the Mistress' Ale.

At one point a bawdern had come in, a trail of prostitutes in tow. Of these painted camp cats, many of the Ganger disappeared. Nils, though quite drunk, politely refused the services of one buxom red haired filly. He belly laughed as he watched a tawny Ganger firmly dig her long finger's into one painted boy's rump and crowed, "Look a here Kapral, I'll wager three months' wage ya taint seen as firm a arse since we first mustered in!"

At some point in the rowdy night, the Gangers took a very drunk Nils to the barn and laid him on a pile of straw. It was now late in the morning and many of the celebrants lay unconscious and peacefully snoring where they had fallen. All about the place, more than one head lay flat on the ale stained tables. Many of the Ganger slept happily with backs to the walls were they last sat, still firmly grasping the Ale mugs in their iron fists.

A horse was curiously examining the man-thing, when Nils came around with pounding head and bleary eyes. He rose and stumbled to dip his head into a nearby trough. The demon of Seti Four had not made its appearance since the night Nils had fallen through the blue midst. Now in the Faerevold, He stood there, thrusting his aching head in and out of the cold water. Eventually the pounding and bleariness of his hangover subsided, and slowly Nils pulled his soaking head out of the trough. He shook out the water from his hair, stretched himself and walked to the open barn door.

A small table with breakfast had been set for him. He found a stool, sat and applied himself with vigor to the pile of steaming eggs, ham, and fried potatoes. He also, drank deeply from a large mug of what the Faerevolder called Kai, but he recognized as coffee. He was nearly complete with his meal when a tall Ganger walked through the courtyard of slumbering celebrants and stood before him. Saluting, the lean cavalryman said, "Ganger Sved Larzmon, escort to His Lordship, Lord Hine Skrapmond."

Nils sloppily returned the salute and asked confusingly, "Lord Skrapmond, who is that?"

The Faeder Ganger replied, "That be you, Letnat."

"And where would you be escorting me to?"

"Ta your'n Hine, sir," Came the laconic reply.

"That is Hine Skrapmond?"

"One an ta same as your Lordship"

Nils shrugged his shoulders. He wiped his mouth with a rough napkin, rose from the table and said, "Then escort on. But first, I need make payment to the mistress for…"

The soldier asked, "Yer promotion soirée?"

Nils grunted, "Yes."

The ganger said, "Na need "ta worry on ta account. I spoke with her. Seems ta lads an' lasses of Hand Zander Fells has stood ta coin."

Nils grunted acceptance of these facts, took one wobbly step forward, and then stumbled face first into the dirt. Sved Larzmon reached down and with a long strong arm, pulled Nils to his feet. Keeping a firm grip on his charge, he guided Nils out of the courtyard. Eventually they made their way through the town and toward the quays that lined the port. Still moving on wobbly legs, in the distance Nils could see the flocks of gulls winging over the glistening water of the Great Ost Mor. Sved laughed, "Ha. Ya may be a fighter, but ya na one for ta Mistress' ale."

By the time they reached the quays, Nils had found his feet and was able to walk under his own power. As was the Ganger custom, Nils walked a few steps ahead of Sved who remained within easy earshot of the strange Taerevolder. If Nils got off the desired course, Sved Larzmon would grunt out a quick "Right! Left! Straight!" under his breath. Nils would then correct his line of march. In this way, the two made their way to the end of one of the crowded docks. At its end was tied a long, low sailing vessel. It was here they stopped and Sved came forward and boarded the Mor Trader Skiva.

A stout wooden gangway extended from the ship's side to the dock. Sved quickly mounted the plank and disappeared behind a mass of barrels, bundles and goods stacked for shipment on the vessel's main deck. He was on board for some time and Nils had a chance to view the transport. Obviously, he was meant to get on board at some point. He searched his memory and the closest he could come to in comparison was a Mississippi River packet steamboat, with its low keel, wide sides and high pilothouse. Except in this case in place of a water wheel, engine house, and multi-storied passenger decks, there were three sail masts set amid-decks, spread evenly from bow to stern, a large rudder aft, and a low set of compartments, ten on each side, amid-ships.

Nils could see a few passengers silhouetted in their cabins. A group of children rather shabbily dressed, stood in a small open place near the aft. This was the steerage area and above it was the bridge and wheel. Everywhere were stacked bundles and barrels. Even the top of the passenger's cabin house was covered with them. Nils review of the vessel was interrupted when Sved suddenly appeared and stormed down the gangplank, cursing, "I ha' na heard o' such! Na ta rooms afford ta realm's officer as some Lordship has 'em all sequestered!"

Nils took in this news and said calmly, "But, we will board."

"A course, ya' nit!" Sven shouted, then remembering Nils rank said evenly, "Ah min "yo pardon sar."

Nils smiled and said, "No need. Let's board and find what berths we may."

Then with a respectful bow the tall warrior saluted and said, "After you sir."

What berths aboard the trade ship Skiva Sved had acquired proved hard to find. What they lacked in the amenities of the cabins was made up for in that they were dry and out of the wind and spray. Many of the children had not been so lucky, as when it rained or the wind blew, the mass of young boys and girls stood or lay huddled together under what small shawls and capes they had on their persons. Nils and Sven were fortunate in another way; all Gangers had right to board at any house or vessel. Their meals were often simple, crude, and meager, but were more than that given to the others in steerage.

One night, as they sat wrapped in their cloaks taking some warm stew and hard bread for their evening meal, Nils observed how one of the older children would now and again enter the cabin area. He asked Sved, "Do they take their board in the cabins?"

Sved gruffed, "P'haps, After "Deys done a bit o service."

Nils asked, "What do you mean?"

The Faeder Ganger spat in disgust, "Na telling 'asure sar, but dems is going in ta trade demselves for whatever scraps as dey can get." Forfeitured, dems younguns is been indentured for seven year dey is.'"

Nils, shocked, asked the young warrior, "How did they come to such a hard way? You mean to say their parents have sold them, whored them out?

Sved answered slowly, "Aye, some 'as sure. But dems bunch is orphaned, wi' dads and marms dead. Famine or disease some took. Most were kilt out past the steppes or in Geldenherm. An' now some arse of a Duke or Lord 'as up an' made cause afore the Dias fer 'em."

"And Mai Yana, I mean the Tektor, allows this barbarity!" Nils exclaimed.

"An' wha' choice do she 'ave, hey? Sved answered, and then continued, "'Tis as proper as your commission. Ta judges long past has ruled coin, holdings, or person should be given for service or payment o' debts. Most dees here is what was left, an' lick split, some swine works ta law to na good! "

Unable to continue his meal, Nils set it aside and pondered this revelation about Faerevolder society. What had once been to him a fair and noble way of life now appeared crude, rough and cruel Sved, sensing Nils' mood gathered up his food and walked away. Leaning over a rail, the Ganger slowly sipped the stew and chewed the hard bread. Nils sat alone, yet his thoughts on what this all meant were soon interrupted by a tug on his cloak. Nils looked up and gazed into the pinched face of young girl.

Nervously she furtively looked about, and then asked, "Will you want that, sir? I can trade fer it!

The little lass slipped the corner of a tattered dress over one slim shoulder. Nils got the message; she was willing to give her young body in exchange for food! As he stared at the girl, he could see the hunger in her eyes as she struggled to keep her small lips from smacking at the smell of the now cold stew.

"No. Take…" He did not finish the words before the girl flashed out her hand and grabbed the sturdy wooden cup and bread. Quickly, she hid them under her worn shawl and without another word, scuttled over to a small figure lying on the deck.

"Hey now!" came Sven's voice as he strode forward.

Nils put a hand on the warrior's arm and said, "It is nothing. The child is hungry, and I am not."

Sven finally became exasperated at this stranger's unusual behavior and said, "Ya know na ta customs, Letnat. "Dems foder is paid by their masters. Youse as wasten yourn."

Nils looked hard into the Faeder Ganger's eyes, until the tall warrior blushed under Nils steely gaze and then turned his head aside. Nils angrily said, "It is not my custom to waste anything, Faeder Ganger! As for providing for their charges, I intend to find out who these masters are that refuse food to children."

Without another word, Nils stomped away toward the shipmaster's quarters. Sven stared after him, and then said, "So it's in ta battle he goes. That's a fight a sure."

Sven was quick to follow Nils into the ship's bowels. However, that night aboard the Skiva, Nils was the quicker for having reached the thick door to the Captain's cabin. Sved found it shut tight and could hear the voices of Nils and the Captain in heated debate. Back and forth, the arguments went until Larzmon decided he had enough of waiting and placed his broad, well-muscled shoulder to force open the door. Just as he readied himself to push the heavy entry open, the hatch swung wide and Nils stepped out, saying, "As I understand it, this Lord is aboard?"

"Aye," barked the Captain.

Larzmon's blood froze as the veteran of many grim battles heard Nils coldly intone, "Then-show-me-this-man."

"Step aside, sir, and follow me," said the Captain as he moved past Nils, through the hatch, and along a long corridor.

Nils followed the Captain with Larzmon in the trail wondering what Nils had learned that set his face in a controlled rage. None of the party spoke as the Captain led them past the cabin doors that lined the ship's narrow passageway, ten cabins on each side. At the end was a large door, here the Captain stopped. He turned and said to Nils, "He is at the head of the main table, entertaining the other noble folk onboard."

Nils' face was etched in stony determination as he said, "Five minutes is all you have to ready your men."

"More than enough time." Replied the Captain as he pushed past Larzmon and hurried away.

Nils did not look at Larzmon as he put his hand on the door's latch and said, "If he does not yield, then we kill him and his."

Not waiting for a reply, Nils worked the latch, opened the door and stepped forward. Sved Larzmon followed Nils into the ship's formal dinning room. Tables were laid out in neat rows, each lined with the country gentry dressed in the casual finery chosen for travel. At the end was a larger table set a bit apart from the others. At its center and facing the doorway sat Pa-Val, a large man, his blond hair flowing over the silk robe of sables that sat on his shoulders.

"Ah guests!" exclaimed the man, a smug and vile smile on his face. "Come now, Letnat. Are you late to board or are you maybe lost?" he asked Nils mockingly.

The man's guests at the large table giggled at the insult. Nils noted the remainder of the gentry remained quiet and set their food aside as they observed what was about to transpire before them. Nils sang out, "Neither, I have words to exchange on behalf of His lordship, Lord Hine Skrapmond."

In an instant, the smug smile disappeared, and the man's eyes narrowed as he took in a quick sharp breath. "Then you have found him. I know my servants. By whose leave do you come?"

A small glint of sweat appeared on the man's brow, as Nils said "Upon my own."

Nils took even measured steps forward until he stood directly before the blond man. Nils took a long measure of the man and his retinue that now sat silent before him.

"Do you mean to kill me?" The man asked nervously.

"If need be," said Larzmon from the side of the table where he had positioned himself between the man and any path to escape.

Nils locked the man's eyes in his and asked, "Who here may vouch for Hine Skrapmond?"

From behind, many voices murmured, "Aye, we know the blazon and signet."

"Then perhaps his Lordship would be so kind as to display them?" asked Larzmon.

The blond man bent forward and whispered lowly to Nils, "Coin I have. In my cabin and on board. Yours if I may leave."

Nils coldly said, "I have no need of your coin, however, you may certainly leave."

The large man breathed a great sigh and began to rise from his seat.

"But first", Nils continued, "Before your guests, explain my possession of these small items."

From within his cloak, Nils produced a scroll and a signet. He placed these on the table.

The man collapsed back into his chair and looked desperately about, the sweat now running freely down his face.

Nils continued, "Please share them about. Give all here a chance to examine them."

Then, one by one the items were passed along the large table and among the Gentry until a voice said, "Aye, this be the Skrapmond patent for tenure and signet. And this, my Lords and Ladies, must be Nils Taerevold, their rightful holder."

Pa-Val now slowly rose from his chair, and fell to the floor as if in great pain. He bit his fingernails as he groveled on his hands and knees until he knelt before Nils, silently begging his life.

Nils grabbed the rich silk robe, yanked the man up onto his feet, and ordered, "Get up!"

Nils turned about and grabbing the man by the right ear lobe, marched him out of the dinning room. As he passed through the door he said, "Larzmon, be so kind as to hold my tokens."

Larzmon gathered the scroll and signet and followed them out into the passageway. As they steadily moved past the cabin doors, the man puffed himself up and boldly said, "Move faster afore me mates cut yer throats."

Nils unceremoniously cuffed the man's left ear. Without a word, he hustled the blond haired man out a side hatch and onto the main deck. Here he turned toward the aft, never letting go of his grasp on the imposter. Once at the steerage, Nils felt the man's energy leave him as he recognized six men standing with their arms and legs tied under the close watch of the Captain and several of the ship's crew.

The Captain eyed Nils and said, "So all went to your plan. Now what about these lovelies?

Nils responded, "Are the children billeted as I asked."

The Captain barked, "Aye and at board as we speak."

Nils ordered, "Then keep these people bound and under guard."

Neither food nor drink did the imposter or his companions receive for the next two days as the ship made its way across the Great Ost Mor. Fortunately for the seven ruffians, there were fair winds and no rain. On the morning of their third day bound, the ship made landfall at the small port of Weslon, used mostly for shipment of the livestock and mail that moved to and from the distant sheep and cattle stations that lay scattered in this part of Fyrd Dente.

At dawn the next day, the crew delivered some cargo and exchanged mail with the waiting drovers. Long after the drovers departed and close to dusk, they marched the seven bedraggled ruffians off the boat, leaving them tied. As the ship made way, the Captain took his horn and spoke out, "You may loose those knots if you can. Fail to do so and the wolves may have a fine meal tonight."

Nils and Larzmon filled the remaining days aboard the Skiva seeing to the more ill and hurt of the children. For many were close to death that night when Nils discovered they had been indentured to Hine Skrapmond. At four to a room, most of the nearly thirty waifs' conditions began to markedly improve once they got into warm, dry beds and received regular meals. Yet, three of the little ones died, their small bodies set into the deep waters of the Great Ost Mor. Of the four and twenty survivors, Nils and Larzmon often found themselves in the company of the young girl who had approached him, Brune and her brother Gunter.

Nils enjoyed their company. Brune was a bright and vivacious blond haired maiden of fourteen. She was learned in letters and numbers, and Nils soon found her books and eager tutors from among the Gentry. He asked her instructors not to reveal his identity to the young maiden. Gunter, although only four, was an active, curious boy who soon had Sved Larzmon teaching him swordsmanship.

The children took their meals at the ship's board at a time separate from the Gentry. Nils and Larzmon continued to sleep and eat in steerage. For Nils refused any offers from the Captain, crew or Gentry to usurp their berths saying, "Nay, kind sir, (or madam). I indeed be the Lord, Hine Skrapmond, but Larzmon and I are first and last Ganger, and need ruff timbers and not soft pillows for our beds."

At this, all aboard let them be. Although Larzmon once grumbled to a crewmember, "Timbers fer pillows me arse!"

THE LONG HARD ROAD

Seven days after depositing the ruffians, the ship made anchor at Leak-Mor, the easternmost port of the realm. Leak-Mor was a major transshipment point between the realm and the Osterlings. Here, the Greafs Leak kept their manor and held court. Many of the Greafalins lined the dock when the crew threw out the mooring lines' to the eager dockworkers that made her fast. Soon the gangplank was lowered and the Gentry disembarked as a line of stevedores moved the cargo.

Among the mass of well-wishers and greeters was Gim Bayz with two equally ugly men. Soon he heard the story of the Lord Hine Skrapmond. Spitting at one lady's feet he said to one of the two vile looking companions with him, "Kern, get yerself on the road to Weslon. With any luck, Pa-Val and his idiots will still be alive. Find them and get to the Barony."

Then to the other he ordered, "Ger Kan, hie yerself to the lads and make a surprise for this new Lord.

Eventually, Nils, Larzmon and the children disembarked. Nils presented his tokens to the harbormaster asking, "Where may I hire swains? I've cargo to go with me."

The harbormaster directed him to a nearby livery. They went there and after some inquiries, found two horses and swains enough to be ready on the morrow. Nearby was a small inn, and in it they found a kindly old innkeeper with rooms enough for the children and Larzmon.

Nils was just finishing counting out the coin for the room and board to the old man behind the counter when Gim Bayz entered. Bowing, Gim Bayz announced, "Steward Graef Kanervald at your leave my Lordship".

The old man averted Gim Bayz' stare as Nils turned and recognized the squint eyed alehouse owner. With a quick motion, he waved the bent man up saying, "What is my Greaf's need to send the Manor Steward to great me?"

Gim Bayz' pale, dark eyes revealed nothing as he quietly hissed, "None other that finds me here these days in advance of our Graef and his new Lordship."

Nils said nothing and soon Gim Bayz continued, "May it be so bold as I have made some arrangement for you in a more suitable place."

Nils shook his head and said, "I thank the Greaf's Steward for the kindness. However, I have just contracted with this innkeeper for a room. Humble it may be, and as you say, less appropriate."

Gim Bayz, hissed, "Ahss you wishsss." Then bowed, stepped back and silently left the inn.

Larzmon turned to Nils and said, "Again, your rudeness wears thin! And just where is this room?"

Nils kept his gaze on the now empty doorway by which Gim Bayz left, saying, "Rather to be rude, than sleep in any place that snake has found. As for my room, Innkeeper, do you have an empty hayloft in your barn out back?"

"Aye" said the old man.

"Then that problem is solved," said Nils.

The next day they set their course along the Ostern Swain road toward Graef Kanervald. Larzmon in charge of five heavily laden swains, each pulled by two sturdy oxen, and filled with the cargo Nils had been charged to deliver to the Graef. The swains' oxen were nearly as unruly as their skinners. More than once Larzmon was forced to put them in line as he said, "Knock o lil' sense in their 'eads."

In addition, on each swain, the children rode on top of the cargo, Brune and Gunter in the forefront. Larzmon had also acquired saddles and trappings for the two worn horses. He rode on a knock-kneed stallion and Nils on a swayback mare as the small caravan made its way out of Leak-Mor.

The ride eastward on the Ostern Swain road was uneventful. The lone exception of once having made delivery at House Kanervald to the Steward as was custom, Gim Bayz insisted the swains should remain. Eventually, Nils said, "By the Maker! Take four and hold me liable for the fifth!"

Where upon, Gim Bayz made Nils place his signet in wax upon a receipt for the swain, and surrender his patent and ring of Lordship. Then Gim Bayz allowed Nils to cram the small remaining supplies and all of the children into the single swain. Once settled, they headed toward the rising sun, seeking Hine Skrapmond. As they made their way east, Brune pointed to the north and said to Gunter, "There is Hine Smythe."

Nils was riding ahead, and Larzmon overhearing her, looked her in the eyes, placed a finger over his mouth and shook his head. Those nights they camped under the stars, the children sleeping peacefully near the swain while Larzmon tended the fire. Nils now took advantage of the quiet pace to inquire of Sved more of the history and customs of Faerevold. To this request, Larzmon eagerly agreed, telling Nils how after the great rendering of the beings, few were there now remaining in the realm and how the Great Maker left it in human hands.

"Of the faithful and of true heart mortals that had refused to indulge in the devourer's wickedness, the Great Maker named five: Linde, Zand, Gelde, Dente, and Rohde. Among them, he portioned Faerevold, charging each to protect the land, husband the beasts, and judge the people. Before leaving Faerevold, the Great Maker sat down two immutable laws: the First—"Each Faerevolder is to be Steward for the others as they would be Stewards for themselves.", and second—"None should engage in the devourer's sorcery nor set it as god."

He continued, "To the Five, he also granted great wisdom of human hearts and skill in speech to judge well those left in their charge. Their first task was to create a suitable form of government. The Five Great Landkrieser took council of themselves and applied all the knowledge they had learned and wisdom the Great Maker had granted. Many days they sat debating together within Gelde's halls until they reached agreement, producing the Ka-Non of Duties and Privileges."

"A Huskarl was formed and an Archon named as First Steward of the Realm. Power was to be shared between the Huskarl and Archon in the form of a Court and Council. The Landkrieser were to name the Graefs. Lords, Ladies, Graeflins and Freiholders were all to be given a place."

When Nils asked how the Faerevolder enforced the Great Maker's Laws, Sved replied, "It is clear you are new to Great Maker's mercies. In faith, we are all stewards of each other. How we fulfill our commission is left to us. It is always a choice, to remain true or not, to do good or not. To follow the words of the Great Maker is a hard task one takes freely."

Long was the road to Skrapmond and Nils learned much more of Faerevold and the Great Maker from Larzmon. Many fortnights had passed and now they were nearing Skrapmond and the eastern-most holdings of the realm. Since dealing with his usurper, Nils had slept soundly each night. Yet one evening as they lay camped by the road, he tossed and turned and finally got up from his bed robes and walked over to the horses and oxen staked on a line near the camp. Nils was surprised to find both the skinner and Larzmon standing there, both attentive to the night air. He asked, "What is it?"

Larzmon raised an arm, his hand open, and the sign for quiet. For some minutes, they stood there: Nils listening and Larzmon more feeling for something that lay out in the darkness. Eventually, Larzmon lowered his arm, and turning to Nils whispered very quietly, "If we wern't in ta Ost, I'd say Vilder-zerk."

Nils' hair raised on the back of his neck as he now placed the night's unease in its proper place. Without hesitation, he whispered, "Then to arms lads. It's two up and one down every four hours. Stay close to the swain and the children."

"An me oxen?" The skinner asked.

Larzmon replied, "Better dem, ta us nor ta young 'uns."

At the notion of losing his precious oxen, the skinner looked at the Faeder Ganger in horror until Larzmon grinning said, "A course you can a stay out here wid' em on your ownsome if you like."

The men spent the rest of the night in restless anticipation of an attack that did not come. Neither Nils nor Larzmon found they could sleep. The skinner, left in slumber with the children, happily snored the night away. Before daybreak, they woke the children. After a hasty breakfast, they loaded the swain and were well off along the road just as the sun rose in the east to greet them. Brune noted they did not stop for their customary mid-day meal, the skinner pressing the oxen forward relentlessly over the low hills and valleys of the Ost Swain Road as if something was pursuing them. She also noticed how Nils and Larzmon now rode around them in a wide circle to the flanks, front and rear, wearing mail under their cloaks and carrying bows strung with arrows.

Near nightfall, they crested a small ridge and intersected a smaller track running to the north and south. Here Larzmon stopped them and after Nils rode up, pointed to some small buildings in the distant south and said, "Hine Skrapmond". Without a further word, they turned south and headed for the faint lights that began to twinkle in the falling dusk.

Nils now rode to the rear as Larzmon led the way southward, the skinner snapping the oxen into a quick pace with his long whip. The children grew fearful as they went without dinner and noticed the manner in which both Nils and Larzmon continued to look nervously toward the north. Their young hearts were gladdened when they came close to the first farmsteads, thinking they had reached the Hine's Manor house. However, what little comfort they found soon passed they saw boarded farmsteads, for Larzmon had ridden ahead giving warning of danger close by to the Freiholders.

On and on they continued, through one farmstead or small hamlet after another, never stopping. The children were fast asleep aboard the swain as the moon rode high in the night sky. Brune awoke when Nils galloped up and said to the skinner, "Get aboard and whip them hard."

With a quick hop up, the skinner sat next to Brune in the swain. He applied the whip with dexterity and quickness the young girl had not witnessed before. Just as the swain picked up speed under the oxen's trot, the shouts of men pierced the night air. Needing no more encouragement, the oxen broke into a mad run, causing the skinner to sit on his whip to hold the reins.

The swain bumped along at a rapid pace, the children now all awake with fear in their wide eyes as the cries of the wild men echoed ever closer and closer. Brune found and held Gunter's hand, more to calm herself then him and the other children. She loudly said, "Now buck you up. Look at our Lord Nils and Larzmon. They ain't afraid of no old dogs in the night!"

Indeed, both now rode at the swain's side; their horses' easily keeping pace with the running oxen. Yet the sound of many men came ever closer and when Brune looked behind she screamed, "They're here!"

In one quick move, Nils and Larzmon shifted positions in their saddles and two twangs sang out into the night, each finding a brigand's throat. After this, the sounds of the boasting men's howls died away, and the oxen eventually slowed their pace to a steady walk.

Larzmon rode up, slapped them in the rear with his bow and shouted to the skinner, "Keep em moving!"

With quick snaps of the skinner's whip, the exhausted oxen surged forward along the dark and winding road. Larzmon, satisfied with his instruction rode ahead leaving the swain and Nils behind in the dark. Within the hour, the oxen began to falter, first slowing to a trot then a steady walk in spite of the skinner's fearful application of the whip. Nils rode up and restrained the skinner, saying, "They and you have done all you can. Keep what pace you may."

Larzmon returned to the swain, his horse blown. Both he and Nils looked at the brigands grouped behind them on a small rise to the north. With a silent nod, Larzmon drew his sword and spurred his exhausted steed forward. Then placing his bow and remaining arrows in Brune's small hands and drawing his sword, Nils said firmly, "These are for the last need."

The girl nodded understanding as Nils turned once again and rode toward the north, hot tears streaming down her face. Eventually the oxen simply stopped moving. Brune watched in horror as Larzmon fell under a gleaming scimitar and Nils collapsed into a ditch; having received a sharp blow to his un-armored head. Brune witnessed the skinner get down from his perch, take a small knife from his belt and slit each animals throat saying, "I'd 've em dead an' cold afore tos beasts gits em."

Gazing down on their fallen bodies and the great pools of blood that gathered about them on the ground, he looked at Brune, and then swiftly passed the knife across his own throat. The man's hot blood sprayed Brune's face and hair. Beyond tears and alone she looked at Gunter and the other children, counting their number and the sixteen arrows Nils had left.

She then dismounted the swain and going to the dead skinner, retrieved his knife. Now resolved to do what she must she prayed, "O Great Maker, receive these and me into your care."

She first went to her brother and pulled back Gunter's head by the hair, revealing his bare neck. She raised the knife, her mind unable to control her now quivering hand. She closed her eyes and slowly regained the mastery of her rebellious limb, stopping its wild shaking. Yet she could not move it down and across the lad's neck. She strained and grunted, and yet the knife hand would not move. Sobbing out a great cry, her eyes flew open as if by focusing her gaze on the blade, she could force obedience upon her outstretched arm. However, the knife was not there, fallen somewhere as a great mailed fist held her wrist. A deep voice growled in the darkness, "Now, now, little one lets have no more of that."

The last memory she had of that awful night was of the Graeflins surging north past her, brandishing bright torches and sharp steel.

Brune lay inside a low farmhouse; she raised herself, leaned over the open windowsill, and breathed deeply of the uniquely fragrant country air of spring flowers mixed with livestock. If not in her native farmstead, she was at ease in her natural environment. In this place, she quickly re-gained her strength and vitality. The fight on the roadway last night now lay nearly forgotten, a distant memory of her maiden's mind in the bright sunshine that dappled on the fallow fields. A firm knock on the door announced a visitor. Brune pulled herself from the window as the door opened revealing a tall, grey haired man.

Though he wore the simple brown homespun of a country Freiholder, she found him strangely familiar. Perhaps it was his features of face and grey eyes that resembled those of Larzmon. The memory of the young Ganger flashed before her and brought a small tear to Brune's eye. Yet, she saw this was not the hero that now lay dead on the road, but perhaps an old steader come to fetch her for some purpose—one of many she may have seen in her journeys. He stood before her, his grey eyes gazing at her for some moments as his mind searched for some old memory. Finally finding it, he smiled at her and said in a gruff voice, "'Tis Brune o Kapral Smythe."

Brune realized she knew this man! He had been the one who somehow had restrained her from the awful deed she had resolved herself to. She bowed politely and said, "Aye, hail and well met."

The man made a short bend at the waist toward her, and gesturing with his open right hand indicated she was to accompany him. He then turned and walked out of the room. Brune dressed herself, wrapped her shawl over her slim shoulders and followed him. Quickly passing through the small cottage, they made their way toward a horse and a small pony, both saddled and ready for travel. They mounted and after seeing the lass could indeed ride, the old man spurred his steed to a canter as he led them out of the farmstead.

At the road, they turned and galloped south. Along the way, Brune's sharp country girl's eyes noted the poor condition of the Hine. The place had the look of a great battle plain, for everywhere she looked, she found abandoned farmsteads, their buildings burned or falling into ruin. Once-rich fields stood fallow, choked with weeds and debris. Offal and rotting animal corpses filled the small rivulets and creeks. Of the pigs, cattle, sheep, and chickens that normally one would find, she saw only a few scrawny beasts.

Any ideas she entertained that the steadern had somehow laid provisions for themselves disappeared when they slowed their steeds to a walk so as to pass a group of men, women and children trudging along the road, their backs bent with heavy loads. None of the destitute group looked up to note their passing, yet Brune noted their starved and poor condition and could not avoid recognizing their burdens as the haunches and flank meat of the recently slain oxen. In a flash she understood these people had risked the night in order to salvage what food they could before the wild beasts or others got to it. Sad indeed had become Hine Skrapmond and greater sadness awaited her ahead.

Much like most of the ancient Manors, the house and court of Hine Skrapmond lay inside what had once been a stone keep. Built in days long past as a strong defense against the Ostlings before the long peace, its high tower was now long broken. Tents were pitched before the old ruins. A black standard gently billowed over the largest of these, the form of a red tiger on its center rippling as if it were trotting through the fields. Brune and the old man reigned in and dismounted. He firmly took her by the arm and in this way; she followed his lead as he headed for the large tent where her master waited.

She had never seen His Lordship Hine Skrapmond but easily recognized his standard. Since the Battle at Geldenherm, she had learned to fear it and him. For Steward Gim Bayz had made cause before the Dias for indenture and apportioned her and the other children to him. Brune only knew him as a cruel master, well able to starve or send her out for use. Why she had been spared along the road, she could not fathom.

As she and the man passed the two steaders standing guard and entered the tent, she wondered to herself, *What use could the Lord have of me now?*

Rather than a richly embroidered sedan or the accoutrements of silk, rich jewels and fine food Brune imagined finding in a Hine House, she found His Lordship's court was closer to that of a Hander's command. Within the tent, sparse furnishings sat on the bare ground. Maps of the Hine were posted along the tent's walls. At the tent's far end was a long wooden door suspended over two large barrels. Several steaders stood patiently in line or huddled around the rough table.

Brune's growing apprehension was eased somewhat when among the steader, she saw Nils listening intently to some discussion between two of the farm folk. Once each had said his part, Nils spoke and the steader clasped hands in mutual agreement, made slight bows to Nils and left the tent. As they exited, the old man cleared his throat, catching Nils' attention. Excusing himself from the steader who moved toward him, Nils came over and greeted the pair saying, "High noon and mid-day mess already passed, before you come to his Lordship's court?"

The old man silently saluted. Brune took note of the new bandages binding Nils' wounds from last night's battle. Then she smiled wide and ran into his open arms crying, "Ganger Nils, I should have known they would not get you!"

She sobbed great tears as she angrily hit his chest with her small fists, bruising her hands on the mail cuirass he wore. "You, you…."

He held her close, gently patting her back as her ineffectual blows and tears faded into small, short sobs. Once recovered, she pushed herself away from him, declaring, "I have come to present myself. Is his Lordship nearby?"

Standing, Nils took her by the hand and led her to the table, saying, "He is closer than you think. Now wait here and I shall fetch him for you."

Nils left Brune standing alone at the table's edge as he went around one side and stood with his back to her. She watched as he took up a black coat of arms, draping it over his armor. He strapped his sword to his waist and turned to face the young lass. Brune was not the only one in the tent to gasp in amazement that day as Serzian Domo Jens Larzmon announced, "His Lord Nils Lordship Hine Skrapmond! Approach and make your cause heard!"

Brune curtsied and giggled, "My lord!"

BRUNE'S LOT

It was late in the evening as the last petitioner left Nils that night. Brune had long returned to the Larzmon farmstead and now Nils sat alone in the flickering lamp light reading a scroll that lay on the table. The old man silently made no noise as he entered the tent and made his way to the table. Nils did not look up as he tiredly said, "My court will commence on the morrow. You may bring your cause forward then."

When the old man did not reply, Nils looked up from the scroll. He saluted Nils, then drew the sword at his side, knelt and presented the blade saying, "I am Jens Larzmon, father of he that laid slain on the road, once Steward Hine Smythe, and Serzian Domo Hand Leak."

Nils stood, came around to the kneeling man and placing his hands on his shoulders said, "You fought by my side at Geldenherm. I accept your service."

Jens Larzmon rose and sheathed his blade. Nils motioned him to some stools and said, "Come sit with me, for Great Maker, how I can use a good man! There is much I need to learn of this Hine."

Therefore, it was throughout the night Jens Larzmon told Nils all of what had transpired in Hine Skrapmond after Dom's arrival in the many years past. Nils learned that at first Dom appeared in Leak, claiming to be a drover come to purchase livestock for a distant Farmstead near the border with Fyrd of Dente. After securing a room at one of the finer Inns, Dom made the rounds of the various auctioneers, inquiring as to quality of the breeds and such other matters as befitted a drover's nature.

As his coin was plentiful and he was liberal in giving ale and board, none seemed to take serious note that he never purchased any livestock. That fall, Lis-Yan, Landkrieser Fyrd of Gelde sat first as Archana. She visited Leak Mor late in the season, and as the ice was forming on the Great Ost Mor, decided to winter with the Duke at the Graef Manor.

Winter had come and passed, the spring finding Dom ensconced in the Graef house. Jens Larzmon would not elaborate on the stories and rumors that Dom seduced the Duchess of Leak. Only saying following the Duchess' sudden death, the Lady Archana Lis-Yan made a rapid return to the Raffer-Mor. Within days, Dom with Gim Bayz in tow presented certain scrolls containing the Archan's signet to the Steward Graef Kanervald.

At the end of that summer, Gim Bayz, at the head of a vile looking column of Ganger, announced Dom, His Lordship, Hine Skrapmond. In those days, the land was rich in crops and livestock, its people having prospered over the years. Nonetheless, the old Steward was summarily dismissed, and the household staff displaced. Upon Dom sitting in office, a bitter and harsh winter blew early into the land. Many crops were lost in the field and whole herds perished in the open pastures due to the sudden freeze.

As was their custom, many of the steader and drovers of the Hine had laid up goods and foodstuffs in good days as caution for dire times. Enough of such there was to see each family into to the coming spring, and the hope of the new plantings and foaling. Nevertheless, Dom sent out parties of armed men who compelled the Graeflins to give up their winter stores. Those farmsteads and drover stations that refused the Lord's demands were burned out, the survivors driven into the bitter snows.

Dom made decree that any such as had left the Hine were considered forfeit of their holdings, and banished from aid or succor. He quickly annexed their lands, apportioning them to his. After witnessing their neighbor's fate, the remaining drovers and steadern complied with Dom's never ending demands, even to the point of giving their land and persons as mark when unable to pay. To keep his farmstead, Jens entered the Kaeder under House Zander-Fells.

Pointing to a map, Jens Larzmon explained how it was in this manner Hine Smythe had been incorporated into Hine Skrapmond. Late into the night, Jens explained how Dom placed many steads as mark for loans from the bankers, indenturing the families to distant places. Others he joined to the Hine, greatly enlarging its area.

As dawn broke, announcing the new day Nils learned how over the intervening years, Dom, and the Steward Gim Bayz, had raped the land leaving many streams fouled and the fields over-trodden with weeds. The abused people continued to dwindle until that now scarcely one in ten of the original Graeflins remained in Hine Skrapmond. As for the recent additions such as Hine Smythe, the lands had yet been untouched and the people remained prosperous.

Nonetheless, the recent war had caused an increase in the Landtieth, leaving many a stead family to tighten their belts. The Graeflins thought the payment of the Ganger's precious horses was a blessing in the countryside, keeping some store of grain and food in the steads. What was proving hard was the loss of coin, iron for tools, and the muscle power that went to build the small army forming at Rafermor.

The last insult recently discovered was the Hine treasury was gone, apparently stolen the day before Nils' arrival at Ost-Mor. Once finished, Jens Larzmon sat silent as Nils absorbed what he had heard. Finally, he asked the old man, "And is there not even seed or brood stock remaining?

Jens Larzmon replied soberly, "None here."

Nils continued, "Tell me, Steward, what of these new acquisitions? This Hine Smythe, could there be sufficient means within it to give us some hope of replenishments? And of the Graeflins, are there some that may take up the plow or herd here?"

The old man answered furiously, "Aye, but not unless ye intend ta demand 'em at sword point."

Nils rose and looked out the tent's opening at the growing morning light and said, "The days of his Lordship making demands are over. But, I think some may respond if asked with kindness by the Steward Jens Larzmon."

Laughing, Jens replied, "Ha! Indeed they may! But the word must be sent anon else, we be missing the planting!"

Nils declared, "Then send word through out our holdings that any Freiholder that can, may present themselves at the crossing of the Ostern Swain road within the fortnight. There, Lord Nils, His Lordship Hine Skrapmond shall have lots drawn for farmsteads and stations. Send word to Leak at Ost-Mor, Weslon and any other place within five days march as well."

Within days, the Ost Swain Road was filled with Freiholder making their way to crossing to Hine Skrapmond on foot, horseback or by swain. By the end of five days, a small camp had established itself at the cross roads, full of the hopeful to receive the promised free lands. Each day the camp increased in size as more came in for the lots.

The buzz of great excitement now coursed though the Fyrd of Zand, drawing the attention of merchants, ale masters and various camp cats and other hangers-ons to the camp, giving the place a carnival atmosphere. Much coin was passed over the tables in the great ale and food tents that had been thrown up in the camp. Even the bawd mistress from the brothels at Weslon and Leak-Mor set up places where each sold their wares.

Inevitably, drunkards began to clog the road and break into the tents of the simple farm folk. Fights broke out, and many a stead wife refused comfort to her man after having discovered he had spent good coin on one of the bawds. Nils sent Jens Larzmon and a contingent of sturdy Smythe lads and lasses to the camp to impose some sense of order.

Three days later, Nils was disturbed in his tent when a steader stumbled in, firmly dragging a red haired young lad by the wrist. Niles asked, "What means this?"

The steader shouted, "Cause it is, As 'dis kungon was a steal'n ta misses lay'n hens!"

Nils carefully regarded the steader and his prisoner; a half starved young man of perhaps fifteen years. He pushed the maps before him away, sat back in his plain wooden chair and said to the lad, "How now you come to thievery in my lands?"

The boy answered sullenly, "How now you keep a prince of the Ostlings from his people?"

Nils said to the steader, "Release him."

Then raising his hand commanded the steader, "Go to the hen house by the barn and take those three layers you deem best as payment for your loss."

The steader bowed, and after giving the boy his best evil eye, left him with Nils. Nils inquired, "Then how did one of the royal House of Ostlond find itself in my court?"

The young man showed his pride and scoffed, "Your court is a ratted tent! My father's lowest servants have richer goods than you."

Nils unperturbed asked, "And how is it such a wealthy personage as yourself came to stealing chickens from a poor steader?"

The boys face froze and he fought to control the anger as he responded, "Captured I was while traveling along your roads to Raffer-Mor as ambassador for my father, of the Ostlings. I make it near four years since I was taken."

Nils raised his eyebrows at the young man's story then asked, "Who did this to you? By what tokens did they know you? Where did they keep you?

The young prince pulled back a tattered sleeve from his left arm and revealed a three headed serpent, the token of Ostling royalty, tattooed on his fore arm. Holding the exposed arm up, he said with clenched teeth, "One called Dom and it was to his prison in Kanervald I was thrown."

Nils rose and coming around the plain table put his hands on the boys shoulders and said, "Truly, he is become a great evil! What is your name, boy?"

The proud young man replied, "Rolf of Klan Mak Doanalt, First Prince of Ostlond."

Nils knelt before the young man and said, "I am Lord Nils on behalf of my liege; accept our humble apologies for the insults you have suffered and the hurts you have endured while in Faerevold."

The young man began to reply, but collapsed on top of Nils, exhausted and too weak to stand. Nils gathered the lad up, washed and bound his wounds, placed him in his bed, and put a small pot of rabbit stew onto the fire. Once well heated, Nils took the pot from the heat and gently spooned its contents into the lad's mouth. As Nils was cleaning the pot, the young prince declared, "You cannot hold me!"

At this he fell into slumber. Nils finished his chores and made himself a bed in the barn. The next morning, he found the young prince and his sword missing. Mounting his grey mare, Nils set out after Prince Rolf. The lad's tracks were easy to spot, leading eastward through the steaders toward Ostlond. Three days later, Prince Rolf found himself before Nils. Only this time Lady Rosa Hine Patten was sitting as judge. Another steader had made cause before his lady and after consulting with Nils, the Lady Rosa proclaimed, "Payment to be made by our Lord Nils at Hine Skrapmond. You, young man are under our Lord Nils' protection."

Five days before the lots were to be drawn, Nils sat astride the Grey mare at the broken bridge that had once crossed the S'iflan River, connecting Ostlond and Faerevold. The River S'ifaln runs between the two lands along a high and wide chasm, its ragged steep sides averaging one thousand feet and its width one kleg distant. The bridge site was at the narrows; the S'iflan being a mere fifteen hundred feet wide there and the one place along the border that was suitable for crossing.

On the Ostlond, side was King Bruze with a large retinue and a host of archers and spearmen. Unlike the plain browns, greens and gray of the Faerevolder Graeflins, the Ostlings wore a wild mix of tartan trousers and kilts, their long red hair and beards braided. Many of the men (there were no women in the group) carried short round shields, mattocks and axes. Rolf rode to the edge of the broken span and hailed the Ostling host. After some passing of what Nils made out to be hand and arm signals, the lad returned to Nils' side and announced, "My father begs me cross alone. Your kind (meaning the Faerevolder) is not welcome in the Ostling Lands."

Nils and Rolf rode from the high bridge and following a narrow path, wound their way along the cliff's edge until they reached the shore. Here the water was shallow, allowing one to cross by either swimming or walking. Rolf and Nils dismounted and Rolf embraced Nils, saluted him in the Ostling manner by gently placing the palm of his right hand on Nils' forehead, and then without a word, he mounted his horse and entered the water. Once the lad was across the S'iflan and safely in his father's arms, Nils mounted his gray mare and turned to depart.

His leaving was interrupted by the sound of a single horse splashing into the stream. Nils turned and saw King Bruze sitting alone on his horse near midstream. The king motioned, and Nils rode into the water as well. Not quite in the middle of the stream, the two men regarded each other. The red haired, blue-eyed man with many scars on his face took in the measure of this Nils of Skrapmond his boy had hastily told him.

Nils was considering that despite the stark contrast in Faerevolder and Ostling dress, how similar young Rolf was to his father when the king spoke, "You be Nils of Taere I hear. Because of what you have done, the First Prince has spoken very well of you. This Dom, of him we demand his head."

Nils sighed, "If it were mine to give, I would do so and gladly. It is not, he sits in vile darkness in Zat Erzern in the Iron Mountains, sending his vile creatures to make war upon the Faerevolder."

At these words, the King grunted, "Dark tidings. Truly, I swear my sword shall drink the blood of the dark master that sits in Val Dunkerz."

Nils responded, "May it be so."

King Bruze then turned his steed and returned to the Ostlond side. As he left Nils still in midstream, the man's gruff voice shouted, "We accept. It is time to repair this bridge. By your liege's pardon, I shall send workers and masons to make it so."

Within a few days of Jens arrival at the camp order was restored, the bawds made to keep in their area, and the worst of the ale masters sent packing. On the 12th day, Nils had returned from the border and rode out to the cross roads, stopping by the small Larzmon Farmstead to see to Brune and Gunter's needs, the other children having been quartered with other families in the Hine. That night, she begged him to allow her to accompany him saying, "There is not like to be another day like it!"

Having relented to her pleas, the next morning Nils mounted his steed and Brune her pony. Together they rode to the crossing. The Smythe lads and lasses, or the Smythe Crew as they called it, met them well outside of the camp. Wild cheers and hurrahs for Nils greeted them as they rode into the now choked crossroads. The Smythe Crew formed a flying wedge around the pair, and in this manner, they pressed through the mass of persons that now surrounded them. Nonetheless, it was slow going, as Nils did not allow the Smythe Crew to indulge in any butting of heads nor rough pushing back upon the Freiholders.

Eventually they made their way to the center of the crossroads. There, Jens had built a large platform high above the road. A single stair in the front allowed access, and on its center was erected a tent. Here, Nils and Brune dismounted and climbed the stair. When one of the Smythe Crew unfurled the sable banner with the red cat of Skrapmond, the crowd burst into another round of loud cheers. Nils waved, and then entered his tent, leaving Brune and Jens Larzmon to follow him.

The tent was smaller, yet laid out much as the one back at the Hine's Manor house. As Nils and Jens huddled over some scrolls, Brune was drawn to a large map. On it, each available farmstead and station was outlined and indicated with a number. In a large box were tiny bits of paper rolled into tight cylinders. On a nearby table lay, Brune saw, other pieces of paper with numbers on them. Taking one, she went to the map and searched it over until she found its location. She sighed, "To be Freiholder, and to be able to cast for you. It must be...wonderful."

She returned the paper to the table and left the tent. Unknowing to Brune, Nils had witnessed the scene. Jens Larzmon finished telling Nils how one steader had gotten several stitches in his head when his mistress found him drunk in the road. Nils smiled at the story then motioned Jens to follow him out of the tent. On the edge of the great platform, Brune sat, idly twisting her hair as her legs dangling over the side. Nils asked, "Jens, at what age may one be declared Freiholder?"

Startled at a question to which every Faerevolder knew the answer, Jens exclaimed, "Why at birth, my Lord."

Nils walked over to Brune and put his hand on her shoulder. She turned her head to look into his face. Sensing the Lord had something of importance to tell her, she shifted her thin hips and stood up. Seeing the Lord on the platform, many of the Graeflins drew near, wondering if he was to announce the lots to take place today, (as some hoped), or he was to deny the whole affair (as others feared). Instead, he simply said in a loud voice, "I name Brune, daughter of Kapral Smythe, Freiholder."

She and Jens Larzmon stood there shocked such a thing could happen! Never had someone indentured been released before serving the full measure of the mandated seven years! Nils returned to the tent and closed the entrance behind him. Jens stared at the closed tent door, looked down at the girl, and croaked, "Now that demands ale!"

She quickly followed him down the stair and through the camp as he made his way to a nearby ale tent. However, before going in she stooped by a booth containing slips of paper. The guard watched as she hastily wrote "Brune Smythe" on one and dropped it into the nearby locked box. As she entered the ale tent, she heard the guard cry, "May the great Maker get ye the land lass!"

At dawn, the Smythe Crew stood around the platform, clubs (Nils had made them stack their spears) and shields at the ready. The guards brought forward the locked boxes. Once the boxes were set on the high platform, Jens Larzmon came forward, counted them to ensure all were present, and read the Lord's rule for the lots, "Names to be drawn at random. Only one name allowed drawing a number, each indicating the landholding. All the new landholdings to be registered with the Baron at Graef Kanervald."

The large map hung behind two large barrels suspended between legs set on the platform. Their sides enclosed in wire with a small open door. An axle ran from one leg, through the barrel and into the other leg. A crank was attached to each axel. Jens then unlocked each box and emptied its contents into one barrel. Once finished, out of the tent came two guards with the large box Brune had seen the day before. Into the second barrel went the small rolls of numbers. Jens closed and secured the barrel doors. He stood aside as Nils came from the tent and onto the platform. The crowd began to murmur and Nils held up his hand. Once they became silent, he called, "May the Graef Leak come forward."

The crowd parted as His Lord the Graef Leak made his way to the platform, followed by four Faeder Ganger of his house. The Smythe Crew allowed him and his escort to pass and mount the stairs, quickly sealing the gap behind. Once on the platform, Nils bowed to him and stepped to one side as the Faeder Ganger positioned themselves near the barrels. The Graef signaled and a Faeder Ganger rotated the barrel's cranks, causing the contents to tumble and spin. Minutes passed as the crowd watched the barrels turn, mesmerized by the flying bits of paper. With a swift slap of the Graef's hands, the Faeder Ganger quit turning the cranks, allowing the barrels to slowly stop their motion. Once stopped rotating the barrels hung on their axels, gently swaying in the morning breeze. The Graef then called, "One at a time if you please."

A tall, young drover with sandy hair and green eyes stepped forward, the Smythe Crew allowing him access. The Graef directed him to the barrel containing the names. Jens opened its door, and the young man reached in and drew out a single slip of paper. Jens signaled he should read it, and after ensuring he could pronounce the name, the drover shouted, "Bette Lin".

A great squeal of delight erupted from the crowd as a middle-aged woman rushed forward. Once on the platform, she was directed to the barrel of numbers. Breathlessly she drew one and unwrapped it, screaming, "Three and forty it is!"

On a large scroll, Jens entered her name next to an entry corresponding to the number she clasped in her hand. He then showed her the land's location on the large map where she made her mark on it. One of the Graef's valets then came out of Nils' tent carrying a small scroll. This he gave to Nils who passed it on the joyous woman who left the platform with the young drover.

Next came up a young girl who drew an Innkeepers' name who was rewarded with a distant drover's station. Then another who drew a Ganger's name, she received a farmstead. On and on the process flowed throughout the day. At dusk, the young drover's name was selected. He in turn drew a station near Dente. It was under torch light when Brune's name was picked and she drew a Farmstead. Finally, the naming barrel stood empty, the crowd around the platform having long dispersed. Nils and Jens took count of the lots, presenting the tally sheets for the Graef's signet. All told, some one thousand, two hundred, six and thirty numbers had been pulled. Yet nearly two thirds of the map remained un-marked. Jens said, "Not as good as you had hoped."

Nils replied, "It will have to do."

HEALING THE LAND

After the lots had been drawn, the camp at the cross roads swiftly disappeared as the new owners made their way to their new lands, intending to register with the Graef Kanervald after the planting. Within a week, Nils received reports of plows tilling long neglected fields, drovers building corrals at the stations, and the streams and ponds cleared of the reek and vomit that polluted them. A gentle summer with fair rains blessed the Hine so that come the harvest Nils was pleased to find the barns and corncribs full, and each Farmstead with a good supply of wood stacked neatly for fuel.

Some had surplus enough to take to market at Leak-Mor, earning coin or trading with the city folk for dress cloth, tools and other goods. Even at her young age, Brune had managed to bring in a full harvest of potatoes, beets, and onions, plus establish a good herd of milk goats and a flock of chickens. When she and the other Graeflins of the Hine arrived at the Manor house (greatly repaired over the summer) to pay Landtieth to their Lord , Nils welcomed them in the grand hall but refused payment saying, "Jens Larzmon has seen to our needs."

Jens had indeed been busy that summer. First setting workers to the restoration of the Hine House, and second gathering what help he could get preparing the Manor's fields and lying in the crops. Nils worked in the fields with the hired hands, wearing the simple brown homespun and wide straw hat of a steader. Much improvement was made to the Hine's Manor House, its tower walls repaired, and a new roof emplaced. Much more remained to be done to the place. Entire rooms remained full of rubble and filth. Yet, Nils could sit at court in the hall, even though he still slept in the tent that now stood at the House's rear within the newly repaired walls.

Similarly, only a small number of the Manor's fields were planted, mostly in fodder and grain for the horses and the few other animals Jens had gathered. Truth be told, that winter His Lordship was much poorer and worse off than the Graeflins of the Hine. In order to pay for the few repairs and seed as he obtained, Nils made his personal holdings mark to the bankers in Leak-Mor. As the snows now gathered, he and Jens stood in the barren barn and consulted the accounts, looking for some fiscal relief. Earlier that week, Nils had received one of the banker's demands for payment; partially made in the form of shipping off the last of the precious chickens and cattle.

The snow let up the next day and Nils took the opportunity to hunt. Long he searched for any suitable game, his bow at the ready. Having shot a doe, he found she had died on one of his Freiholders Farmstead. Technically, she was the steader's, but as Lord Hine Skrapmond, he could gainsay any landholder within the limits of the Hine. After some discussion with himself on the matter, he recovered his arrow. After carefully dressing the animal, saving the edible organs, he decided he was not above the smallest point of the law and delivered it to the Farmstead's mistress. As the winter night closed in, he returned to the Hine House, wondering how he would explain the day's events to Jens.

When he reached the ancient keep, he noticed a number of horses and an oxen standing in the corral. Many swains were parked nearby. Nils muttered, "A troop of Faeder Ganger come my way."

He dismounted and relieved his tired horse of the saddle and accoutrements. Once set in her stall, Nils measured out what remained of the mare's fodder, and then replenished her water bucket. He entered the wall through a small sally port, passing into the keep by way of the scullery and cookhouse. In the kitchen, he removed his knit cap and winter robe. He stopped to straighten the homespun tunic he wore over his still soiled leather breaches, and scrape the mud from the black ridding boots that reached over his thighs.

Once he was as presentable as he could then make himself, Nils made his way to the Manor Hall. There he found Jens Larzmon explaining to the members of the Faeder Ganger troop that his Lord was most honored to garrison them here for the winter, but they should know the impoverished nature of things as the Lord was in fact a rather poor man.

Nils walked over to the meager fire that blazed in the hall's hearth, the flames eagerly consuming more wood than he allowed himself to be used in one week. The Troop's Captain stood before the heat warming her hands. Nils also extended his cold hands and said, "Hail and well met, Suze Li."

She likewise greeted him and said sharply, "Skrapmond, a good name for the place as Jens will likely provide us the scraps from your table."

Nils replied, "No, Captain I promise. You shall enjoy all our mess has to offer. I ask only you understand our situation here."

Suze-Li was about to respond when the troop's Serzian caught her attention. Politely excusing herself, she received the gray haired woman's whispered report, "Tis true ma'm. Me an' the Kaprals done turned things out. Other than the two old nags in ta barn, ter taint no livestock about. What fodder dems got is scarce enough for demselves. Ters taint but dust an' mice in ta larders and pantries."

Suze-Li asked, "No sign anyone's been looking in the swains?"

"No ma'm," the Serzian sternly replied.

Suze-Li dismissed the Troop Serzian and Kaprals, and returned to Nils' side. In a low voice she said, "Truly, it is as I have heard. You have denied yourself, refusing the Landtieth due your House."

Chastened at her confirmation of his dire condition he replied, "Guilty as charged."

Suze-Li then smiled at him and called, "Jens, Serzian! Come along. Nils, you'll want a cloak."

In a few minutes, Nils and Jens stood outside as Suze-Li and the Serzian directed the covers be removed from the swains. Most contained barrels of foodstuffs and casks of ale. One was laden with strong boxes. At Suze-Li's order, the Faeder Ganger hauled and rolled the barrels into the keep, storing them in the kitchen and pantries. They carried the strong boxes into the hall.

Once the Faeder Ganger emptied the swains, she led them back into the confines of the warm hall.

Standing in their cloaks, Nils and Jens watched as the Faeder Ganger wiped and rubbed away the layers of grease and mud that covered the strong boxes. They soon made quick of the task and stood back from their work. Each strong box was blazoned with a sable shield and a red tiger. Clearly, this was Hine Skrapmond property.

With a nod from Suze-Li, one of the strong boxes was pried open. She reached in and withdrew a leather bag, heavily laden with coin. This she threw to Nils, saying, "Near the border of Linde and Gelde, some two months ago, we came across a band of Vilder-zerk and traitors with the swains you saw outside. We killed them all, and after the fight found these and the other contents now resting in your larder, enough of coin and grub to see one through the winter, I think."

What she did not report was the one lone rider who had escaped the Faeder Ganger attack. Even now as Nils stomach growled at the prospect of food, Gim-Bayz knelt before Dom, presenting the sword of Bruze to his master.

That night, Nils and Jens enjoyed the first full meal they had in weeks. After the ale and story telling, the Troop Serzian reported she had found suitable billets for all in the keep's environs. The Ganger then dispersed to their various places, some in the barn, and others in the not so badly broken rooms of the keep. Jens Larzmon reported he would remain in the hall, as someone trustworthy must guard the hoard of coin. Later, as Suze-Li lay under thick fur robes next to Nils in the tent, he kissed her hands and said, "I cannot thank you enough."

With a wolf grin on her face, she opened the covers, revealing her body to him and said coyly, "I think I can help you come up with something."

THE PROMOTION OF SUZE-LI

That winter, Suze-Li's troop remained at the Hine Manor House. Brigands had taken to raiding along the length of the Ost Swain Road. The Tektor had commissioned the Faeder Ganger to capture and hang all ruffians and highwaymen they found between Leak-Mor and the eastern edge of Hine Skrapmond. Jens Larzmon obtained permission and sent the swains laden with half of the Hine's treasure under escort to Leak-Mor. With ready coin from the strong boxes, the old Serzian purchased fodder for the animals and whatever sundry food stuffs as was desired. Jens called on each banker holding Nils' markers, paying each in full, to include the usury due.

On their return, Jens sent the swains forward while he detoured to the north toward Hine Smythe telling the Serzian, "I have business in this direction."

That night when Jens did not return with the swains, Nils commented to Suze-Li over dinner that the Hine included Smythe and although not exactly sure as to Jens' reason to go there, was confident the old Serzian Domo needed to attend to the Hine's affairs. Two days later, Jens arrived at the head of a small cart loaded with bundles and carrying a woman and a young lad of about five. That night Nils' mess was treated to Mistress Larzmon's cooking, for the woman was Jens' wife, Helge.

Throughout the winter, which was mild that year, Suze-Li's troop vigorously patrolled the Ost Swain road, and soon the hosts of brigands that preyed on the country folk disappeared. The swains rolled back and forth between the Keep and Leak-Mor. They brought in supplies as needed, but mostly hauled the tiles, lumber, and clay shingles required for the keep's repair. By spring, the Ganger had made much improvement to the place. In addition, with chambers cleaned and readied for Nils, and the kitchen and Steward's quarters restored, the entire troop could now be billeted inside the old barracks near the gatehouse.

Stonemasons, carpenters and various workers appeared with the warm days of spring. Jens recruited some twenty field hands who put the entire Manor sted under the plow. The young drover from the land lottery agreed on a count of coin to provide a steady number of beef on the hoof. Soon, with the pigs, chickens and other animals Mistress Larzmon found room for, the Keep's larders, cellars and pantries were full.

Deciding the presence of so much coin would present a great temptation, Nils and Jens had the remaining strong boxes filled. Minus some small bags for the Mistress's petty cash, the boxes were loaded on the swains. These Suze-Li again provided escort for until the hoard was deposited with the Graef Leak's banker; whom Jens found most trustworthy. That night, Nils, Suze-Li, and the escort found rooms with the old Innkeeper. While at the sumptuous board, a messenger arrived and presented a scroll to Suze-Li.

Nils noticed the mixture of joy and sad concern that played on her face as she read the scroll's contents. Setting it in her valise, she motioned the messenger to an open chair, and then carefully placed her hands in her lap. Nils, now accustomed to her moods, recognized she had something important to say yet did not want to blurt it out asked, "Captain, what news?"

She smiled and replied, "My Lord, it is the best and the worst of news. I have reached my majority and am now made Lo-Kagon and am to command a Logas of Faeder."

At this announcement, cheers, calls for more ale, and hazahs for the new Lo-Kagon erupted from the Faeder Ganger. While the uproar continued, Nils leaned over and asked, "And are you to go on campaign?"

The look in Suze Li's moist eyes confirmed Nils' words. A splash of cold ale rained down on her head as the Troop's Serzian called, "Ale, ale, ale. A bath of ale for the boss."

Suze Li smiled, grabbed a mug and downed its contents in one long swallow. She grabbed another full mug and doused the Serzian, which set off the Ganger in a cacophonous stream of shouts, catcalls, and a veritable rain of ale everywhere. Nils would remember the moment as one of the happiest in his life.

⋊⋌⋋⋌⋉

The next morning, Nils, with newly loaded swains and the escorts returned to Hine Skrapmond. Suze-Li remained at Leak-Mor, awaiting the arrival of the next ship to carry her to Raffer-Mor and her new command. The Ost Swain Road now hosted frequent travel between Leek-Mor and the eastward lands. From the congestion of caravans and herds, under Faeder Ganger escort moving west along the road, Nils easily marked the Tektar's preparations for war. Often, he was obliged to give way on the road to make room as they passed, and the moon rode high in the night sky when he and his small party reached the Hine's Manor House.

Jens Larzmon was waiting at the corrals, having set torches alight to guide and assist the latecomers. As they arrived, the skinners guided the swains into an area near the corrals, the Ganger dismounted, and Nils led his horse to one of the young stable hands that now inhabited the place. After quickly dismounting and handing over the mare to the lad's care, Nils hurried toward Jens, wanting to share his mind on his observations of the great traffic that was now on the road. As Nils strode through the small gaggle at the corrals he caught sight of Jens engaged in rapid conversation with the Troop's Serzian and a well muddied Ganger he did not recognize.

As he reached them, the Serzian rolled up a scroll, shouting, "It's orders! Kaprals, get these mounts fed and watered! They'll be leaving in the morning!"

Jens gestured for Nils to follow him and entered the keep. In a few moments, Nils found him in the hall standing by the hearth. The old man nodded when Nils relayed what he had seen on the road, and then said perfunctorily, "The Serzian will be taking the steeds to Leek-Mor come the dawn."

"Then the Troop is to war," Nils flatly intoned.

Jens then revealed the full extent of the contents of the scroll now in the Serzian's firm grasp. Dom had broken the truce and raiding Vilder-Zerk had swarmed into Fyrd Dente. Because of the dire shortage of horseflesh in the realm, not only the Troop's steeds were to go, but also all steeds within the Hine including Jens' young gelding and Nils' old mare were to leave in the morning. Only one in three of the Troop's Gangers were to ride on the morrow, the rest to be dismounted and formed into Kaeder.

After Jens delivered this news Nils gasped, "Reduced and without orders! Left on our doorstop until the Tektar decides what to do with them! And who is leading these Kaeder?"

Jens gave Nils a scroll and a gold ribbon with a silver bar, a captain's badges of rank. He then slapped Nils on the shoulders saying, "Congratulations, you've been promoted!"

Within the week, all repair and refurbishment of the keep ceased. Nils named Jens Larzmon Steward of the Hine and focused on forming the displaced cavalry into infantry. The former equestrians grumbled and cursed their fate, feeling as all elite soldiers do in similar circumstances that somehow they had been shamefully dishonored.

Following one unsuccessful morning of shouting orders to no affect to the disgruntled Ganger, Nils recognized his hand was forced and sent for Brune, his most astute and loyal Graeflin. When she arrived, he gave Jens the Serzian Domo's rank badges and made Brune Steward of the Hine.

Brune moved into a small room next to the Steward's quarters saying, "'Tis but for a season and 'ta mistress Helge needs her place."

The next day, Jens put on the wide scarlet sash of the Serzian Domo, bade his young son Val be a good lad, and kissed mistress Helge farewell. Shouldering a well-worn campaign haversack on his back, he made his way to Nils' command tent. With a gruff salute, and his no nonsense manner, Jens gave greatly needed advice to Nils, particularly in the selection of solid noncoms as the Serzian had taken the best of the Kaprals.

At the first opportunity, Jens left Nils in the tent engrossed in a long history of various Faerevolder battles and campaigns. As only a Sergeant Major who knows his business can, Jens gathered the Gangers together, and then force-marched them without rest or water stops some thirty klegs distant from the keep. At the end of the foot-sore journey and before he allowed them to make camp, he proceeded to knock sense into the demoralized soldiers;

saying, "Yas think yas been hurt! Sluggards, be grateful you're not Zerk fodder on the steppes!"

After a fortnight of Jens' tender training, the ganger returned to the keep and Jens ensured each loaded the curved long sabers, lances and other cavalry accoutrements on the swains that set out for Leek-Mor and the coming campaign. However, he also made sure each retained their personal weapons: mace, axe, and small bow being the most common. Still, while on guard duty or alone in the mess, many grumbled the loss of status and rued their fate in the loathsome Kaeder saying, "Death afore dismount. That's my policy!"

Other than his reading lessons, Nils had received no instruction as to the Kaeder's organization, weapons, or tactics. After consulting with Jens, he sketched out the Troop's basic organization of ninety Kaeder formed into three sections, each to be headed by a Letnat and two Kaprals. These, plus a Serzian equaled one hundred of foot for a full strength Troop of Kaeder. For arms, spears and large shields were to be provided.

Some of the Gangers were adept at using the small steader hunting cross bows, and Nils directed bowyers and fletchers to be employed producing one for each soldier with a supply of one hundred bolts for each Kaeder's use. As for tactics, Nils decided on three basic formations, the column, the line and something new to Faerevold, the square.

In those days, Skrapmond became a beehive of military activity as each day former Faeder arrived on foot or in swains to become Kaeder. By mid-month, some four hundred converted Faeder Ganger had reported to the Hine. Their numbers easily overwhelmed what the ancient keep could support and Nils turned over entire fields to become parade and training grounds. He established tents as temporary barracks and mess points. He also found a great need for proper sanitation and fresh water, so he had swains loaded with great water barrels and ensured the latrines were dug far away from the wells and streams.

By early summer, Nils and Jens forged a competent fighting force. By no means had the former horse soldiers enjoyed their conversion into a lower status (in their eyes) as infantry. However, in spite of their emotions they remained disciplined professionals and under Jens' capable hand, soon adapted their significant martial skills to Nils' demands. Some moved rapidly through the ranks. The former guardsman Galen demonstrated a near native ability for the work, and Nils commissioned him as Letnat.

INVESTITURE

After mastering the tactical nuances of infantry, Nils began to focus his energies on the important matters of logistics and reconnaissance. One morning a messenger rode in, leading a saddled steed tied by a tether. Nils learned Garm had come to his own lands, and now sat as Lord Graef Kanervald. The Hine Lords and Ladies were to receive their investments at his court at the earliest date. Nils informed Jens of this development and made ready to leave after the mid-day mess. Two days later Nils arrived at the Graef manor.

Like House Skrapmond, Manor Kanervald retained its keep. Here the similarity ended for the Manor sat in a castle and had been much increased in size and opulence by Dom. A valet greeted Nils at the stables. After being relieved of the precious mount, a house servant led Nils to one of the Manor's many chambers. On the bed cover lay clean linens, a silk shirt of light blue with a high color and billowing sleeves, a pair of cream colored calf skin trousers, silk hose, a wide belt of brushed black leather with a silver buckle, and short sable jacket with a red tiger embroidered on its left breast. In an alcove was soap, a brush and tub of steaming water for his bath, something he was in desperate need of, having not indulged in the finer points of cleanliness since Suze-Li's departure.

A chamber maid came in and bade he remove his muddy and worn ridding boots. Going to the alcove and pulling the dressing screen in place, Nils stripped off his much patched and soiled clothes; settling himself in the hot bath water with a great, Ahhhh!."

After gathering up his tattered homespun and holey boots, she wrinkled her nose in his direction and announced, "The Baron will see you at your convenience but begs you not stay over long in the bath."

The chamber maid left Nils alone in the tub. After scrubbing off some two months of dirt and grime, he pulled himself out of now cool water and dried off, his skin flushed lobster red from the bath's heat. In the alcove, Nils found a toothbrush of boars bristle, combs, and scissors. With these, he diligently scrubbed his teeth, and with the aid of a thin silver panel polished to a mirror, trimmed his scraggly beard. Once dressed, Nils realized he had no boots. He searched the room, and not finding them went to the door to call for the chamber maid. On the doorstep was pair of newly made high black riding boots. Nils took these, and after drawing them over the silk hose on his feet, noticed how perfectly they fit.

Nils found it all a bit amusing, standing in line in the large Manor Hall with the other Lords and Ladies dressed in similar costume. They all wore the same silver buckled belt, blue silk tunic, calfskin trousers and high black riding boots as Nils. The various colored and patterned jackets they wore, being the fashion in those days when displaying their Hine House Coat of Arms, distinguished each. At the end of the hall stood Garm dressed as his petitioners, but in the Manor's colors of red, a golden mace held by a mailed fist at his breast.

As each one made their petition to their Graef, the Lord or Lady would give their Hine the signet and patent of tenure to a valet who then passed them to Garm. They then knelt before the Baron, who announced their titles and placed the tokens in their hands. In this way, the Lords and Ladies Hines received vestment and authority.

When it came his turn, Nils advanced to the old warrior and bowed. Garm returned the bow, and reached out his right hand announcing, "Your Lordships, this is Nils sent to Hine Skrapmond. He presents no tokens, yet I extend my hand to him and beg you treat him as peer until his cause is settled."

Nils bowed again and stepped to the side, allowing the next petitioner access to the Baron. At the end of the day's investitures, the Manor Hall was cleared and a large table set for a banquet. During the sumptuous meal, Nils sat at Garm's right hand at table. Most of the talk that night centered on the

Faerevolder defeats during the current campaign, the prospects of the herds and harvest, and the small raids and ambushes that plagued the Fyrd.

Nils had little to contribute as his life was now consumed with the Kaeder Ganger. One item did get his attention when he heard one of the Hine Lords describe how he had recently come from Raffer Mor. The Tektar, Mai-Yanna had declared martial law, and he further explained how the she had assumed the title of Strategon Domo. Now the Landkrieser, Barony and Lordships had full authority to administer capital punishment within the boundaries of their land holdings.

Garm had also listened intently to this news, considering its meaning. His attention from these serious matters was soon diverted. He was pleasantly surprised when her Ladyship, Lady Rosa Hine Patten, her massive breasts close to bursting from the tunic she now wore open at the neck, leaned over the table toward him, and bragged, "I expect to fill two ships this harvest! One for the sheep flocks and another for my grain!"

Garm drained his wine goblet and happily chirped, "Well done my Lady!"

Hearing this, the Lords and ladies offered congratulatory toasts. All but Nils began to vie for Garm's attention as one after the other shouted out wild claims of the huge herds, mountains of wool, and tones of grain destined for Leek-Mor at the end of the season. Then one drunk and loud Lord mockingly asked Nils, "What can Hine Skrapmond boast?"

Hearing this, Garm slammed his fist on the table with such force and violence the plates shook and many wine goblets fell over, spilling their contents on their owner's laps. He shouted, "Enough! He has raised something more valuable than all of your imagined crops and herds!"

Garm then abruptly stood from the table and furiously strode out of the hall, signaling the end of the soiree. Without the dessert course or an evening of dance and flirtations, or the continued gossip and politicking, the hushed guests meekly made their way to their chambers. Last, to leave Nils drained his goblet's contents and slowly strolled out of the Manor Hall and into the clear summer's night air.

The sky was full of the alien bright stars whose names Nils had yet to learn. A cool breeze moved over the rising fields of corn and oats. In the heather and pastures, Nils half listened to the lowing of his Baron's cattle. In these few quiet moments, Nils often considered his situation and thought deeply on how and why he had come to Faerevold, whose strange people he found in spite of their imperfections many admirable attributes.

Nils was attempting to untangle the conundrum of indenture when Garm approached. He stood by Nils for sometime then said flatly, "Hine Skrapmond is no more."

Nils shook himself out of his reprieve and asked, "How do you know this for sure?"

Garm responded, "Gim Bayz, Dom's Steward took its tokens as well as others when he fled to the Iron Mountains. It is true. I have it from one of his underling's mouth, a certain Pa-Val I believe you are familiar with."

His body shaking, Nils asked, "He is here now?"

"Aye" replied Garm as he pointed toward a distant tree.

Under the light of the full moon, Nils saw a man sitting astride a horse under a large tree. Two of Garm's men stood nearby, their features indiscernible as they positioned themselves on at the horse's head and the other at its rear. Nils watched as the horse's head was released and the man at its rear raised a whip. With a quick SWACK! The whip snapped and the horse bolted forward, leaving Pa-Val dangling by the rope attached to his neck and one of the tree's thick branches. For some minutes, the brigand's legs kicked and his body quivered as he slowly died from the hanging he so richly deserved.

With his ending, Dom lost his last thrall and spy within the Faerevolder lands. Now, Dom was blind and deaf to all of Mai-Yanna's doings. Hence, although he had known of the raising of Suze-Li's Hand, Dom knew not to his everlasting doom of Nils' investiture, and the raising of his Kaeder.

As was the custom, Garm left the corpse of Pa-Val hanging and swaying in the wind for a fortnight before having it cut down and burned. The ashes scattered among the various trash heaps and piles of offal on the Manor's Farmstead.

After the hanging, Garm said, "Several mason's swains passed through here five days ago heading east. Are your repairs so needy at Skrapmond?

In all the fuss of the day Nils had forgotten to tell his Baron of his meeting with King Bruze. After hearing him out, Garm growled, "It is about time! It is good we trade with them as we are in desperate need of it in these dark days. Very well you did by tending to his son, the First Prince. Naught but good can come of this I wager."

He then led Nils into the Keep, past the Great Hall and after lighting a lamp, continued down a series of stairs. He stopped at the armory, gave Nils the lamp, and pointed to the chests laid in neat rows and the stacks of shields, mail, and weapons saying, "The Herald will be here in the morning to blazon your new arms. Spend as much time as you wish selecting arms. I suggest you begin in those chests as the Maker knows what Dom's creature has in them."

As Garm made his way up the stairs, Nils asked, "And what of you? Don't you need a light?"

With the Ganger's characteristic wolf grin, Garm chuckled, "I need no light to attend to the two full boats awaiting me!"

Nils set the lamp on a high shelve. Opening the first chest, he whistled, "Like father, like daughter."

><del>⌁⌁</del>⋖

The next afternoon, as new groups of petitioners were gathering before the Great Hall's doors, the Herald spoke to Garm, "He has chosen. The Blazon was long lost in ancient days."

The Baron barked, "Good!"

As Garm looked out an open window, Her Ladyship, Lady Rosa Hine Patten with her hair ruffled and cheeks blushed, grimaced from the soreness in her thighs as she gingerly made her way to a waiting carriage. The carriage passed his window and Garm and Lady Rosa waved at each other. Greatly satisfied with themselves they smiled and sighed, "I still know how to ride my ponies."

The Herald bowed and left the hall by a side door. Garm took his position, and the procession of petitioners began anew. The last in line received the tokens from their liege, and Nils had yet to appear. Garm grumbled and fumed as he and the petitioners waited for the sign to adjourn to the evening's banquet. Small coughs and the swish of tiny fans echoed softly in the hall.

Garm, never a patient man, was about to give the signal when Nils entered and the room fell into a sudden hush. Garm was not alone as he stared at the arms Nils wore. It was dark blue with an eight-pointed pale green star on the left quarter. The stuff of fables and legends had come alive, for Nils presented the tokens of Hine Perion to the Barony. Of Nils, there had been no more sign at the investiture's adjournment, having excused himself from the liege's table before desert.

From the Baron, none could receive word of Hine Perion beyond Garm's laconic replies of "A rich land I hear and known for its root crops."

Much gossip passed among the Hines that night at the dance. Some asked, "What did this mean? And were the legends true?"

Others wondered, "Have we really seen the Perion?"

Yet a few others buzzed, "What of it? A plain man he is, no more than you or me."

The next morning found Garm in the barn grasping his knees and sucking in great gasps of air before Nils, dressed in his old, but now clean, home spun. Once Garm recovered of himself, Nils learned that after taking breakfast, and laying his costume on the bed before he left the chamber, the chamber maid had found the items. She carefully folded the rich cloths and placed them in a pommel bag. She had then run to Garm, who after hearing her explanation grabbed the bag and raced to intercept Nils in the barn.

Understanding they were his to keep, Nils took the pommel bag and tied it firmly to the horses' saddle. It had begun to rain, and as a parting gift, Garm produced a hooded cloak of light green color. This Nils put over himself and mounted. Seeing the escort was also ready, he saluted Garm and rode into the wet day. The rain did not last long; the sky broke into the clear well before mid-day. The warm sun quickly dried the two riders, and they rode the remainder of the way in the comfort of a rich Faerevold mid summer.

Summer passed and hints of autumn floated through the air as Hine Perion continued to prepare for war. Upon one dog day, a message arrived.

Nils had received commission as Lo-Kagon and his Logas of four hundred Kaeder were now ordered to the Raffer-Mor. Within the week, all was made ready and Nils marched onto the Great Ost Swain road, turned his face west, and headed toward Leek-Mor.

What took riders a few days travel, the infantry spent a week or more to traverse. The early harvest was beginning and Nils' Logas arrived at the docks the same day two ships anchored. The ships' Masters had sped ahead from Raffer-Mor in anticipation of the greater coin they could command by being one of the first to return to the capitol with the new crops and livestock. Finding the vessels suitable, Nils commandeered both and loaded the four hundred aboard. Beholden to provide transport to the Ganger, the ships set sail at the earliest tides and winds, reaching Raffer Mor five days later.

Begrudging the extra coin they had anticipated, the two ships' Masters were not long in their disappointment in now being last, taking what leftovers, and small coin, from the late harvest as they may find at Weslon. Once disembarked, Nils sent Brune word to pay them both double what had been anticipated. This she promptly did, causing one old salt to remark, "Sometimes being last taint all bad!"

At the Raffer-Mor Nils gained audience with Mai-Yanna. As Tektar and Strategon Domo, her court was taken over with the various Strategon and Hander of her military staff, and few of the frilly courtiers Nils recalled when last before the Dias. When he stood before her, he noticed how much the vivacious lady had changed in the intervening seasons. Her once raven hair was now streaked with grey; her face was haggard with long lines on her once fair cheeks, and dark shadows lay under her eyes.

After receiving his salute, the exhausted Tektar did not raise her eyes to him as she placed her signet in the hot wax, saying, "We recently regained Geldenherm Citadel, and the garrison is in great need of supplies and reinforcement. A Logan of foot is your command. Serve us well, Lo-Kagon. Your Logan is to leave on the morrow as escort for the swains and to garrison the citadel. Do you have any questions?"

Nils took the new commission from her extended hand saying, "No."

"Hail and well met", she replied.

He saluted her, turned, and marched out of the hall.

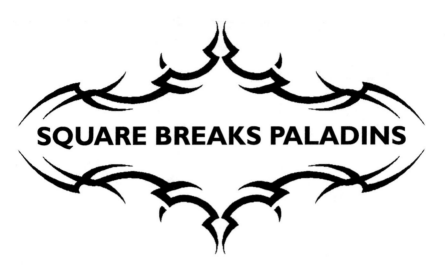

SQUARE BREAKS PALADINS

In due course, winter passed and spring came to Faerevold. Nils established a garrison at Citadel Geldenherm, putting the troops at hard work repairing and improving its defenses. Suze-Li was now Ganger Hander in command of a full regiment of cavalry. She was on patrol in the wide spaces between Zand, Linde and Gelde. Nils had been relieved of his command by another Lo-Kan and returned to Raffer-Mor where he found to his great delight he now commanded the Lo-Kan which contained the original troop he had trained at Hine Skrapmond, and with Serzian Domo Larzmon in its ranks.

Within one of the palace's council chambers Mai-Yanna, Zander-Fells, and Nils were assembled. Nils watched as ice and snow melt dripped rhythmically from the windowsill. They had been debating various councils of war since early before sun up, and now Mai-Yanna was speaking, "It is done. Garm carries the call to war. He scours the land for any and all that may bear us arms. Dom and his traitors may hold the roads to Geldenherm. The steppes are yet ours."

Zander-Fells then spoke, "Nils. All seek your council. Do you wish to consider war with us?"

Nils, still looking out the window responded, "I am at the Tektar's service."

Mai-Yanna took up a scroll from a table, "Then here is your commission. A Lo-Kan of foot is yours to command in battle. Serve us well Lo-Kagon."

Nils turned from the window, took the scroll and saluted, "As you command."

Mai-Yanna returned his salute and then turning she said, "I name our Lord Zander-Fells Strategon Domo. He commands all that is ours in the name of the Tektar. What is your council?"

Zander-Fells responded, "Geldenherm's peril is a grave situation. However, it is not as grave as it is to Dom. To seek battle, he may come to us by one of two ways. The first is through the steppes and over the fords. The second way is through the Rohdernvald and across the great Aerkan desert."

Nils interjected, "He will gather what strength he has at hand and attack Geldenherm, preferring not to lose time and troops in the desert."

Mai-Yanna looked at Zander-Fells and asked coquettishly, "You will not let him campaign so easily?"

With a wolf-grin, the Strategon Domo replied, "No. Suze-Li now watches the steppes and its roads to the Iron Mountains. We shall send Nils' troops into the steppes."

"You intend to hold Geldenherm," she said rather than asked.

As rapid as it appeared, the wolf-grin disappeared as he flatly said, "Yes. He must have the place as it controls his line of march, and if he intends to move quickly against us."

The steppes are the vast, open area that lies in the middle of Faerevold. Far to the north lies the Great Aerkan Desert, while at the western edge runs the River S'iflan, bordering the Ostling lands. To the far southwest lay the Kraags that bordered Fyrd Dente, a line of tall mountains perpetually covered in snow and ice. Far to the east stands Citadel Geldenherm and farther beyond are the Iron Mountains and Zat Erzern, Dom's lair.

A single, well-worn road wound its way from Raffer-Mor through the steppes. As Nils and Anadan rode at the head of a long column of infantry and supply wagons, Nils began to consider the importance of Geldenherm;

whoever held it controlled access to the steppes and the road he was now moving on.

"I think you made a poor bargain," said Anadan from atop his mount.

"Why do you say so?" Nils replied.

"There is no guarantee you will survive this march much less hold Geldenherm. Dom's thralls will not let you live if you fall into their hands. And there are those among your ganger that will slit your throat at the first sign of failure," the old man continued.

Nils smiled wryly, "Then I must not fail nor allow myself to be captured by the enemy. He thinks he can win this with her?"

Anadan asked, "What do you mean?"

"Ka-Tayana." Nils answered.

Then he hesitantly continued, "He wanted me when I was with him. I tell you this. Dom has brought the plans for a terrible weapon from my world and into this one.

"And?" asked Anadan.

Nils answered, "And it is not him alone. There is a thing darker and more powerful than Dom which lays in Zat Erzern that overlooked our escape."

Anadan replied, "One of the Val Kiren, and ancient enemy."

Nils and Anadan then rode silently along together for some time after this brief exchange. Finally breaking their long silence Nils said, "Dom and this thing in his hall will not succeed as long as I live and she remains true. As for those others out there, they may try to take my head."

Nils spurred his horse and trotted forward where he dismounted and began to stride along the trail, leading his horse by the reins. His Serzian Domo, Jens Larzmon walked next to him. The long columns of infantry and wagons wound behind along the dusty trail.

Deep in thought, Anadan turned his steed aside from the surging columns of infantry and returned to Raffer-Mor.

Within Zat Erzern, Dom and Ka-Tayana stood before the dark lord. The Dark Lord extended a misshapen chalice to Dom's lips, "Dominare, our right hand. Drink and take her as our bride."

Dom, sipped from the chalice, and said, "I do take her for your great and everlasting power."

The Dark Lord then extended the chalice to Ka-Tayana, "Ka-Tayana, Evening Emerald, be our bride of the flesh and soul."

With a slight turn of her head, the young maiden said, "I cannot."

Great was his anger and rage as the Dark Lord threw the chalice down, spilling its contents on Dom's boots demanding, "No one rejects us! Why this refusal?"

Ka-Tayana responded meekly, "Dominare is indeed most seductive. Yet, he has given me no boon for my maiden head."

Taken by surprise, Dom asked, "What boon do you speak off?"

Ka-Tayana addressed the Dark Lord directly, "The head of this Nils that fills Lord Dom with such great lust."

The Dark Lord asked his servant, "This is true? You desire another?"

Sheepishly, Dom admitted to his master, "Yes."

Ka-Tayana insisted, "Bring me his head, and I shall come to you eagerly."

The Dark Lord proclaimed, "Done. Dom, do not fail us."

A fair morning had come upon the Steppes, and the sun rode hidden in the disappearing grey mist. A gentle breeze stirred the dry grass as Nils and the four hundred Kaeder Ganger of his Logan surged forward over the steppes in long, orderly columns. The extended line of heavily laden swains plodded steadily forward as the Faerevold infantry marched in their disciplined formations. The soldiers' arms swung in easy rhythm with the measured stride called out by the Serzians and Kaprals as each booted foot hit the earth. Their rough voices rang over the Kaeder Ganger formations with lance, ax, and sword lightly resting on strong shoulders, rolling the cadence, "Heyt! Dvu! Tree! Chert!"

The old warrior's face spread wide in a crooked grin as he thought upon what lay stored in the swains among the foodstuffs, equipment and other supplies destined for the garrison at Geldenherm. For in addition to their visible kit, each Kaeder Ganger had an extension to their spears that added about another three feet to its length, a nasty surprise Nils had in mind for the first Vilder-zerk he ran into. As he strode alongside of Nils at the Logan's head, Serzian Domo Jens Larzmon grunted under his breath, "Any enemy scout could easily determine the manner of these arms."

"Let them. There will be few, if any survivors I wager." said Nils.

Through the sea of tall prairie grass, they marched in ranks of three. Nils was in the lead with the banners and heralds. Behind him followed the units of his Logan. Two columns formed the head. A company of 120 crossbowmen was next. The swains and a pack train of mules followed. In the trail was the third column. The faint outlines of skirmishers accompanied each flank.

Nils stopped and signaled a halt as smoke and dust rose in the mirage of the distant horizon. The sun's dim light mixed into a faint golden-red haze as Faeder-Ganger whipped their mounts furiously toward him. The mounts were flecked with salt, their eyes wide and red in panic. Most mounts carried wounded and dying riders. Other were without riders. Many of the horses and riders displayed open wounds as bright red blood flowed from where dark arrows pricked them.

Nils commanded, "Hold the column!" Serzian Domo and commanders on me!

The troop commanders ran up to Nils. Jens Larzmon pointed at the growing dust cloud before them and said, "Riders from Suze-Li's Hand."

Nils flatly intoned, "What's left of them."

One Fader-ganger, Baer-En galloped up to the standing group. Although wounded and exhausted, he easily slowed the glistening black horse's pace. Other riders continued to rush past the column's head, slowing to a trot as they reached the swains and last column. Nils ordered Baer-en, "Whoa there! Hold your steed!"

Baer-en pulled up before Nils and saluted.

Nils ordered, "Can you report, Faeder-Ganger?"

Baer-En saluted and reported, "Aye. The Lady took some 'o dem black'arts this side 'o Geldenherm. Near 20 klegs back. They was a small band at first, then it seemed they came from everywhere at once. Two, three hander all mounted rolled over us like a flood. We scarce chopped our way through and broke out."

Nils forced a sudden sense of dread down his throat and asked, "And Lady Suze-Li, where is she and the rest now?"

Baer-En responded, "Five maybe three klegs behind, insisted on commanding the rear guard in person."

Nils relaxed and inquired, "How many more are there of you? Where is the remainder of the Ganger?"

The embattled horse soldier answered, "My Lady 'olds most of the third Logan. We lost 'ta trains; we's all that's left o' da first an' second."

Nils turned away, wanting to keep the shock on his face from panicking his command. He gathered control of his raging thoughts of Suze-Li lying dead on the steppes or worse. He scanned the area before and around him, spying a knoll rising in the distance. Quickly he decided on his plan and said, to Baer-En, "Gather together what you can at our trains. The surgeon and farriers can help, as they are able. Serzian Domo, see to it."

Jen Larzmon replied, "Yes sir."

The old Faeder-Ganger continued. "There's more, sir."

Nils asked, "What?"

Baer-en spat, "Dem riders weren't no Vilder-zerk. Dems are gone-overs."

Nils asked, "Faerevolder traitors? Are you sure?"

Baer-En was un-used to a Lo-Kagon of infantry not believing the word of a Faeder-Ganger. *Did this officer not know that even a Hander of infantry stood below the lowest Faeder-Ganger in rank?*

The grizzled veteran considered correcting the foot soldier of his error but noted the steel hard determination in Nil's face and said, "Sure I'm sure. I'd known that Gim-Bayz since he gave a run at my misses 'afor we had our little one. He's ride'n a'hed tose other black'arts."

At this news, the Serzian Domo saluted and escorted Baer-en and his mount to the rear. Nils never realized the salute was for the Faeder-ganger, and he scanned the horizon as more wounded and exhausted Faeder-Ganger continued to ride in.

Having made his decision, he turned and faced his officers. "It's hard work ahead of us gentlemen. Lady Suze-Li is holding off a large body of the enemy between here and the citadel."

Pointing to the knoll, Nils continued, "There is a small rise to our front. We'll take that and hold it."

Kaptan Galen asked, "How many of the enemy?"

Nils replied grimly, "Enough for everyone, more than enough."

Under the watchful eye of the Serzian Domo, soon all of Nils' infantry were stretched in a long line along the top of the knoll, the low ridge commanding the road. Spears and shields were at the ready. Thin lines of cross-bowmen were thrown out to their front, acting as screeners. The Faeder-Ganger gathered in small groups near their comrades at the trains. The surgeon, farriers and aides busily tended to both wounded human and animal. From the distance and through the skirmishers rode Suze-Li and the remains of her broken command to Nils. She halted her horse and shouted, "Nils, hail and well met!"

Nils could not suppress the wide smile on his face as he saluted her, crying, "I am glad to see you alive."

Suze-Li dismounted. She and her mount were covered in mud and blood. Her cuirass was dented in many places. Blood seeped from under a dirty rag that bound her left hand. With a nod, she directed Nils to walk with her away from the formed soldiers. Once away some paces, she commanded, "What do you mean to do here?"

Nils replied, "I am to reinforce and provision the garrison at Geldenherm. And you, how did you come by my march so far from the Iron Mountains."

She said, "War, and the orders that drive us all on its tail. Aye, even the Great Aerkan Desert could not stop the riders from Our Lord Zander-Fells. We were to take our rest and provisions at the citadel. Then meet Lord Zander-Fells at the fords."

Nils continued, "These Vilder-Zerk and traitors, where are they now and how many?"

Suze-Li responded proudly, "Some 10 Klegs back. Near four thousand lay back there dead or licking their wounds. Most are now on foot, some on horse."

Nils considered her information carefully for some time, then said, "I mean to fight them here."

With a professional eye, Suze-Li looked over the terrain and Nils' disposition into order of battle on the ridge. "This is a good position. But it is futile for you to stand here."

He asked her, "And where else shall I stand? You know the road I walk."

As a drill master would instruct a raw recruit, Suze-Li said, "Your infantry has little chance in the open."

Lo-Kagon Sicharis looked at the hurrying formations of his soldiers, and considered Abrams' last words at Seti Four. He responded, "You are the senior officer on the field, do you take my command and order a retreat?"

Stepping back, the Faeder-Hander considered Nils' response. No longer was he Anadan's strange foundling. Nor was he the stout, brave fighter at Geldenherm that she had met, trained, and allowed a place in her heart. He had become something she immediately recognized, a leader. Yet she was loath to allow him to throw away his command easily as she carefully said, "No. Consider this. Burn your wagons and flee before they swallow you whole."

He responded, "And what of the wounded?"

Suze-Li's words roiled over his ears. He could not make sense of what she was saying, as in his mind, he was in another battle. Instead of facing Suze-Li, Lieutenant Colonel Abrams glared at the plebian. Nils had spoken no words when the ground erupted under him and what had once been Abrams' tall and lean form disappeared in a fine red mist. The force of the explosion blew Nils high into the air. Nils remembered lying in a crumpled pile on Seti Four.

He was deep in the memory, when Suze-Li lowered her voice and repeated flatly, "Do you not hear me? I must save what I can. We all must."

Awakening to her, Nils said, "Dom knows you are to his front and he is pushing his horse ahead in hot pursuit. He does not know I am here. When he digests that little piece of news, I intend to give him a nasty treat."

Angry that this fool of man would not see reason she blurted, "Your flanks are exposed!"

Red faced, he turned to her and hotly said, "Go! The wounded may stay with me. Gather what you can and get to the fords. If you hurry, Our Lord Zander-Fells may find us alive when he gets here."

With tears in her eyes, Suze-Li mounted and rode to the rear, passing the Serzian Domo as he walked up to Nils. Jens Larzmon reported, "Sir. The skirmishers are in."

Nils removed a small telescope from his saber-tasche. He scanned the distant horizon, and then fixed its view on a horde of mounted Faerevolder traitors and Vilder-zerk riding hard and fast. They carried their bloody weapons at the ready. On top of pikes, and tied to their saddle pommels, many displayed the severed heads of Suze-Li's Faeder-Ganger.

Nils said, "Damn they're riding fast. Give the command to form square. Split the archers into four groups, one behind each side of the square. Make sure the trains and wounded are in the center."

Before carrying out Nils' command Jens asked, "What of those Faeder-Ganger with us?"

Nils responded as Suze-Li returned afoot to Nils, "Get those men spears and axes, and tell them to hold the trains."

Serzian Jens Larzmon returned to the lines shouting, "Form square! Form square!"

Nils replaced his telescope and without looking at Suze-Li said, "I thought you were leaving."

She grinned at him and said, "Better to perish a hero and fool here than be caught on the steppes as a coward. By The Great Maker, this is good ground!"

Turning to her, Nils gave her his biggest smile and said, "Very well. If my Lady will please, dismount her riders and gather them within the trains. Watch the Kaprals and have your Faeder-Ganger do as the infantry."

Nils looked past her at the disciplined ranks. The infantry were forming into a large block of spears and shields around the swains and wounded. Nils said, "Our best and only chance is to hold our lines. We cannot let them get in."

Suze-Li walked by Nils' side as the two made their way into the well-ordered ranks of infantry. She grunted, "We shall not live it down. Faeder-Ganger to fight on foot when good steeds are at hand."

Nils said firmly, "If you wish to gain victory with me and one day tell a great and glorious story to our grandchildren, and then you must."

Then in front of the massed troops, lowly Kaeder and high Faeder alike, Suze-Li grabbed Nils and kissed him full and hard on the lips. Just as suddenly, she released the surprised warrior and bolted into the square.

Breathlessly he managed to choke out, "Keep those mounts unhurt and ready. You may get to use them again!"

If Nils was temporarily unable to command due to Suze-Li's sudden embrace, Serzian Domo Jens Larzmon suffered from no such affliction shouting, "Form square. Form square.

To Kaptan Galen standing alone atop the ridge surveying the enemy amassed below, Jens politely but firmly intoned, "Kaptan, beg your pardon, get back in line with your troops. You'll do not much good out there."

Galen and Nils returned to their troops while, to their front, the horde of mounted Vilder-zerk and Faerevolder traitors men drew scimitars. They shouted as one and charged pell-mell toward Nils' command. From behind his soldiers, Nils commanded, "At the ready. First rank, kneel, present!"

Nils' forward ranks knelt with shields to the front. The infantry attached their spear extensions and presented a forest of glinting spears on long shafts to the on-rushing horde. Nils commanded, "Archers to the front, let fly."

A hail of deadly bolts rained into the charging mass. Many of the enemy and their mounts died and fell with bolts and war cries in their throats. Nils, walked to Suze-Li and gave her a spear, and taking an extra one from the Jens Larzmon put his foot firmly behind its butt and said, "Put your foot on it. See like mine."

Seeing what he intended, Suze-Li mimicked Nils' actions. The Faeder-Ganger similarly armed, followed her example. The cross-bowmen continued to slay Vilder-zerk and enemy Faerevolder at will as large gaps appeared and filled within the mad charge. Nils said in a calm yet loud voice, "Steady men. Kaptan of Archers, loose your bolts as you see best. Send those beasts to hell."

Bolts zipped forward as the charging mass hit the lines of bristling spears. It faltered then broke away from the bloody spears. Its wings separated from the main body and swarmed the flanks only to meet more razors on long poles.

Repeatedly, the shrinking mass charged the compact square, only to be repulsed and then shake itself free from Nil's iron lines. The confused and angry mob swarmed and swirled around the grim soldiers as it attempted to encircle and roll over the steady ranks of Faerevolder Kaeder and Faeder.

Here and there a Vilder-zerk or traitor managed to break through or catapult over the lines and into the square's open enclosure, only to meet the crossbowmen's' flashing swords and axes. Wounded Faeder-Ganger also dispatched a lone Vilder-zerk or two as they held their formations near the trains.

Finally, several of the Vilder-zerk and traitors dismounted, and attacked on foot. In a frenzied melee, both sides grappled in vicious hand-to-hand combat. Every weapon was present: axes and daggers, maces and swords, chains and darts. If a member of the two sides lost their weapon, they tore at their enemy with bare hands and teeth. Eventually, a harsh blast rang over the steppes, and the few remaining Vilder-zerk disengaged and struggled away. Alone, their Faerevolder companions continued the attack and perished under the weapons of Nils and Suze-Li's Ganger; many of whom began to seek out and slay the few wounded enemies.

Nils ordered, "Hold! Hold your weapons! Bring that wounded one here to me."

Two Faeder-Ganger drug a badly wounded man to Nils. From the remains of his mouth, the traitor Gim-Bayz spat blood and broken teeth at Nils, gurgling, "Bastard son of a bitch. You will die for this."

Nils carefully regarded the man's wounds and dryly replied, "No. I'd say you would be the one doing the dying today."

Gim-Bayz spat out more frothy blood, "Dom said you were a fool. Do you think that is all the Lord Dominare has? There are many, many more for bastards and shit eaters like you."

Nils asked, "Really? I do not see this Dom and his many minions?"

With an evil gleam in his eyes, Gim-Bayz chortled, "Oh they are close, but still far. You find him, you find your death."

Then in a final spasm, the man gagged, and died spitting blood and teeth. Nils stepped back and said to Suze-Li "Close enough to hurt us but too far away to be in this fight. What do you think?"

Suze-Li replied, "Close, that's maybe three to five klegs."

Looking long at the distant horizon from which the enemy had come she continued, "Too far, that would be twenty or thirty."

Nils regarded how Dom had risked and lost his most potent force; the enemy cavalry lay slaughtered in piles before his victorious troops. He also considered that there had been none of Dom's infantry in the battle, and somewhere in the distance, there were likely some nine regiments of foot.

So much infantry was a force he could not contend with and survive. He noted the sun's position in the sky, and making his decision commanded, "Gather all the wounded. Take what swains you may need for those that cannot ride and get to the fords."

Suze-Li asked, "And our dead?"

Nils locked his eyes on hers and said firmly, "We'll take only what we can use and carry. Gather all of the broken wood and our dead here. Fire is the best I can do for them this day."

NILS FINDS A WARHORSE

The Sergeant Major strode through the debris of the battle. Stoically he trod through the muck of blood, severed limbs and spilled intestines, careful not to trample on any remains, either Faerevolder or traitor. Upon reaching Nils and Suze-Li, he briskly saluted them and said, "Sir, my Lady, there is a Faeder-Ganger sore hurt who refuses to leave the field."

With an exasperated look, Nils sighed, "Take some men and compel him."

The Sergeant Major, unruffled by Nils' curt response continued, "Done tried that. Got us a Kapral stuck in the surgeon's wagon with a sore head and Kaptan Galen nursing a great black eye."

With a broad smile at Nils, Suze-Li interjected, "That would be old Baeren or none at all. He is passionate about his Lilly."

Reading the Sergeant Major's demeanor and seeing the evident glee in Suze-Li's face at his predicament, Nils resigned himself to his fate, and summoning his command voice said, "Let's see this Baer-en and his Lilly."

As they approached the Surgeon's wagon, Nils noticed the pale light shown on the tall grass and soft purple reflected in the distance. Little time did Nils have to consider the natural beauty of his surroundings as his party wove their way in and out of the many swains full of the wounded ready to move southward. Nils thought to himself, *Too many.*

Then he saw a severely wounded Faeder-Ganger standing defiantly next to his mount. Recognizing the man as the Faeder-Ganger who first gave him the report of Suze-Li's battle, he thought *Baer-en, or no one.*

As Nils stopped and looked upon the old veteran and his mount, he could clearly see Baer-en's grizzled face carved with steely determination and sad resolve. Lilly, his mount, did not move, the mare gingerly holding up a foreleg that displayed a broken spear shat protruding from her otherwise silky raven colored leg. Although clearly badly hurt, she emitted only a small ninny of pain.

Suze-Li spoke first, "Baer-en. Let the surgeon tend to you. We need your sword arm for another day."

Eschewing any salute or other formal sign of military respect, Baer-en growled, "Nay ma'am. Stand away. Perish ta thought 'o me part'n from poor Lilly when she needs me most."

Nils asked, "How did you get this? You were both hale when I saw you ride in and give your report."

Baer-en switched his attention from his commanding officer to Nils. He spit out some blood and a broken tooth, and answered, "It was after we got our wind back up. I went to the lincs like the rest 'o usns and fought a'foot. Gat me more 'an a few 'em."

Pointing to the wounded mare, Nils asked, "And her?"

Baer-en puffed up his chest and his face shown with the twinkling eyes and crooked smile of a proud parent as he said, "Seems when that mess broke in ta the surgeons, she gat 'ta blood up an' took to knockn' in their 'eads wi' her hooves. She stepped in a hole as dat Gim-Bayz was get'n away. That's hows we gat here."

As quickly as they had come, the smile disappeared and the twinkling in the eyes faded into a smoldering determination, he continued, "An' nows me an' Lilly's goin' ta stay."

Nils placed his hands behind his back and paced back and forth for some moments. Eventually he cocked his head toward Baer-en as he continued to pace and said, "I see your situation clearly. You can get to safety with a fair chance to live. But Lilly, she's too hurt for the farriers to do much out here."

Baer-en then dropped his chin on his chest and said despondently, "Right y'ar sir. We could make a run at it if'n we was in a good hold. But we ain't, an' we cain't git to one. So we is a stay'n."

Coming close to the grizzled veteran, Nils stopped, turned to him and whispered conspiratorially, "If I could make a way, would you at least try?"

An astonished Baer-en answered, "Me an' Lilly?"

Then, as if reading Nils intent he said in a low tone, "I no see how. But, If'n ya could, we'd try it. Sure."

Nils straightened, and then commanded, "Sergeant Major. Get a detail and gather some of those spear shafts from the pile. Bring that busted swain over here. I'll need the woodsman and his kit."

The Sergeant Major looked at Nils and Old Baer-en and seeing they had set upon some-to-be-soon revealed course replied, "Yes sir."

✥

It was deep into the night as the stars shown brilliantly above the Steppes in the high, clear sky. A blue hot fire shot flames into the air as it eagerly consumed the remains of the dead Faeder and Kaeder Ganger. Out of the glare of the fire, wild animals fought among themselves as they feasted on the fallen enemy.

Grim was that fire, yet of good use was its light to Nils, Suze-Li, and the small group of Ganger standing watch. The woodsman had finished the last work on a splint of spears, wheels and rope. The surgeons had removed the spear shaft, and then cleaned, stitched, and dressed Lilly's fore leg.

Nils instructed the surgeon's assistants as they and Baer-en endeavored to place a makeshift sling around Lilly's neck, "Keep her head. The farrier will bind the hurt leg to the saddle."

Baer-en said, "Aye."

He looked up from the task then asked, "How's that contraption go'n 'ta help?"

Galen, whose troop had supplied the infantry that formed the rear guard responded, "It will fit so her good leg is on the outside. Once it's strapped on, the cart wheels will take her weight."

With the sling set in-place, Baer-en's face showed more than a bit of amazement and respect for Nils as he said, "I's a never believe it a'fore."

As the farrier gently lifted Lilly's broken foreleg into the sling, and tied it firmly in place, Baer-en said, "Lilly, hush now an' up ya goes. Ta's ma girl. Sush, shusa girl."

A cold wind began to blow from the direction of Geldenherm, causing all to gather their cloaks tightly about themselves. Seeing that everything was as ready in the dire circumstances would allow, Nils placed his face in the wind. He stood and shivered as he felt an ominous force gathering somewhere beyond the distant cold wind. He commanded, "We had better leave now. We've been here near four hours."

Baer-en asked, "An' just ow' am I supposed to git outa here?".

Nils faced him and responded, "Better a Faeder-Ganger ride. Take my horse. No Lilly I'm sure."

With a quick nod of agreement, Baer-en mounted Nil's horse with some difficulty. Baer-en was sore wounded in many places, but the old warrior was loath to complain them as the party headed south away toward the fords. The fierce blaze continued for some time, casting flickers of light about the battlefield until near dawn the next morning, it too faded and disappeared in the dark. At dawn, the enemy found the hasty crematoria smoldering on the ground. Dom sat in his carriage as Vilder-zerk kicked the embers and searched the trampled and scorched ground. The Vilder-zerk overlord stood by, his scimitar drawn. "They will be at the fords by now."

Dom said. "They had horse and infantry."

He then commanded the Vilder-zerk overlord, "Back to the Iron Mountains."

THE BURDEN OF COMMAND

Long and hard had been the columns' return to the fords. In the gathering twilight, the remains of Nils and Suze-Li's commands stood in groups around their standards. Nearby were assembled the Lord Zander-fells' cohorts standing at attention in battle order. Each Faeder and Kaeder Ganger held a torch high. Galen crossed and stood waiting by Zander-Fells' side.

In the distant dark they heard, then saw the rear guard pass by. The torches flickered off Suze-Li's dented helm and dirty armor as she led the small, ragged group across the fords. With heavy step, the exhausted band crossed the rippling water. Last in line, Nils led Lilly. Hurt and as worn as the others, she held her head high and splashed her hooves into stream as they made their way. Behind her and tied by a long rope, came Nils' horse carrying Baer-en. Unlike the proud Lilly, Baer-en rode hunched over in the saddle, tightly grasping the horse's mane.

Once across, the massed Faerevolder troops sent a loud crescendo of shouts and cheers into the night sky. Their faces streamed with tears in the torch light as Zander-Fells reached out his right arm and said, "Come Nils. You have done more than could be hoped."

The Strategon turned to Galen, pointed at Lilly and Baer-en, and said, "Get these two to the surgeons."

The Strategon had furnished the Spartan command tent with the tools of war. Armor and weapons, maps and charts, and camp furniture adorned its interior. The light of candles and lanterns flickered on the charts and maps hanging from the walls and spread across a rough table. A simple bedroll sat on the edge of a rough cot in one corner. In another corner, Mai-Yanna prepared a steaming pot of Kai over a small fire. In the tent's center, Nils and Zander-Fells sat at the table hunched over one of the maps.

Zander-Fells moved a finger over various locations on the open map and said, "Geldenherm was near lost to the enemy. He has retreated north and west of the plain, making his camp near the foot of the Iron Mountains. He controls the far west as we control the east."

He left a finger on one spot and continued, "We are as hard pressed as he. He knows we must consider withdrawing the garrison at Geldenherm.

Nils, despondent at this summary said, "Then the campaign for this season is over. Our stand at the ridge was a fools' waste after all."

Zander-Fells answered, "Not so Nils. Your actions on the steppes cost Dom far too much. He is without any horse and now, whoever holds the middle wins. If we move fast, we can still reinforce Geldenherm before Dom can act."

Zander-Fells did not finish his words, for without announcement, Serzian Domo Jens Larzmon entered the tent. He approached Nils and whispered in his ear. Having delivered his message, the Serzian Domo exited the tent as unceremoniously as he had entered.

As when awoke aboard the U.R.S.S *Sergeant York*, Nils, felt as if his heart had been wrenched from his body. He sank into the small wooden chair. Terrible were the Jens Larzmon's words. Nils did not believe he could longer carry such a burden as had now been laid upon him. First the disaster at Seti Four, and now the losses upon the steppes. As one dazed, slowly, he rose from the table and reached into his saber tasche. From deep inside, he removed a dirty scroll. He handed the scroll to Mai-Yanna and said, "My commission Tektar. Despite your faith in me, I am unfit for command."

He saluted and stepped toward the tent opening. She halted him coolly saying, "Do not be rash Lo-Kan. If I were to reduce you for your actions, I would have done so earlier. You not only defeated the Vilder-zerk in the open steppes, you wrested the initiative out of Dom's hands."

Nils stood silently, torn between the Archan's words and his own deep sense of failure. Zander-Fells then stood and spoke, "You should be proud, as your officers and troops are."

Nils turned and faced the two. Tall and strong, they appeared to him, with fell wisdom in their eyes. He said, "Yes, I am proud of what they did. However, at what terrible cost should they have to bear for my pride? Good soldiers were lost out there. Baer-en did not live to sit in honor within his hold."

Upon hearing this, Zander-Fells and Mai-Yanna went to Nils and placed their hands on his stooped shoulders. Hot tears flowed freely down Nils' face as Mai-Yanna said, "Now you truly know what it is to command."

Zander-Fells continued, "There is always a high price that must be paid in blood and death. It is what we do. Our lives are forfeit the moment we accept service under the colors. The trick is to make the enemy pay out his and to keep ours."

Then Nils perceived that like Randal Clark, the two shared the bitter truth of command. He saw the wisdom in their words, and it seemed to him that he could likewise endure what he had freely laid upon himself. He continued too openly weep before the two; receiving the forgiveness he had so long denied himself. Then his wet eyes dried, and then smoldered as he recalled the courage and fidelity of Baer-en. He said flatly to the two, "Then may I suggest a way to make Dom pay a very high price."

Late winter now again lay about the Raffer-Mor. Nils stood alone in a familiar, yet empty courtyard as he considered the last year. He had gained much praise for his gallantry, and promotions followed in the wake of in the many engagements and skirmishes with the enemy following the fight on the steppes. The garrison at Citadel Geldenherm had been relieved, reinforced and supplied. The Vilder-zerk now sat huddled in their lairs deep in the Iron Mountains in the far west.

He was a Faeder-Ganger and a Strategon in his own right, wise in council and resolute in battle. Indeed, one from his old days in the STERNZCO firm would scarce have recognized the middle-aged clerk that found himself naked in the Great Aerkan desert so long ago. Back and forth, the two sides had struggled for dominion of Geldenherm Citadel, until with winter's approach; Dom ceded the battlefield and withdrew to his hold westward, into the Dark Vale.

Nils gathered the folds of a rich fur robe closer to his neck and murmured, "Much Dom has lost, yet he remains a dangerous foe. Even now he is building another army with which to rampage."

Nils' silent breath formed wreaths above his head. He was standing on the well-trampled snow, reviewing the assembled sword-scarred training quintains and targets. Like the unspeaking sentinels that stood on watch, uncomplaining in the freezing air and deathly quiet, the training dummies stood in the snow, patiently waiting the next round of warriors to be.

Nils noted that much like the training arena at Geldenherm, piles of wooden shields, swords, axes and blunted spears stood in the corners. He closed his eyes, imagined the area soon host to veterans giving instruction to the young men and women as they vigorously applied sword, spear, and ax to the unbending wood. An approaching page noticed Nils closed eyes and said to himself, *It is as they told me. He can even sleep standing.*

The page's step crunched in the soggy snow as he made his way to Nils. Close he came to the seemingly somnambulant Strategon, then remembering his lessons, the page stopped at a respectful distance from Nils and said, "My Lord, the Tektar presents her greetings and begs you retire to bed less you freeze your…"

Nils interrupted the young lad with a wry smile and laughed, "Canoochies off?"

The page smiled widely as he bowed to Nils and replied, "Her words sir, not mine."

Nils continued to laugh as he walked to the bowing page, and asked, "We wouldn't want that now would we? Is there anything else?

The page straightened and said, "She commands you select a steed at the corral as it is un-seemly that you are not mounted as befits a Strategon."

Nils growled, "Humph.". I suppose so. I'd rather keep the sledges moving west with every horse and ox at hand."

Undaunted at Nils' curt response, the page continued, "She also reminds you of the matter of your staff. You may select any from the keep's household you deem fit."

Nils slapped one glove covered hand on the boy's shoulder and said. "Last spring, all I needed was two good legs and my own council to command. Now I must worry over a horse and an entourage. Tell the Tektar I am off to the corrals."

The Page again bowed as Nils left the courtyard and its silent sentries behind.

In the corrals, the young stable hands led splendid horses around the auction circle. Many steeds had been lost in battle and prime horseflesh was in great demand. Fierce was the bidding among the Faeder-Ganger for these steeds, and both Lord Zander-Fells and Lady Mai-Yanna stood in the docks and won bids for fine mounts.

Alcoves and doors leading off to barns and sheds surrounded the corrals. So intent on the bidding were those in the docks, none noticed the latecomers that stood or sat within the alcoves upon the piles of straw and hay gathered there. If directly looked upon, alone or in twos and threes they could be seen, worn and gaunt Faeder-Ganger wearing rusty and dented armor, with little coin or hope of finding horse suitable for war.

In one small alcove to the side of the auction corral, Suze-Li and Nils silently stood in plain robes, hiding Nils' rich accoutrements and Suze-Li's rank. They spoke not to each other while closely watching the auction's progress. Suze-Li had said little upon their meeting that evening. It seemed to Nils she could not hide the despondent air that hung about her. Yet it was she that broke the silence that had laid between them as a thick wall divides neighbors as a fine roan was led into the corral. Scarce had the horse began to walk when the bidding broke out, when she nodded in the direction of the roan and lowly said, "One should pick a good steed before the best are taken."

Nils responded, "If one was so inclined."

A Faeder-Ganger in one of the alcoves managed to out-bid his comrades for the well-muscled roan and Nils asked, "How is the daughter of Garm these days?"

Since their first meeting at Geldenherm, Nils knew Suze-Li was a warrior of action and little patience. Indeed, he considered these traits as some of her more attractive attributes. Therefore, it came to Nils as no surprise to hear the exasperation in her words as she said, "As best as can be expected given my commission. And what of Nils of the Taerevold, now a Strategon?"

Then, seeking to change the subject he replied, "Some things were much easier when I was just plain Nils. Is your father here as well?"

Suze-Li answered, "He is much concerned with the matters of the Graef and the raising of the cohorts. As you see, mounts are precious few."

Nils averted his attention from the auctions and said, "I do regret the loss of your Hand."

Nils did feel remorse and sadness for Suze-Li's situation, for as he continued to campaign and had grown in military prowess, rank and responsibility, she had remained static in her station. Yet she begrudged him not, for even when at the steppes she recognized a greater ability within him for war craft than was hers. The hurt she felt was for the remains of her Hand. There was no time nor means to renew its former strength, its few survivors having been re-assigned new duties or amalgamated into other units. Meantime, the Tektar found Suze-Li other duties before the Dais and it was deemed more pressing she fulfill those than leading and fighting.

She said sadly, "It had to be done."

Her mood seemed to brighten as she continued, "Once word spread of your plans for Geldenherm, the volunteers seemed endless. Every day more come in."

Nils asked, "Were not the fields rich in crops? I hear the mares foaled near unceasing."

Suze-Li said, "Yes, our barns and stables were overflowing once came the harvest. Little did we expect such blessings as the misty spring seemed to hold us little promise.

She fell silent for a little while, and then continued carefully as she remembered Nils' rank and station, "It is today's demands. Even one such as I cannot find a decent mount, nor room and board in the press about this place."

Nils noted the change in her demeanor and tone, and said, "Come with me. After a warm dinner we can discuss some ideas I have to relieve us of our current dilemma."

Suze-Li asked shockingly, "Dinner? With a Strategon in his tent? I am no common camp tramp that leaps into the first bed offered her."

Nils, glad to see and hear the pride and fight in her retort, replied, "Nor should you be. There is a small inn where the ale is cold and the food good, hot and plenty of it. Not very fancy apartments, but clean. And the mistress keeps both a wholesome house and an honest count."

With that, and brooking no further conversation between them, Nils took her firmly by the arm and briskly walked out of the corrals.

⤜⬩⬩⤛

Originally, the family Raffer had established a small fishing village and its docks on the west banks of the Ost Mor. Near this place, the Archons of ancient and happier days first built the Raffer-Mor palace. It was a simple lodge where they escaped, if even for a short time, from their duties and the incessant intrigues of the court. Near the old Citadel Rafferherm, they pursued the hunt in the lush forests nearby, or punted along the banks of the Ost Mor. Such joy they found there, the Archons began to stay longer and visit more frequently so that, save for the fell hard times of bitter winter, they kept house and held court there. Yet, the high Dais remained at Geldenherm.

As in all things regarding governance, the retinue of the court found reason to accompany the Archons. Over time, the simple hunting lodge grew into a grand palace. Glorious was its design and construction, its rooms and apartments filled with fine furniture, its walls covered in intricate and beautiful tapestries, its windows made of stained glass. And the Archons, perceiving the ancient Citadels as rough places unfit to house their court, removed themselves and established the high dais at Raffer-moor. Only at Geldenherm was the well of justice; the place set aside for the rendering.

Soon the small fishing village housed the carpenters, masons, plasterers, painters and workers of all kinds during the Raffer-Mor's building. As the

Raffer-Mor's importance changed and grew, so did the size and complexity of the town that supported it. The quays were expanded as more trade goods came and went across the Ost Mor. Many homes the retinue built, and schools for their children and surgeries for their ills as well. The town became filled with the court and courtiers and became known as Stewardton in homage to those who managed the affairs of the Archan's court.

In time, in addition to the Faere-Ganger High Command in the old citadel, Stewardton became home to the Faerevolder centers of governance, learning and commerce. Freiholders, soldiers, archivists, merchants, and folk of all sorts lived there; many were those that traveled to Raffer-Mor to conduct business of their own or that of the Archon. The town was divided into many wards. One for the Faerevolder's garrison, one for the traders and merchants, another for the stewards, and so on. In a section below the citadel and near the edge of the old swain road leading to the west was the ward that held the corrals, farriers, tanners, and saddle and harness makers. Not far from the garrison and stables was a cobbled-stone lane whose sides were lined with rows of taverns and alehouses.

The lane's end was the far border of the Stewardton along the swain road. Here sat the Blue Dog Inn. The Blue Dog was an old, large stone and rough timber building that had been added onto and modified by generations of owners. The original structure faced the swain road and stood three stories tall. Its ground floor was made of well-laid stones from the old quarries near the Iron Mountains, now long lost to Dom. The next two levels were of large oaken logs, hewn to fit at the corners. A steep roof of gray slate capped the place.

Two wings had been built along its sides, one of brick stretching low along the lane and its opposite extending toward a small garden that separated the Blue Dog from its neighbor, the Sawhorse Tavern. It was through its single door facing the lane most folk entered the inn. In days past the traffic along the Swain Road had decreased as many Faerevolder found boats and barges better fitted for the transport of trade goods, people and such. Now and again herds of cattle or other livestock would pass by on their way to the corrals. Yet, the wide, double doors that faced the Swain Road fell into disuse, as the Inns' customers came from the docks and into the Stewardton proper.

Hard times had befallen the mistress of the house as her man had gone off to war, and their young son, Doer-En, needed tending and what schooling she could manage. For she could ill afford to pay for help and often needed him to assist when those few boarders would stay. In need of money for food and fuel, she had mortgaged the place, the note being long past due and the banker preparing to take possession.

Dire were their straits when Geldenherm fell as its refugees fled, seeking shelter at Raffer-Mor. Scarce became lodging in Stewardton and many were turned away regardless of the amount of coin offered. Nevertheless, at the Blue Dog, the mistress cleared out the attics and made rooms in the barns, charging a discount for their let.

She often said to Doer-En in the heavy brogue of the farmlands where she had been bred and raised, "Tose as despert still needs a roof o'er their eads."

The inn's common room was full, and Nils and Suze-Li sat at a table drinking ale from wooden tankards. The remains of their dinner sat on the plain wooden plates before them. On the roads and hard-pressed had Suze-Li been in fulfilling her commissions. Long had it been since she had sat at board and drank her fill.

The simple meal of roasted mutton, potatoes, and onions had been a feast for her. As Nils promised, it had been plenty, hot on the table, and more than good. Bustling about the place, giving quick instruction, greeting customers or collecting the fare was Mistress Baer-en. She was a portly woman and wore a brown smock and a deep blue apron tied about her sumptuous waist. Her flaxen hair was streaked with grey, and sat in a tight bun at the back of her head.

Her face was flushed red as she vainly wiped sweat from her brow with a quick sweep of the damp napkin she held in one meaty fist. When presented with the fare, a drover at a nearby table complained, "Agh, as not worth a bag of brass Gran pennies, was this grub."

The Mistress, wise to the sharp dealings of his type, retorted, "'An no 'a better you'd have at the corrals. Ya cheet'n pinch. Yous et it, now pays up or it's afore the constables for ya!"

The chattering room fell silent, and seeing more than one grim Faerevolder finger his weapon, the drover thinking better of his ploy, got up, threw a pile of coins on the table, and beat a hasty retreat out the door. After finishing with the drover, she continued her rounds. Yet, the conversations remained murmured as, she came and began to clear the dishes from their table. Nils said in a loud voice, "Mistress Baer-en, a fine meal indeed."

At this, mugs were tipped in toast and the rough chatter began in earnest.

Looking at the food left on their plates, she admonished Nils and Suze-Li, "Scraps is na ta' leave an 'ta table when there's nigh a pinch in 'ta markets. Wid' dem commissary agents a pay'n gob 'o gold for every thing 'ta be 'ad."

Undaunted by the woman's direct manner, Nils asked, "Speaking of which, what is my due?"

With a hurried bustle of action the mistress answered him, "I na 'ta tally sheets 'pon me person. Pray I present your debt another time?"

Not be dissuaded, Nils took from his belt a large bag of coin, and pressed it clinking into Mistress Baer-en's hands saying, "Even my credit must come to an end. Who knows the fortune of war or the path of The Great Maker, eh? Now relieve me of this bag of metal and the worry of my marker. It is too heavy for me to carry on campaign. Count the remainder to my credit."

She clutched the bag to her large bosom and her face beamed gratefulness at his generosity. For she knew by its two ten weights, the contents paid for Nils' room and board many times over. Then, as was her constant worry, the thought of future days to come jumped to her mind and she said, "But what of your rooms? I've no boarders after the army leaves. An' this lot o' merchants and drovers is not as likely to pay as well on account."

Nils stood and placed his arm around the mistress' shoulder and whispered into her ear, "That will not happen over night. In the meantime, this young lady needs a place. Let her have mine. There should be more than enough in that bag to cover the board as well."

Under her breath, shockingly the portly woman asked, "She is to move in tonight?"

Nils said, "Yes, and she may have my rooms after I'm finished moving out."

Satisfied that all was to be done in its proper fashion, for she did pride herself in running a respectable house, Mistress Baer-en said with a feigned huff, "I should dare say so in my house!"

With that, Nils and Suze-Li took their leave, gathering their cloaks and passing by two Faeder-ganger waiting in the drifting snow by the door. Chocking back a tear, the Mistress said quietly to herself, "A finer one there is nay about these days."

Then deciding to delegate the remainder of the table clearing to one of the many servers, she yelled over the crowd, "Hey Jacko! Git this wiped an' cleaned! D'are's more a-wat'n for un at da door."

In the space between the Blue Dog's two wings, and near the garden were set the inn's stables and a small corral. After leaving the common room, Nils and Suze-Li had retrieved what little gear she had placed in the barn. Now they walked about the corral under a clear, open night sky filled with the twin moons and a host of strange stars that Nils still had not learned. Quiet had Nils been after leaving the common room, yet Suze-Li sensed some matter of importance or worry over the upcoming campaign laid on his mind.

She had more than fulfilled her commissions, yet chaffed at not receiving another, desiring to return to the battles. If not as a commander, then as a plain Faeder-ganger for her sword was ever sharp and her arms ached to use it.

In the cool night, Nils remained silent, and she perforce decided to speak her mind to him. She said, "You mean to keep me from the campaign. How small and spiteful. My sword arm is as strong as ever."

Nils stomped his feet in the snow and laughed, "Don't I know it little teacher."

He gazed into the distant dark with its alien stars and said, "This is not about you or me. It is about how we each fulfill our commissions. Look around. The Raffer-Mor is bursting with too many people and not enough supplies."

Catching his tone and thinking his intent, she interrupted, saying, "Now I am to be your quartermaster?"

Nils stopped walking, caught her eye, and holding it said, "That and more. I need you to establish a training camp for the young gallants your father is gathering from the Landkreiser Fyrds."

Seeing all hope of battle dashed from her again, and being a good soldier, Suze-Li sighed as she asked, "And where is this camp to be?"

Knowing he had her obedience to his designs, Nils continued, "As near the fords as you can make it. Set your camp and build us an army. Select solid non-comms. Look for the ones most like Jens Larzmon and Garm."

She replied, "These new ones are not the youth of the Landkreiser, rich in coin. Steadern lads and shop girls with no more than the clothes on their backs answered the call. Who shall pay their costs?"

He said, "After I leave, go to my…your rooms. There you will find instructions that will answer your questions and coin enough for the troops."

In dismay she asked, "Leave, tonight? And without a mount?"

With a laconic yawn he said, "I have a mount."

Suze-Li then took his arm and said, "I was at the corals and you did not pick any."

Then remembering his rank, she loosened her grip and said, "And we walked here."

She readied to say more but at that moment, the high whinny of a battle steed came from the stable. Doer-en, son of Baer-en and the most precious item The Mistress held in her heart, stepped through the barn door and into the pale light. He was a tall, young lad dressed for travel, and wore tall riding boots over his thick trousers and a hooded cloak over his jacket. The cloak's hood was thrown back and, but for his mother's golden hair, he close resembled his father in body and movement. In his gloved hands, he held two sets of reins, leading two mounts behind him, and tied to their saddles, a train of four heavily laden pack mules.

In the moon light, Lilly's coat glistened as she proudly carried her Faeder-Ganger's weapons and shield. The other horse, obviously Doer-en's, carried bulging saddlebags. Suze-Li's astonished gaze was fixed on Lilly. Scarce could she believe this was the same stead that was so grievously wounded at the Battle of the Steppes. Yet, here she was made whole again and ready to carry her rider to war.

Nils asked, "Doer-en, son of Baer-en, is everything ready?"

The tall lad gave a short bow and said, "Yes sir. Everything is packed as you ordered."

Nils then took Lilly's reins, stepped lightly into the stirrups, and sat high in the saddle.

As Doer-en mounted the other horse, Nils leaned over and said to Suze-Li, "When you report your affairs to Our Lord Zander-Fells and the Lady Mai-Yanna, please inform them that I have both a mount and a staff."

He bade Lilly walk with a short, "Hup!"

Nils and Doer-en silently rode past her and out of the corral, disappearing into the dark night. As they passed into the pale night, Suze-Li, asked in a small voice, "Can I not do more than what you have given me?"

Faint was the outline of the pack mules trailing behind, when through the pale night air Suze-Li heard Nils' voice ring out, "Even the smallest thing one does is of great importance. There will be many opportunities for battles. For that we need an army, an army that you will build."

IN THE VAL DUNKERZ

D awn slowly crept into Dom's dark vale, revealing a golden sunrise lying just beyond the eastern horizon of the Val Dunkerz. Upon the Zat Erzern tower's ramparts was assembled Dom's army. Armed and mailed Vilder-zerk huddled behind the massive walls. The few of these that looked out upon the vale stared in dismay at the mass of armor and spears that glittered before in the fair sunrise.

Uncountable in their majesty, the Faerevolder and Ostlond pride lined the vale from the high northern ridges to the southern escarpments. Their lines filled the vale and disappeared in the distant horizon. The cohorts of infantry and mounted Faeder-Ganger stood in row upon row facing the Dark Tower.

One hundred thousands was their count that day that marched to the Iron Mountains and now were prepared to give Dom battle before his very doors. That winter, the masons had repaired the bridge over the S'iflan. As the last stone was set, the Ostlings crossed. Passing through Leak-Mor, and taking ship over the Ost Mor, King Bruze Mak Doanalt had landed his seventy thousand above Stewardton and crossed the steppes. Hot burned the Ostlings for revenge for the hurt Dom had made upon the First Prince, Rolf.

Suze-Li had acquitted her commission very well, gathering and building Nils' army. Among the grim and determined Faerevolder formations, crews worked catapults and trebuchets into position. They loaded massive boulders and smoldering embers into the great machines. Among the smoke from the heated shot, the Faerevolder warriors' breath rose evenly into the early morning air. They cradled their weapons like newborn children. The power of their arms displayed its glory in their muscled arms and legs. Vain folly rested easily on every bronzed and intense face. The Handern standards and battle flags snapped in the breeze.

Nils sat astride Lilly at the front and center of his army as he calmly surveyed the final preparations. Faint shudders of anticipation for battle rippled along Lilly's gleaming flanks. Nils reached down and patted her, more to calm his own growing eagerness, for like hers his sinews were stretched near beyond breaking for battle. Yet Nils maintained his outward appearance of calm, knowing how his demeanor, more than his words, kept his troops energies contained until the moment of release.

He thought to himself, *Now. Now is the time.*

Doer-en rode up to his side and pointed to the North and reported, "Our Lord Zander-Fells is on the field. See he rides this way."

Nils looked in the direction Doer-en pointed and saw Zander-Fells and three riders cantering toward his position. Noting his lord had acknowledged his presence and message; Doer-en dropped his arm and turned to Nils. In a nervous voice he asked, "Was it like this on the steppes where my sire fought?"

Nils sighed and responded evenly, "All battles are very similar, but unimaginably different. Your sire, Baer-en, and I were fewer that day, much fewer."

Doer-en continued, "I have heard of Dom's mastery of shack-mackt. Now he has the advantage."

Nils smiled at the young man, for though still young in years, Doer-en had long ago come into his manhood by earning his spurs during Nils' campaign against Dom from Citadel Geldenherm to this place, fighting and killing more than a few Vilder-zerk. Nils responded, "Perhaps. I still have a few chips to put in the kitty. We shall see how he turns his cards."

Zander-fells, Anadan, Garm and Suze-Li had halted their horses next to Nils and Doer-en. Suze-Li leaned forward in her saddle and asked, "Cards, sir?"

Nils saluted the group and said, "Dom is playing shack-mackt from some dark hole behind those great iron walls. Even now, I do not think he has realized that I am playing poker."

Anadan asked, "Poker? What is that?"

Nils answered his old friend and mentor, "A different game entirely."

At this, Zander-Fells directed the question at the forefront of his thoughts, "Then you are ready?"

Zander-Fells face showed his dismay, as Nils did not answer his superior officer; rather, Nils turned to Garm and asked, "Garm, did you bring that which I requested?"

Garm, as gruff as ever answered, "Of course I did. Not that I had to hide the thing in my saddle bags."

Anadan now smiled wide and said, "Then let us get to it."

Anadan dismounted and gave a quick nod, after which Zander-Fells, Garm, Suze-Li, Nils and Doer-en followed his example. Garm rummaged into the deep recesses at the bottom of one of his saddlebags, then finding what he sought, retrieved a bundle from its interior. Doer-en brought over a standard's staff and held it out as Anadan and Suze-Li very carefully unfolded the bundle and attached it to the long pole.

Once finished with their task, Doer-En extended his long arms to their full length and thrust the standard high above his head, its folds snapping in the breeze. The red lion leapt running upon a field of green, dappled in the standard's folds as Zander-Fells revealed himself before Dom's dark walls. Nils stood at attention and saluted Zander-Fells, saying, "This is your field to command Oberst Strategon."

From the center of the Ostlings rode King Bruze, saluting the group he said, "The tide is ready."

Now our Lord Zander-Fells looked about himself and saw the army and its leaders ready and eager for battle. With his crooked wolf-grin, he gazed at the grim battlements before them and cried out in a loud and proud voice, "To battle, ha-zah."

As one, the shout rang out from the Faerevolder host as "Ha-zah, Ha-zah" echoed within the dark vale. Long the gathered host shouted for war, and then once their voices fell silent, Nils signaled and the siege engines began to work. In moments, the massive machines began to hurl their loads of stone and fire onto the Zat Erzern's ramparts. Its walls cracked and burst apart as fire engulfed those screaming Vilder-Zerk that had been unable to avoid the crashing doom that fell upon them.

From deep within, the Dark Lord stretched out his power, enchanting spells of destruction upon the attacking host. First, he reached out for those crews operating the machines that were inexorably pulverizing Zat Erzern's defenses, attempting to stab their minds and souls with a venomous spell of death. After a few minutes of scouring the battlefield, he found them and quickly shouted the words of power. No sooner had he done so than the very poison he had sent out returned to his mind, nearly crippling him. Only rapid reflexes had raised his defense and saved him.

Repeatedly he tried to find a mind he could kill or injure. Yet, at each attempt, something repelled his efforts. Chastened, but undefeated, he began to focus his mind and will in seeking the one whose power shielded the massed host from his evil attacks. Then without notice, a grip of pure energy seized his mind, ripping apart its meager defenses.

In the midst of the host, Anadan stood silently murmuring to himself, his eyes wide open as he deflected first one and then another of the beast's casting spells. Anadan did not seek out his foe, knowing where the evil in the Iron Mountains now lay. Rather, set his trap and patiently waited for the beast to run into it. And race into the vice it had done. As Anadan began to strip away one layer of the beast's defense after another, it cast vainly about, panicking in seeking an escape. Then, using all the strength it could muster, it emitted a high and sharp screech of pain and broke free from Anadan's grasp.

Zat Erzern's foundations shook, its inner walls cracked and began to fall. The door of Ka-Tayana's cell sprang open, she ran out, into the dim passage, and up the nearest flight of steps she could find. In his audience chamber, Dom watched helplessly from his steamy pool as large chunks of the keep's ceiling fell and crushed his retinue. He jumped out of the hot bath, hastily put on trousers and boots, racing about and dodging the falling debris. In his haste to save himself, he forgot to strap on the sword his thrall had given him. He jumped over the dead body of his voluptuous slut and sprinted down an un-lit corridor toward his master's chambers.

Again and again, the volley of stone and fire smashed into the ramparts. Under cover of the blistering barrage, Zander-Fell's standard flew in the front of the assaulting Faerevolder. Still, some numbers of Vilder-zerk stood firm at their posts, launching swarms of dark arrows that hit, killing infantry, rider, and horse alike.

As he neared the gates, hurling boulders crashed down the tower's iron doors, slashing open a wide, gaping hole. Over the rubble and into the breach, Zander-Fells with Nils and King Bruze at his side, led a sea of Faerevolder and Ostlings, rushing into the breach and falling mercilessly onto the waiting Vilder-zerk. Behind came Anadan, carefully picking his way through the masses of dead and dying.

Fierce and likewise useless was the Vilder-zerk defense as the on-rushing host would not be denied and broke over them, slaying Dom's minions underfoot. Unable to stem the rushing tide, the surviving Vilder-zerk broke their ranks and fled into Zat Erzern's inner walls and chambers. Indeed, many more of the vile beasts perished under the press of their rout as were slain by Zander-Fell's troops. Now under the lead of Suze-Li and Garm, to the left and right they now fanned out, flowing into the rampart's chambers and seeking out their foes.

The sounds of the raging battle faded from Dom's chamber within the vile tower. Dead and dying Vilder-zerk and humans lay littered and bunched in heaps on the chamber's and hallway floors. Near one heap, Anadan cradled Ka-Tayana's golden locks in his arms, as she lay unconscious on the cold stone floor, a small line of blood trickling slowly from her mouth. Near another bunch, Doer-en finished killing a Vilder-zerk that had attempted to impale Anadan with a pike.

Garm entered the chamber; his armor dented with blood and muck smearing its once gleaming shine. He quickly looked about, seeing with one glance Ka-Tayana's sprawled figure and Doer-En's dispatch of the last of the enemy in the place. Still holding his sword, dripping with Vilder-Zerk blood and gore, he ran to Anadan's side. Anadan was talking in the soothing voice of healing as he cooed to her, "Now, now. Come along with you. Your father is here."

Ka-Tayana eyes fluttered, then came wide open. Nils and King Bruze strode into the chamber and Anadan asked her, "Can you walk, lass?"

Nils surveyed the scene before him and asked hoarsely, "Where is Dom?"

Ka-Tayana nodded, rose up on one arm and answered him in a weak voice, "He left some moments ago."

She pointed toward a darkened chamber and continued, "Down that hallway."

Nils commanded, "Doer-En, on your life take her out of this place!"

Soon, Doer-en had covered Ka-Tayana in his cloak. Then helping her to her feet and holding her tightly about the shoulders and her slim waist, he escorted her past the gathering Faerevolder and out of the chamber. Close behind followed Garm, still watching over his charge.

Anadan did not notice the amazed look King Bruze and the Faerevolder gave Ka-Tayana's emaciated figure as she left the chamber. Rather, his attention was focused on the passage Dom had fled into. Grimly, he stoically stepped toward the passage's opening and said, "Now for the end of this."

The strong arm of Nils halted Anadan's progress as the Kunkern-Kint held the old man back from his intended course. Nils said, "No Anadan, this is my duty. Take these men and rejoin Our Lord Zander-Fells."

Anadan replied, "You do not have to play this part. Leave it to me. Live out your days in peace and honor in Faerevold."

Nils retorted, "Live in peace? For how long? Your redemption is nigh. You know as well as I this evil must be dealt with once and for all. Down that hall is Dom. I intend to finish what he started, and besides, wasn't it you who taught me each kindt to its vold and each vold to its kint?'"

Long had Anadan pondered over this Nils and his presence in the Faerevold. Now he could only look at Nils and say nothing. Far beyond Anadan's understanding had Nils come, and now farther he must go. Then, of sudden, the Great Maker revealed his mind, and our Lord Anadan perceived who Nils was and why he had been brought into Faerevold. What more, Anadan saw in his mind's eye, clear as the new morning that had greeted them this past morn, what Nils must now do, or perish in the attempt.

Anadan then moved his gaze from Nils and looking about the debris of battle-axes and swords scattered on the stone floor. Carefully and silently, he noted and rejected the weapons before his eyes as his head rotated past them. His head snapped back and he leaned forward as he focused on a sword, still sitting in its scabbard on the stone floor. In three long and quick steps, Anadan reached the sword. Picking it up, he dusted the scabbard and read its inscription. He said, "This will do fine. He may regret leaving this behind."

Anadan drew the sword, the flash if its gleaming sides and sharp edges sparkling red and blue in the dim chamber. As the fell light sparkled along the blade, King Bruze exclaimed, "The razor of my house! Long had I believed it lost!"

With a self-satisfied grin, Anadan walked back to Nils. As he did so, he held the King's eye and silent agreement came between them. King Bruze nodded as the sage placed the sword hilt in Nils mailed hands and said, "Then, well met."

They grasped each other's arms and then parted. With no other words spoken, Anadan turned from Nils and left the chamber, taking King Bruze and the remaining Faerevolder with him. Nils entered the dark passage.

Dom stumbled along a dark passage. He held a weak torch as he bounced off the wet and clammy walls. Often, he would trip over the worn cobblestones, falling to his knees, and then struggling to his feet. Ahead of him, he focused his energies on a red glow that throbbed in the distance. Dom forced his bruised and bleeding body forward.

Finally and near exhaustion, Dom reached the source of the red glow. Its light furiously pulsated out of the native rock. He put his hands out and leaned forward. Yet, his master had given the throbbing glow a power to deny entry to those he wished. So it was the glow refused Dom's attempts at entry to the chamber beyond.

Dom eventually fell to his knees as he continued to feebly push his way through. By some forgotten piece of wizardry, or a failing of the Dark Master's powers, a small gap lay between the throbbing barrier and the stone floor where Dom now found himself. Through this tiny gap, Dom pushed through on his belly, a smear of slick blood marking his path into a wide, circular chamber.

His voice cracked as with a scarce whisper, Dom cried out into the dark, "Master. Please do not leave me."

High was his anger and furious the Dark Lord was toward his servant when Dom found him; the incarnate evil hissed, "Fool of a man, and I the greater! Your meager excuse for a brain cannot even begin to phantom the smallest part of the disaster you have wrought upon me."

Dom lay prostrate before the rising wrath before him, and quivering said, "I understand, my Lord."

The Dark Lord shouted, "You understand nothing! You beg me not to leave when it was you who left us."

Dom continued sheepishly, "I did all as you instructed. I wooed her in every sense."

Short and brutal came his master's response, "Her? That candied trollop. What of him? Your lust blinded us to his true nature."

Confused at his master's reply, Dom, now very frightened, said, "You mean to save yourself. Yet, I shall remain until your time comes again."

The Dark Lord responded dismissively, "Why should I do so? The Evening Emerald is beyond my grasp. You saw to that when you pushed your affections on him."

As it was with Anadan, understanding flashed through Dom's mind. Then, he stuttered out, "Nils is…"

With an angry growl, the Dark Lord cut off Dom's words, shouting, "The Evening Emerald! Bagh. What is the use? You shall remain behind. But, I will not burden myself any longer with your incompetence."

The beast leapt upon Dom, seizing his servant with one dark claw. He drug Dom out of the chamber and back into the passage. There, he held Dom's right arm against the cold rock, and taking a steel rod, drove it through Dom's open hand, pinning him to the rock wall. Stepping back, the beast slavered gleefully as it said, "Remain until the binder is bound, until the binder unbinds."

He scurried back from Dom, and threw a ball of blue fire at the rock wall, opening a gap in the red glow. Without another look at Dom or further words, the beast exited through the hole. Soon, the red light began to pulsate and then fade as the opening began to slowly close in on itself.

Days, years, only moments. None could tell how long Dom lay pinned to the wall. His pitiful cries echoed into the passage behind him as the red light faded and the passage closed behind his master. Still, Nils walked slowly, but resolutely along the dim passage. He held the sword in both hands to his front, expecting ambush at every turn of the passage or one of its many narrow places. He stopped and peered ahead, seeing the dim red glow and sensing the beast nearby, navigated his way forward by the light from the fading red light. Within a few steps, Nils heard Dom's weak sobs of anguish. He quickened his stride and soon he found Dom impaled upon the rock. Nils said to him grimly, "Your life is forfeit."

As one defeated and denied succor from his liege, Dom said, "Take it and be done with me."

Nils raised the sword and placed its razor edge on Dom's neck saying, "I should take your life. A small recompense for all of the needless hurt you have brought into this land and onto its peoples."

Yet, something held Nils from killing Dom. Another power seemed to be at work within him, as his arms quivered, neither thrusting the blade forward nor withdrawing it. Eyes wide in panic, Dom stuttered, "You hold, sir?"

Nils, keeping the sword on Dom's neck responded, "You are that thing's. It is not for me to deliver the justice you so richly deserve."

Dom looked at Nils, his eyes widening as he said, "You mean to go into the void? The abyss will swallow you. It is his making and its paths are his alone."

Nils replied flatly, "That is not what I've heard."

With a gasp of disbelief, Dom retorted, "You think you're smarter than me? Very well, you will find no pity beyond this time and space once you enter his world."

Nils then said slowly yet firmly, "Pity? What would I need of it? In spite of all of your temptations and best efforts, I have survived. The desert, the rendering, the ice and snow, and more blood and gore in battle than anyone should have to witness."

Nils turned from Dom and stepped toward the now almost closed gap and announced, "Here I am, ready or not. I do not understand any of this. Not from the night in the hotel until this very minute. But I do know in my heart that the way back lays this way."

Dom could not believe what he had heard Nils say or what Nils now contemplated. He weakly intoned, "Back. Go back to your dreary little existence in that cesspool?"

Nils responded, "Yes, it may be as you say. Nevertheless, it is our home. Not this place."

He said no more to Dom as he thrust the sword forward. With it, he slashed a hole in the throbbing red light, entered the shrinking portal, and disappeared. As the heel of his trailing foot passed through, the portal snapped shut behind him.

Alone again in the dark, Dom spat out, "Be finished yourself. Nothing mortal has ever gone into the void without his leave and returned to tell of it. Be finished yourself."

NILS MEETS HIS DOOM

Nils stood in the total darkness that enveloped him. A faint trace of the red glow trailed into the darkness. Looking at the wisp before him, Nils said, "Got you."

He began to follow the withering and coiling tendril of red light into the darkness. Ahead lay the beast, the Dark Lord. Nils steps did not falter nor did his determination fade as this knowledge, rather he quickened his pace toward his doom.

Far in the vile bowels of evil the beast had made for himself, was a solitary chamber. Time to time, the beast would long leave it abandoned. Yet, ever it was here the Dark Lord would retreat to make his strategies, cast his deceits, or now recover his strength. The beast had been sore hurt when his powers failed him, and the iron gates fell before the Faerevolder.

Now, the Dark Lord slowly paced about his throne. Carefully considering and weighing out the meaning of the other power that was at work against his designs. The Evening Emerald was a power, yet a power to be used by others. It mumbled, "The old man, Anadan?"

It thought perhaps the sage had found a way to harness it to his own use. However, this power was something else, something older. Something that was oddly familiar; the beast could not grasp its form.

The red glow cast a rough reflection of the beast in its true form as it paced to and fro. Its head, if one could call the form that, sat at what could be considered its hunched shoulders. It was a knotted and twisted malignant mass that sprouted fragments of hair, bone, and horn. Maggots and filth dripped from its rotting tusks. Its body was that of a crooked bird. Spindly legs moved akimbo in their uneven and halting strides. Its long, thin, leathery arms tapered and ended in claws.

A wide metal band encompassed its bulging neck. Fastened to the metal collar was a long chain of thick links, extending down the beast's back and trailing behind its steps. The beast stopped its pacing in front of a tall, stone throne and turned. Sibilant was its words as it slowly hissed, "As it was foretold. The Evening Emerald comes to me of its own choosing."

Nils stood in the beast's lair and looked at his doom, carefully considering its horror. Then he said, "I am here. As you can see, Ka-Tayana is not."

Gleefully the beast laughed in its serpent's speech, "It thinks it doesn't know what it is? It thinks it is not what was written and now shall come to its destiny?"

The beast stepped close to Nils, opened its rancid arms and said invitingly, "Come, man thing, share with us."

Nils had long ago passed his toughest tests. This one was the easiest to negotiate, as he was no longer thrall to his passions. He said, "The only thing I am willing to share with you is this."

Nils thrust the sword deep into the beast's chest. Badly wounded, the beast jumped back, pulling the sword out of Nils' hands. Its claws closed on the sword's hilt and with a howl of deep pain, pulled out the sword and dropped it on the cold stone floor. Black blood oozed from its open wound. Hissing, it cried, "Where did you get that?"

Nils replied flatly, "Anadan found it in Dom's play room."

The Dark Lord howled, "Again and even apart from me, that man finds a way to grieve me!"

Nils moved quickly and recovered the sword. With another quick slash, he cut into one of the beast's extended arms. Nils stepped back as green puss and maggots spewed out from the new wound.

The beast cried, "Endless and supreme power was yours, my gift to you, Evening Emerald. Now, by my will you shall suffer an eternity of cold pain."

Nils replied to the great tempter, "Power. What would be the good of it? Your lust for souls and worlds cannot be satiated. You would devour all of Taere and Faere and still hunger for more. This ends now."

The beast snickered at Nils, "Do you think you can come into my abode with that little pin prick to challenge me? I cannot die. You, little man, can."

The beast's visage then sneered and as if unhurt and it struck at Nils' face with a sharp claw. Surprised at its energy and strength, Nils fell, bright red blood flowing from the open gash on his face. The Dark Lord's form grew and expanded so that the throne room filled with its evil. From within the massive dark form, its voice hissed, "Recoil in the horror of me and die."

Nils stumbled backwards, pressing his back on the stone wall. He wiped the line of fresh blood from his cheek and hoarsely laughed, "All this power and the best you can muster is a scratch? I've been bit worse by mosquitoes."

A sudden strength overcame Nils and he leapt up, thrusting the bright sword forward. Within the deep darkness, where none other was witness, Nils and the Dark Lord fenced back and forth. Nils's sword struck the Dark Lord's fangs and claws, rending its body. The Dark Lord lashed back, slashing Nils' armor and flesh. The beast grasped the chain fastened to its neck and whipped it around Nils legs, pulling him down and onto his back.

Nils thrust the sword, cutting out one of the beast's eyes, the putrid orb hitting the stone floor with a flat squish. In return, it dug a claw into Nils' sword arm. Pain seared through him and Nils cried out as the arm went cold and numb. Nils grabbed at the fresh wound on his arm, vainly attempting to keep his lifeblood pouring through his fingers. The Dark Lord shout out a victory howl, and taking Nils by the hair, drug him to the throne where it sat heavily on the stone.

Wounded, sorely hurt and sitting on his throne in victory, the beast's claws loosened their grasp and Nils slumped in front of the great evil. Nils, weaken seized the moment and crawled away from the exhausted enemy. On all fours, he made his way around to the back of the throne. There he likewise collapsed. Nils fought off the call to fall into darkness and still awake, he noticed a large buckle with a heavy bolt sitting at the throne's back. He grabbed it with his bloody hands, and weakly raised himself up. Then, he smiled.

From the throne's front and in the darkness came the beast's voice, "I am tired and I hunger. Your soul will taste bitter, yet I shall feast."

Nils staggered from behind the stone chair and across the distance to the chamber's walls. He watched as the Dark Lord extended his fangs and began to raise itself from the stone throne, a thick green slime drooling over its lips.

Nils asked, "Didn't whatever you claim as mothers ever tell you not to be greedy?"

The Dark Lord sat back, curiosity in its question, "Mother? I am as I have ever been. Alone. This my being, my darkness."

It then stood, placed its chin in one dripping claw, thinking.

Nils began to slowly crawl toward the room's opening. He stopped as the beast hissed, "The abyss of souls is mine alone. In the early days before the time of Taere and Faere there were others in the dark."

Nils set the trap for the beast by asking, "And what happened to them?"

The Dark Lord was quiet for some time, then chuckled, "I was hungry, oh so ever hungry. I hunted them and devoured not only their flesh but their power as well. With each kill I became larger, stronger."

Nils then sprang the trap, "What of the Great Maker?"

A great howl of pain and anger rolled and echoed through the beast's throne room. Hisses broke into its words, "Hiss. There came a time when I could not find any other in the dark. Hiss. Hiss. I hunted everywhere and found none. Hiss. Then, I passed through a door and into a garden full of light and such sweet prey. Hissss."

Nils inquired, "Wasn't their flesh enough?"

A long "Hissssss" reverberated in the chamber.

The beast responded, "How dare you speak to me of what is enough? Evening Emerald you shall be mine either by gift or force."

Then the dark lord lunged out at Nils, stretching its withered arms and claws to grasp and impale the mortal standing before its power. As the Dark Lord thrust himself forward, Nils stumbled backwards. The chain extended, clink-clink-clink, through the bolt, and wrenched the Dark lord's neck and head back. The Dark Lord's fangs snapped at Nils' neck as it recoiled, then lunged in fury and anger toward Nils again and again.

Using his arms and legs, Nils retreated closer to the exit and said, "You may not die. But you can be bound and bound you are."

A cold and vile tone filled the beast's voice as it said, "You think you have defeated me? Bagh! One will come and free me. I am not done with the likes of your race."

Nils reached the passageway. Then he lifted himself up, and stepping through it, turned away from the throne and its occupant, passing into the dimly lit passage. He turned around, watching the beast struggle against the chain. Again and again, the great tempter extended its claws behind itself, vainly grasping for the sword that was firmly threaded between the chain links high against the buckle that sat at the back of the stone throne. As he watched, the rock wall snapped closed before Nils, separating him from the Dark Lord struggling on his throne.

Nils turned away and walked toward a dim light, not unwholesome as the red, but a pale white that gave Nils hope and strength. He was bruised and hurt, his face and body crossed by many slashes and cuts. As he walked, he knew not where he was going, yet the light grew stronger and brighter. Eventually, he stumbled upon a fork in the passage. On one hand, the now brilliant light beckoned him, on the other Dom's weak cries echoed in the darkness. With a heavy sigh, Nils dropped his head to his chest and turned toward Dom.

In the passage, Nils stood at Dom's side. As he was standing there, Dom drifted in and out of consciousness. In a soft voice, Nils said, "I don't doubt that in time your master will deceive some poor wretch to find its tortured way here. That thing would ensure he or she would find whatever remained of you and then the doorway."

Nils bent down and, with both hands, firmly grabbed the steel rod protruding through Dom's hand and into the rock wall and said, "This is really going to hurt."

In one swift move, Nils jerked the rod out of the wall and through Dom's hand. Dom sharply cried out in great pain and awakened, "My master?" He asked, and then recognizing Nils cried out, "No, not you!"

Nils said to him, "Surprise, surprise. It's not your lover."

Dom gurgled as he attempted to speak. Nils asked, "Can you stand and walk?"

At this Dom wildly kicked his legs and threw his arms about. Frustrated, Nils sat on Dom until he tired and his thrashing stopped, passing out into a limp ball. Nils bent down and placed Dom over himself, grasping Dom's wrist and ankle in a fireman's carry and said, "It appears I'll have to carry you."

Nils wobbly stood and adjusted Dom's weight. Turning around, he walked toward the fork in the passage. Long Nils had carried Dom, resigning himself to the fact he had missed the fork in the dark. Rancid water dripped from the ragged ceiling, collecting in shallow pools along the passage's floor. Nils struggled and splashed through the dark pools as he carried Dom's limp form. At the edge of one of the pools, Nils stopped and stooping down gently lowered Dom on a dry piece of bare stone.

As Nils sat heavily next to Dom, he heard a crack, as the rock floor suddenly gave way from beneath them. Nils and Dom toppled over each other and fell into a deep chasm. At the bottom, they simultaneously hit an underground lake. Nils bobbled first to the surface. A faint light from within the subterranean lake revealed Dom, still unconscious, drifting downward in the water below Nils. Nils bent and dove under the water, swimming to Dom. With one extended hand, he caught Dom by the wrist and struggled upward to the surface.

With a great splash, Nils head broke through. He gasped for air as he struggled to keep Dom's head above water. Then, Nils released Dom into the water. Dom began to once again slowly sink back under the surface. Nils quickly took off his trousers, knotted the legs, and flipped them over his head rapidly several times, inflating them with air. He then closed the waist with a belt. Nils left the floating trousers and dove again and once more retrieved Dom.

Using the hasty life preserver, Nils secured Dom's arms. Nils now dove below Dom and removed Dom's trousers. He repeated the same action as before, making a second life preserver. Then he took off his shirt and with it, tied himself to Dom. Exhausted with his efforts, Nils sank into the bloated trousers. Unable to keep his eyes open, his eyelids closed and Nils passed into unconsciousness.

Time was lost as Nils and Dom drifted on the dark water, the lake's current moving them at a slow pace. The pair softly snored as the current picked up speed. In the distance, the small roar of falling water bounced over the water. Louder and louder came the sound of roiling water to the slumbering pair.

Nils awoke just as the flashing water pushed him and Dom over the fall. Together, they crashed into the churning stream at its bottom. Under the surface, sharp rocks cut and bruised their already hurt bodies, opening old wounds and making new. Turning and tumbling within the roiling stream, Nils fought to bring himself and Dom to the surface. Nearly out of air, Nils broke through, finding that during their foray into the fall's well, the cold, sharp stones and angry water had ripped apart the flimsy, makeshift life preservers.

Now cast apart, Nils and Dom bounced separately with the surging water. Nils managed to place himself on his back and pushed his feet forward in the stream. A short distance ahead of him, Dom, bobbed and floated along like a corked bottle, sometimes face up and others face down in the water. Nils used his arms and legs to both propel and guide him to Dom.

At a turn in the stream's course, its banks extended and the water's pace slowed. Here, Nils changed his position, flipping himself over and putting his head forward so as to be able to swim to Dom. With some remaining strong strokes, Nils reached Dom. Then, he placed Dom face up, rotating his position so as to cradle Dom's head above the water. In this manner, they bobbled and bounced together as the current once again picked up speed, carrying them toward a distant, grey shore.

The water became ice cold, and Nils' body convulsed and he began to shiver uncontrollably in the frigid water. Together they floated into a thick fog lying on the water. Nils was now unable to see clearly, his eyes having become blurry in the fog. Yet, he sensed the water had once again ceased its rapid movements, leaving him and Dom gently floating. Along the dimly defined shore, Nils could make out flashes of light flickering in the dense grey fog.

The lights' intensity grew and flashed a blurry hot white, and then a mix of red, blue and white before him as the now gentle current softly pushed him and Dom closer to the shore. Unable to keep himself awake and feeling Dom slip from his grip, Nils slid into unconsciousness, the flickering strobe lights slowly fading to a steady pulse of hazy red, blue, and white.

⤝⌒⤜

The rain had begun again, and now steadily pummeled the yellow-cloaked police and rescue workers lined on the shore and in the small rubber powerboats on the lake. The lights, atop of the emergency vehicles parked nearby, flashed red, blue and white in a steady rhythm.

They had been there nearly an hour, having responded to the bizarre lighting strokes that had blasted Rafferty's. There had been no fire, but the hotel's receptionist reported some fleeing guests having seen what was to be believed to have been bodies falling into the lake. A bundled rescue worker tugged the hood of the yellow rain slicker tighter over his head as he looked out over the rain swept lake and muttered, "Not likely."

The floating bundles did not at first catch his attention, bobbing small and crumpled. Then a searchlight passed over them, and the rescuer caught a flash of something, a gleam of perhaps a watch on a wrist or a ring on an extended finger. Not considering he may have simply seen some rags caught floating on the lake, he keyed the microphone at his shoulder and shouted, "Over there. Did you see that?"

Through the radio's static came the reply, "Got it."

The rescuer in one of the rubber boats ordered, "Get some more light over here."

Soon, searchlights illuminated the two figures floating in the water, and soon the rubber boats sped to their target. Upon reaching where Nils and Dom floated, the boats stopped and rescue workers dressed in rubber dive suits entered the frigid water. Another rescuer held the boat's outboard motor in idle as his colleague recovered the two floating people, bringing them aboard the small craft. Along the shore, a police officer spoke into a handset, "We have two in the water. The boat is bringing them in now. Yeah, Yeah. The EMS crew is standing by."

The rescue worker turned his boat, and bringing its motor to full speed, raced to the shoreline. Upon reaching it, he cut back the engine's speed, slowing their forward movement to run the rubber boat gently aground. On the shore, An Paramedic reached over the boat's side. She unceremoniously hauled first Dom and then Nils onto land. Gurneys were pushed forward as she said, "Got them."

Swiftly, the Paramedics placed the pair into separate gurneys and lifted them into waiting ambulances. With sirens blasting their claxon calls, the ambulances drove away from the shore. Within one, Nils eyes fluttered open as a Paramedic covered him with a blanket, careful not to disturb the intravenous drips in his arms. Nils worked out the hoarse words, "Where are we?"

She responded, "Try to stay quiet and calm.

She injected Nils with a sedative. His eyes closed and the Paramedic monitored his condition as the ambulance sped on its way. Later, Nils lay on a bed in a hospital room, his steady breathing keeping pace with the slow, rhythmic beat of the monitors. Close by, Beatrice sat quietly on a chair next to him, snugly ensconced in a thick robe. Looking on his sleeping face, she gently took his hand, and softly said, "I never said thank you."

Nils opened his eyes and weakly murmured, "Thank you for what?"

Beatrice sobbed, "For that day at the country club. You were so courageous then. And now here. They told me what you did for me. And how you saved Dom."

Nils said flatly, "There are some things a man, any person has to do."

A tone of hope crept into Beatrice's voice, "So there are things for me to do as well?"

Nils extended one bandaged hand and gently wiped the tears from Beatrice's face and said, "Indeed."

Eight months later, Nils found himself traveling along a winding, forested road. To the doctor's surprise, he had recovered from his hurts within a few days. Within the week of his return, he reported to his old workspace. Now, the pockets of shade from the morning light dappled the luxury car as it smoothly negotiated the road's asphalt surface.

At the end of the road lay a long, high stone fence. The car pulled up to the set of double steel gates that sealed the entrance. From each side of the gate, strings of barbed wire topped the stone wall. At one side was a guard post; its outside wall displaying a sign that read VOLDREN CLINIC. Here, the driver stopped and lowered his window, passing their identification documents to the guard.

The guard carefully inspected the identification, turning over each document before handing them back to the driver. Pushing a button within the gatehouse, he opened the steel gates. Once opened, the car passed through the gates and followed a red-bricked road, its sides lined with tall trees, hedges, and security cameras.

The car continued its journey until it came to a grand structure built in the Victorian style. It was an old three-story mansion faced with double oak doors and gleaming white boards. A short series of teakwood steps led from its large double doors to the drive. It sat silently, neither a happy nor a sad house. The old place impressed Nils as a reserved person, one that strives to conceal and control its passions.

At the mansion's front, the car stopped and Nils exited. He quickly mounted the wooden steps and entered the doors. Once inside, one of the staff, his coat starched white and demeanor as impassive as the mansion that was the clinic's front greeted Nils. After a few perfunctory greetings, the doctor escorted Nils through a series of antiseptic halls and to a single cell.

Upon entering it, Nils could not ignore the cells' sterility. Its' walls were white, a stainless steel bed, sink and toilet its only furniture. High on one wall, a thick window, enmeshed with wire sat between two sets of thick steal bars. On the high, bare ceiling, a phosphorescent light glowed. Dom sat on the edge of the steel bed; his eyes fixed staring at nothing. The doctor, standing next to Nils said in a cold tone, "He is in a complete catatonic state."

Nils asked, "Can he hear or understand us?"

The doctor replied, "No one really knows what a person in his condition may or may not sense. I'll leave you two alone now. Remember, only a few minutes."

The doctor walked to the door and pressed a button. An orderly opened the door, and the doctor walked into the sparse clinic hallway. Once clear, the orderly closed the door.

Once alone with Dom, Nils spoke, "There are days I'd like to think it all had never happened. Yet here we are. Is this the future you desired? It is not what I wanted."

Dom did not answer, staring ahead blankly with drool dripped from his half open mouth. Nils continued, "No matter. On the steppes I learned we must try and save all that we can. We are now as we are."

Nils took a photo of Beatrice from his jacket and placed it on the bed next to Dom. He flipped it over to reveal the inscription from his grandmother.

"I brought this for you. You do not deserve it. But neither did I and she would have wanted you to have it."

Nils then turned away from the broken thing Dom had become and pressed the button. The door opened and Nils exited. As the orderly closed the door behind Nils, a single tear slowly tracked its way down Dom's face.

><del>~</del><del>~</del><

The beast sat chained to the stone throne in its own filth, a pale light surrounding its twisted form. Anadan entered and stood silently as it hissed, "So, you came to gloat?"

Anadan replied, "No. To offer you the Great Maker's grace. Will you accept it?"

The beast scoffed, "Bagh. Who are you to offer me anything?"

Anadan responded softly, as a parent will when speaking to an errant child, not wishing to scold but instruct, "Can you not see who I am? Have you become so deaf so as not to be able to hear the Great Maker's words? If not for yourself, then for those poor souls you keep imprisoned."

The beast hissed, "You ask too much of me. Hiss. It is my window to the two worlds. If I give it you, what do I receive in return?"

Anadan said, "Faith in my word."

Again the beast scoffed, "Bagh, braggart whore's son! You give me nothing. And nothing do I give you."

To this response, Anadan said, "Very well. So you have spoken. Yet you should know this, a way is made for any to come to the Great Maker. Even now one of your servants has found it."

Anadan then left the beast in its throne room; howling in rage has its connection to Taere was irrevocably broken.

The sage passed through a stone hallway, strolling into a lush garden. Before him was the Great Maker robed in brilliant light. Anadan squinted as he attempted to make out his Master's face as the great one softly spoke, "Enter. Well done, good and faithful servant."

In the darkness that engulfed the Dark Lord trapped in the Faerevold was the sound of small claws scratching in the distance. The beast whispered, "Come. And let us see who eats who."

It was day in the city, the commuters were moving along the sidewalks, the swarming tide of intertwined bodies, and grey faces bundled against another blowing snow. The opulent automobile pulled up silently into the covered parking area, its engine purring rhythmically as it stopped by the door. In its back sat Nils.

Within the parking area stood the security guards, flanking the executive entrance. The car stopped before them and one of the guards briskly stepped forward and opened the rear passenger door. Nils got out and gave the guard a wide, friendly smile, his polished shoes gleaming. He wore a silk suit, a fedora, and brushed calfskin gloves. A brushed camel hair coat lay neatly over his ensemble. Nils said to the guards, "Thank you. Good morning, Charles, James.

He strolled past the guards and into the building. Without fanfare, he entered the plush elevator, the richly uniformed operator holding open its doors. Once inside, Nils nodded and the operator closed the elevator doors.

At the STERNZCO reception area, the elevator doors opened and Nils walked out. There in her desk sat the red-blond secretary, busy with her morning's duties. He walked past her smile, through the set of large oak doors and closed them behind him. In the door's center at eye level sat a brass nameplate. It read, BEATRICE STERNZ, President.

Fin.

BEGINNINGS AND ENDS

lthough the Street had expected his demise for some time, the
Oraton's (the Republic's many and diverse media forums) wave-cast
of Nilsen Sicharis' death, CEO of the mega-corporation known as
STERNZCO, posted as STRN on the Republic's Securities Control List
(R.S.C.L., or Rascal as most referred to it), shot thorough the Republic,
shaking the very foundations of its many provincial capitals and markets.

To say he was both the Republic's wealthiest and most influential citizen
is to state the obvious. Yet, he did not seek out public office either as a Senator
or an administrator, preferring to focus his energies on STERNZCO, his
fellow citizens, and the ever increasing mass of the Republic's subjects. So
intertwined were STERNZCO's financial interests with those of the several
firms, governmental institutions and untold billions of citizens throughout
the Republic, as its fortunes went so did those of its shareholders. A simple
data cast to senator or administrator (very few of these) was all it took for him
to wield his substantial power.

I found no joy in the news of Ms. Sternz's victory and the firm's
vindication. As fate would have it, it fell to me on the morning of his funeral
to go through the old man's trunks and boxes teeming with the now useless
junk of his life. The gang was holding a wake for him at Klingers Bar, and
I'd been invited to honor one of his last requests, drinking pints not in his
memory but to the hope of future days. Instead, I was in a musty smelling,
cobweb filled and rather dusty attic stuffed with trunks and boxes; figuring
if Le Grand Madam—the Grey Lady, as we called Ms. Beatrice Sternz, CEO

of STERNZCO, wanted it done, there must be a reason. I just kept wishing she'd picked someone else.

Sure, I was close to the guy. At first, as close as a fresh out of Harvard MBA just turned twenty prodigy wanted to be to some old fart that acted, looked, and smelled like he was part of another age could be. But somehow he got assigned to me as part of the STRENZCO mentoring program. Like I needed his help; I bloody well got out at nineteen with a 3.875! Then pushing sixty, the man had been recently promoted to one of the low level vice presidential positions in the firm. So I thought, *How quaint. They must have given him a do-nothing title as reward for long service. Besides, what could an old has-been, going nowhere corporate clown offer to someone like me?*

Funny thing is I found out he offered quite a lot. There wasn't one part of the firm he did not have an intimate knowledge of, from accounting and finance, to legal and compliance, to marketing and sales, to operations and production, to warehousing and distribution. It was an odd day some financier, Street analyst, or someone in the firm or industry did not call on him. If it had the tiniest thing to do with STRENZCO, he knew about it. He also had a deep knowledge of a host of other subjects beyond business, being fluent in ancient history, archeology, politics, and on and on.

He was never wrong about anything, never said a bad word about anyone, and never did anything spiteful. He had a knack of saying precisely the right things to me when I was in the midst of making a mistake at the office or a fool of myself with my colleagues. When the need arose, he could fight fiercely in the board room like a trapped lion. He also had a way of ferreting out the back-stabbing, power hungry wanabees in and outside of the firm, sending them packing with their tails firmly tucked between their legs.

He was wise and had a unique air about himself. Other than my father, he was a person with a certain something, something very different from just about everyone I'd ever known before. After a few months of his listening more than talking, retrieving me from the strip bars in the wee hours of some hazy morning, and saving my ass more than once in the office, I found I liked the guy. I really did.

In fact, after my year with him ended, I downright wanted to be just like him. I often found myself sitting with him and soaking in his words as he shared his simple lunch with some stinking drunk or dope head outside on the firm's immense granite front steps when the weather was warm and fair.

When the season turned hard and cold, he'd take his meal inside the common cafeteria, often chatting with the security guards, dock workers, and clerks. Despite his lack of high position in those days, everybody at the firm, and many outside as well, held the old fellow in high regard. Those bitter enemies he had, feared and respected him, giving him a wide berth, loath to confront him. Even Le Grand Madam seemed to sit quiet and pay close attention when he spoke in that soft, often weak and cracking voice of his.

Four years later, he personally called and asked me mind you, to be his assistant when he became Executive Vice President and Chief Operating Officer under the old CEO, Fredric Sternz. Two cycles of the Mars rotation later found me sending a data cast of my new assignment from a Republic Marine shuttle to the STRN-TSCO site director of the petroleum recovery and refining operation where I had been working. When Fredric Sternz eventually retired, it came as no surprise to me that Beatrice Sternz took the reins of the Mars operations and named Nilsen CEO of STERNZCO. I became Director of Enterprise Development for the Valdan Worlds and spent the next intervening years on Valdan Prime building the business.

Now, after the end of his life I found myself in the musty attic above his rooms within the Sternz mansion. During his years as CEO, Beatrice had remained on Mars, leaving the place to my friend and mentor. Truth to be told, his place in the immense stone building was no great collection of luxury apartments. Rather, it was just a simple set of rooms containing a bath, bed, sitting room, and small office positioned just above the kitchen and part way over the garage. Other than the large leather reclining chair and a cat of unknown age and breeding, the most defining objects in the sitting area were the crammed-full bookshelves lining the walls from floor to ceiling, and a ladder leading up to the attic above. In the bedroom was a wardrobe containing his suits, hat, gloves and other clothes. Wedged in a corner of the office was a small wooden secretary and chair, upon which sat a computer and the last items of STERNZCO work he'd put his hand to.

Rumor at the firm had it old Beatrice Sternz kept him there because she was madly in love with the man. It being common knowledge she would stay at the mansion during her many return trips from Mars. However, during my first year with him, after one night of pints for me and coffee for him at Klingers, he got to talking about how he and the Grey Lady met and how they ended up working together at the firm. I came away with the idea she liked to keep him close because he was probably about the only person she could really trust. It seemed they went back quite a few years.

The cat had managed to get into the attic and was coyly sitting by my side licking its paws as I went through the trunks and boxes of his musty stuff, reviewing and setting his things in neat piles. In one, pictures including a very young himself, at maybe seventeen or eighteen years of age wearing the distinct dark blue uniform of a Republic Marine Legionnaire. In one pile I carefully stacked the yellowed correspondence. Yes, the Republic ran on digits, but its Marine Legions still marched on paper! in the heavily stilted language of the military informing any and all of a move, promotion, or some medal. On top of this I carefully placed his discharge.

In all the years I'd known him, I never knew he had joined the legions as a Private, had worked his way up through the ranks, and left after ten years as a Major. As I considered this hidden part of his life, a sudden sadness of his death rushed over me, and I deeply wished I'd gotten to know him a bit better. Other piles contained his personal letters, stuff from the firm, or copies of his degrees in history and business.

I'd grown up around the legions and understood what all that yellowed paper meant. Pops had retired after 25 years at full Colonel. After more than a few opportunities at dodging death, forced moves, and separations from my mom and me, my parents settled down near Jackson Hole in Old Wyoming to knit (her) and fish (him). Six months after moving to the Tetons, pops passed from a sudden and massive heart attack.

It was now past noon, and after spending the morning in the attic where the stuff was stored, I was finished sorting through the trunks and began to feel the need for one of the waiting cold pints at Klingers. So I got up, stretched out the growing knots and kinks in my shoulders and headed for the ladder that poked up into the attic from the sitting room floor below. As I was just about ready to leave, I spotted the cat playing with a strip of pale blue ribbon attached to one small trunk tucked so far back in the attic's eaves that if it had not been for the quick flicker of light on the cat as it pounced to catch the loose ribbon, I'd have missed it.

So I sighed out my great regret of not sharing my sadness of the old man's passing with the gang down at Klingers, turned from the ladder, and went to fish out the small trunk. It turned out to be a stout wooden box, firmly stuck behind the eves. I ended up skinning my knuckles and cutting my hands in more than a few places by the time I got the thing out and into the middle of the attic floor.

After about a half hour of looking, I decided there was no key. So I went to the pile of his old military gear and dug out the Marine's best friend, the well honed and oiled K-bar combat knife he'd carried and, and from the looks of the nicks along the blade, used. At about twelve inches from blade tip to the butt of the handle, it was the perfect thing for prying off the box's brass hinges and lock.

Once opened, I was startled to see smiling up at me from the box's interior, the beaming face of a very young Beatrice Sternz. The photograph of Beatrice lay on top of a large stack of note books, loose leaf paper, and scrolls all bound tightly together with a wide strip of faded blue ribbon. Burgundy red wax sealed the ends of the ribbon which, when I looked closer, was embroidered with the image of a pale green, eight pointed star, having seven even-sized and distributed points circling its sides and one larger and elongated point at its top. I also noted a miniature of the odd-shaped star symbol embossed in the burgundy colored wax seal.

The picture showed Beatrice when she was a skinny girl of about eleven or twelve standing in front of a gazebo, and wearing a large straw hat and what was then called a sun suit. Since I'd already gone through the other scraps of minutia, I took out the stack of documents, popped the wax seal, and began to sort through the box's contents. I set Le Gran Madam's photo aside, thinking to give it to her as it seemed to be a personal item.

On the cover of each note book was a unique icon. A number was also penned in at the top left hand corner of each one. The papers were in packets, each held together by a brass rivet the size of my little finger nail. The scrolls were each sealed with a small piece of blue ribbon in a similar fashion as the large stack.

The first thing I noticed was the material of the scrolls and papers; not paper as I thought, but some type of translucent animal hide I'd never seen before. It was very thin, incredibly pliable and inscribed with a text I did not recognize. The alien lines were written in a form similar to cursive, and unlike the old man's chicken scratches, were laid down with a fine, even hand. On each was an icon matching that of the ones on the notebooks, each notebook corresponding to a scroll or packet of the mysterious hides.

Intrigued with the notion he had somehow come into possession of some ancient documents and their translations, I used the icons to match the notebooks to each scroll and packet, ending up with each notebook matched to a scroll or packet. Remarkably, the top packet's icon matched that of the top notebooks', as did the second, third and so on. Sensing the top notebook contained the beginning of the work, I opened it to find he had scrawled in his heavy hand across its pages the following:

Having received commission from His Lordship, Lord Hine Perion and Smythe, I set forth this tale neither as witness for nor against any person, cause or event laid before thee. The days spoken of that lie here-in are not mine own, but of others, who lived and died, loved and hated, found and lost, made and destroyed long before these present days. May the Great Maker find this imperfect work true to the recollection of deeds and misdeeds done by those who strode Faerevold in those days past and declare, "Well done, my good and faithful servant."

Sam Stone, Chronicler A.N 0154.

>––~–‹

It was very late in the night when I finished reading Nils' fantastic tale. I closed the last notebook and carried the cat down the ladder into Nil's room. I let the cat down and followed it into the kitchen, it wanting to mouse around, and I to find something to eat. On a table was laid some sandwiches and a thermos of coffee. I was adroitly applying myself to these victuals when Ms. Sternz came in.

She walked so softly, and I was so very intent on the food, I did not hear her when she came in. Her slight cough surprised me, and I jerked my attention to her standing in the kitchen's door. She was dressed in pajamas over which she had an old robe tightly tied. On her feet was a pair of nondescript slippers. Her long grey hair fell over her face and cascaded past her shoulders, leaving only the tip of her nose and the bright twinkle of her eyes poking out at me.

She motioned I should follow her, and soon I found myself in a room, seated next to her in front of one of the many fire places in the mansion. We sat alone, me eating and her idly poking the fire's embers. As I finished the last of the coffee, she said, "You were long in the attic. Did you find something of interest to you?

I could not think of anything to answer her simple and direct question to my discovery of the strange items describing Nils' strange tale. Finally, I concluded there was nothing else for it and decided to tell her the truth. Unsure of how she would receive what I had to say, I swallowed hard, and answered, "Nils' adventures in Faerevold."

Her fist tightened on the poker's shaft and she sucked in her breath and said, "So, there is an accounting of his deeds."

The next moment she was on her feet and staring directly at me. In a furtive whisper she asked, "What do you think of it? Can it be true?"

In that moment, I sensed my fate in the firm was in the balance. Indeed, hints of her use of violence were common at the firm, and I felt my very life was at issue. She stood there with her glinting eyes locked on me, yet did not press me as I thought over my answer, then slowly and carefully I responded, "Yes, Nils found redemption there."

She relaxed her grip on the poker, and turning from me laid it in its place by the fireplace. She stood there for some time, her arms placed on the mantle with her head bowed between them. With a great sigh, she turned and again faced me, pulling the loose strands of grey hair from her face into one long stream and holding it behind one shoulder with a single hand.

Without a word, she strode past me. At the end of the room, she stopped and said, "As long as this remains between the two of us, you need not fear me or my people. I and Nils have need of you."

Stunned, I shouted, "Yes of course!"

She smiled at me, joy in her wrinkled face and nodded. Then she asked me, "Do you think Nils was the only to have been in Faerevold?"

Before I could answer she disappeared into the bowels of the mansion. The next day I returned to the big house and was escorted not to the small room, but to a set of locked and guarded doors. After verifying my identity, the guards opened the doors and I found myself in a small library. On one long table was set the notebooks, scrolls, and hide packets I had found the day before. A hand written note signed B. Sternz contained my instructions.

Over the next several months I reported to the mansion and was escorted to the library, and within the year, I had fininshed transcribing Nil's work. Once done, I was transferred to one of the STERNZCO subsidiaries, receiving a significant pay raise and promotion (much to the dismay of my collegues who had taken other jobs).

It has now been six years since the Grey Lady had me go through the trunks in the Attic. I was not surprised when I received an e-mail from her directly. Its message was as clear as it was brief. There is more than one attic in the mansion, each full of trunks and boxes which the Grey Lady invites me return to and explore their contents.

ACKNOWLEDGEMENTS

Students of geometry will recognize an eight pointed star as a form of an octagram, while travelers to the ancient realm of the Barbary Pirates will identify it as a symbol for Morocco. Hence, I experienced no small epiphany when long after penning his travels; I serendipitously discovered the eight-pointed star is an ancient symbol of importance in many of the world's beliefs. In Buddhism, it represents the Eight Fold Path, the Star of Lakshmi in Hinduism, the khatim or khatim sulayman is of especial meaning for Muslims, and in Judaism, it signifies the Sons of Jesse. For those who share the Christian faith, it represents baptism, the Star of Regeneration or Redemption.

In days past, writers could toil alone sequestered from the remains of the mortal realm. In our times, no one inks the pages cloistered in some far way archipelago, and it takes many talented people to produce a book. The difficulty always lies at the start point; with whom does an author begin? I think it safe to say I am not one to wear my faith on my sleeve; however, I first thank the Merciful Lord and God who by Grace paid my debts, and by whom I now live an imperfect life. I also take this opportunity to express my gratitude to my wife and best friend, Christine who not only was my first reader, but also is my closest confident and stalwart ally.

I especially thank my son Samuel and Mr. Jim Bodenheimer whose insights helped Nils enter Taere and then return home. I cannot express enough gratitude to Mr. Robert 'Bob' Spear whose expert advice and wise mentorship truly made this work become a reality. I will always be grateful to the many good people who perused sample paragraphs or listened to my recitation of snippets, and then provided kind criticism and welcome advice.

ABOUT THE AUTHOR

J. Daniel Stanfield was born and raised in Boise, Idaho. He is a retired U.S. Army Officer. First, he was an enlisted soldier and non-commissioned officer along the former West German-Warsaw Pact border. After receiving his commission, he served in a wide variety of Intelligence and Electronic Warfare positions. During his military career, he had the great honor and privilege to lead soldiers, and serve in the Fifth Special Forces Group, with Navy SEAL Team 5, and as a Strategic Intelligence Officer for the Supreme Allied Commander Europe. He holds a Masters of Science and Doctorate in Business Administration, and has a passion for the arcane subjects of social and organizational design, grand strategy, and decision-making. He currently lives near Kansas City with his wife Christine and their menagerie of dogs and cats.

ORDERS

Please send orders with check or money order to:
Syringa Press, Inc.
2109 High St.
Leavenworth, KS 66048
913-648-4058

Item	Quantity	Times Price	Total
Nils' Passage		$14.95	
Sales Tax 8.3% KS Residents			
S&H	$4.00	1 price fits all	$4.00
		Total	

Name: _____

Address: _____

City:_____ State:_____Zip:_____